SO MANY OFFERS

The sophisticated, seductive French nobleman, Etienne de Roncy, offered Miss Verity Cox love without marriage as he taught her the rules of the game of aristocratic amour.

The well-born, well-bred Mr. Bennington-Jones offered Verity marriage without love as he proposed she follow the dictates of good sense rather than the senses.

But the most perplexing proposal of all came from the dashing Patrick Tarkington, who offered Verity a smokescreen of lies she could see right through—and a mystery she had to solve before she could know if her own heart was playing false or true. . . .

THE
NOBLE IMPOSTOR

SIGNET Regency Romances You'll Enjoy

THE
NOBLE
IMPOSTOR

By Mollie Ashton

A SIGNET BOOK

NEW AMERICAN LIBRARY

NAL BOOKS ARE AVAILABLE AT QUANTITY DISCOUNTS WHEN
USED TO PROMOTE PRODUCTS OR SERVICES. FOR INFORMA-
TION PLEASE WRITE TO PREMIUM MARKETING DIVISION, NEW
AMERICAN LIBRARY, 1633 BROADWAY, NEW YORK, NEW YORK
10019.

SIGNET TRADEMARK REG. U.S. PAT. OFF. AND FOREIGN COUNTRIES
REGISTERED TRADEMARK—MARCA REGISTRADA
HECHO EN CHICAGO, U.S.A.

SIGNET, SIGNET CLASSIC, MENTOR, PLUME, MERIDIAN AND NAL BOOKS
are published by New American Library,
1633 Broadway, New York, New York 10019

First Printing, May, 1984

1 2 3 4 5 6 7 8 9

PRINTED IN THE UNITED STATES OF AMERICA

Caroline Verity Cox released the crank handle and heard the contents of the barrel slosh to a standstill. The butter was nowhere near stiff yet, but she would have to leave it now. Minnie had just come scurrying over from the house with the disconcerting news that his lordship and her ladyship had already arrived. Verity glanced down at her coarse dairy smock; it would not do for Uncle George and Aunt Maria to see her thus.

"Minnie, you'll have to stay and finish the butter," she said, reaching behind her neck to undo the smock buttons. "Just keep turning the handle until it becomes stiff."

"But Mrs. Budgitt had me on the potatoes, miss," the scullery maid protested, her bright cheeks and saucer eyes reminding Verity of a hurriedly painted doll. "And then I'm to rub up the silver."

"Don't fuss, Minnie. I'll take care of Mrs. Budgitt."

Verity slid the rumpled smock down over her arms and had begun to step out of it when she saw Minnie's brows shoot up toward her mobcap. Then she remembered; she was not wearing her dress beneath. In deference to the muggy August weather and the strenuous task she had set herself, Verity had slipped off her dress before she began, and had bidden Sarah take it up to her room. Under the smock were her petticoats;

not even stays. "Oh drat," she muttered, and drew on the splattered linen garment again.

Modestly buttoning up once more, Verity wondered how best to avoid the scene she would inevitably precipitate by greeting her relatives this way. By dint of sneaking around the back of the house, using the belowstairs door, she could reach her room without encountering them and make herself decent before she appeared. Then, of course, she would be obliged to explain the long, discourteous delay.

"Minnie," she called out, pointing an emphatic forefinger at the small butter barrel, still at rest, "don't gawp. Churn." It was all too tiresome, the Strathmores arriving so early, and having to feel guilty about something so trifling.

"They will simply have to accept me just as I am," she muttered, and headed out of the dairy, resigning herself to a lordly tirade.

Mrs. Travers had shown the visitors onto the east terrace beyond the french windows of the little yellow drawing room. It was quite the coolest, most delightful spot in the house on a warm afternoon, and it was there Verity found them, seated at the wrought-iron table, sipping lemonade. When Verity entered the drawing room, her aunt and uncle were looking out at the bed of salmon-colored roses to the left of the terrace steps. In the mirror above the drawing-room mantel she caught sight of the stained muslin cap that imprisoned her roughly bundled hair, and she was tempted to back out of the room before they saw her.

No, this is absurd, she told herself firmly, and taking a deep breath, she went outside to greet them.

"Aunt Maria, Uncle George, how lovely to see you." She prepared to offer them a peck on the cheek, but cheeks were not proffered. Instead, she was greeted by mutual consternation as the couple turned in unison. It was going to be worse than she feared. Aunt Maria's mouth clamped down like a nutcracker. Uncle George was too stunned to rise from his chair, but he was not at a loss for words.

"Good grief," he squealed. "Is it an entertainment? Some kind of harlequinade? It *is* Caroline?" he asked, as always ignoring her preference for being addressed by her second name.

Verity nodded patiently.

"Fan me daylights if you don't look just like a dairymaid!"

"That is exactly what I am today, Uncle. Polly's mother took sick, and so I sent Polly home to tend her, and took over the butter myself."

Lord Strathmore stared incredulously at his niece, then cast a quick look of panic at Lady Strathmore. When he spoke again, his voice was stern. "Really, Caroline, you go too far. You do have family to consider. This is monstrous."

"There was no choice, if we were to have fresh butter this evening," Verity said carelessly, then gave a placating smile. "But I did think it would be over and done with before you arrived. Forgive me—I had not intended to greet you in this fashion."

Lady Strathmore leaned toward her husband and laid an admonishing hand on his arm. "Did I not tell you?" she whispered loudly. "It's not a moment too soon."

"There is no excuse for this, Caroline." Lord Strathmore's finger wagged furiously under his niece's nose. "Your father is not a farmer. This business of maintaining a little dairy at Briarley just for your own table is ridiculous. He should close it down and buy his butter from Wentworth—or any one of the county suppliers, for that matter. This is sheer pastoral whimsy."

Verity's brown eyes widened in protest. "But it isn't just for our table. It feeds the Stodds too, and if we shut it down, little Polly Stodd and her brother would have no employment. They cannot work in the mills, you see. They have a chest weakness, and the dust from the lint would be very bad for them."

"No, dammit, I don't see. The Stodd chest complaint has absolutely nothing to do with your becoming totally *déclassée*."

"Besides," Verity continued, and now she knew she was courting disaster, "we simply love the taste of it, fresh from our own Guernseys. It has quite spoiled us for mechanically made butter."

As she saw the purple tide rising from her uncle's snowy cravat and slowly tinting his face, Verity beat a hasty retreat.

"Please excuse me while I make my toilette. Father will be home within the hour, and I shall join you again before then."

After she reached the hallway, Verity broke into a run, taking the broad staircase two steps at a time. Bursting into her room as if the house were on fire, she lunged for the bell cord that hung beside her bed and pulled it three times. She was stepping out of the offending dairy smock for the second time when Sarah appeared from the dressing room, carrying an armful of freshly laundered clothes.

"Leave that now, Sarah," she ordered breathlessly, "and help me dress." Pulling off the tattered mobcap, Verity released a tumbling riot of hair that was just the color of old brandy held up to sunlight. She hurried over to the washstand, while the abigail deposited her burden on the bed, separating dresses, unmentionables, and petticoats into three neat piles.

Sarah turned from the bed just in time to see her mistress swoop over the basin, and she rushed to rescue the dangling locks from falling into the wash water. She stood there, holding the tresses back with a fond, lopsided grin, as Verity soaped and scrubbed vigorously with a face flannel.

"The Strathmores arrived—whole hour beforetimes— had to greet them like this," Verity explained between splashes.

"Tha' didn't 'ave to, Miss Verity. Tha' did it on purpose," Sarah remarked, holding out the towel.

Verity's eye caught a flash of green in the dress pile on the bed as she patted her face dry. "Ah, the green jacquard, that's what I shall wear, Sarah. Something grand to mollify my aunt and uncle."

"Aye, ah can just imagine!" Sarah rolled her eyes. "Tha' looked a proper sight. Now come into the dressing room and ah'll coiff tha's 'air."

"Yes, but you must be quick about it, Sarah." Verity seated herself before the marble-topped dresser with the mounted mirror.

"Yes, ah know, miss." Sarah sighed. "Quick, but perfect." And she began to apply the ivory-backed hairbrushes with a will.

Verity was seldom in repose unless she was reading or sleeping, but she never minded holding still for Sarah while the abigail brushed, curled, and twisted her hair, and did those marvelous things with combs and ornaments. It was not obsessive vanity. Indeed, often she would have Sarah undo the more ornate coiffures and end the long session by leaving it simply well brushed and caught back with a plain ribbon. It was Sarah's company she relished, because Sarah, more than anyone, was Verity's own special link to the past.

Verity's mother had died of typhoid twenty years ago, so she had no personal recollections. Sarah was her memory, for Sarah had served the Strathmore household long ago as a very young girl; Sarah had stood bent just so over Mother's hair, long before Verity was born. Sarah had weathered the storm of the long-ago legendary marriage, had accompanied her late mistress to Briarley, and had become a teeming repository of memories and anecdotes for Verity's delight.

When that fragile beauty the Honorable Caroline Debenham, daughter of the sixth Viscount of Strathmore, had run off and married Josiah Cox toward the turn of the century, it was the talk of the entire county. Not only was it the first time in five generations that a Strathmore girl had married a commoner, but that particular commoner had not even "had the grace to be an Anglican," as Uncle George was still fond of putting it. The truth of it was, Josiah Cox was a dyed-in-the-wool Quaker, and the son of a nonentity. The only redeeming feature of the whole affair, and what had mercifully confined it all to the level of a minor scandal, was the fact that Mr. Cox was wealthy—although, of course, only a self-made man.

In his teens, he had inherited a patch of land from the insignificant squire who was his father. Shortly after, he was obliged to sell it to a neighboring estate as a consequence of the Enclosure Act. With the pittance he received for his land, and the backing of several in the Quaker community, Josiah Cox had managed to secure a steam-powered mill. Ten years later, when he ran off with Caroline, he had once more become a landowner, but this time a landowner of proportions that stood comparison even with the Viscounts of Strathmore. But the grief of Caroline's family had been none the less piteous for that.

Oh, the tears, the vapors, the entreaties that had accompanied the elopement! Sarah had depicted it all for Verity so often and so colorfully that Verity sometimes felt as if she herself had lived through her parents' romantic saga.

It had been Caroline's dying wish that Verity be baptized and brought up as an Anglican—more as an act of reconciliation with her family, Verity gathered, than out of any deep religious conviction. Josiah Cox, who had doted upon his bride in the brief span of bliss apportioned to them, had readily agreed, as he had to Caroline's every wish. He had been her adoring slave. But saving his aberrant passion for the lovely Anglican aristocrat, he was a devout and undeviating Friend.

He had never gone back on his word, always insisting that Verity attend the "proper" church, and never permitting her to accompany him to the Meeting House of the Society of Friends. These twenty years, Josiah Cox had remained a widower, devoting his days to the mills, to the improvement of the poor, and to nurturing his beloved only child in Anglican luxury.

Verity was blessed, she knew, with two very disparate heritages. There were times when it seemed more like a bane than a blessing, she thought, wincing as Sarah worked at the last tangle in her hair. Eyes narrowed, she peered into the looking glass and fancied she could detect both sides of the family in her face.

From Papa came a strong social conscience, and an unexalted sense of her place in the universe; it was reflected in the zealous eyes of amber brown, the assertive chin, and the generally modest demeanor. From Mama came the style; a full lower lip hinted at the unabashed pleasure lover; the thinnish nose, slim arching neck, and lustrous hair were definitely Strathmore traits.

It had been left to Uncle George, Mama's only brother, to see that Papa kept his word, and that Verity was raised, as far as humanly possible, exactly as she would have been raised if Mama had married "suitably." Uncle George had doubled his efforts ten years ago when he had succeeded to Grandpapa's title, and he had done an admirable job, she supposed, from his point of view.

Verity had always felt herself to be the social equal of her lordly cousins; just like them, she had acquired all the airs and graces, all the inimitable high style that only a blend of expensive training and noble blood can bestow. Of course, Papa's wealth had helped too, saving her as it did from the ignominy of ever being considered a poor relation.

To a degree which sometimes shocked her, Verity shared with her cousins a love of exquisite clothes, elegant conversation, and elite amusements. At the same time, from the beloved man she most admired in all the world she had inherited the Quaker's contempt for the idle rich.

Verity loved to dance at the assemblies held in Strathmore House, but here at Briarley, there was no question of dancing and she would never have dreamed of mentioning it to Papa. She was moved by the same reforming zeal that fired her father. But at Strathmore House, "do-gooding" was not a proper topic of conversation except in very special contexts; in fact, it was considered the poorest of taste to mention the needy on social occasions.

Sometimes she felt it would tear her in two, this painful ambivalence. Her Quaker conscience made the dashing young bloods up at Strathmore House seem fearful shallow. But the few eligible Quakers she had met appeared sober-sided to her, and rather humorless. However would she find an acceptable husband? she often wondered. Whoever would put up with her? How would it be possible to marry at all without either scandalizing the Strathmores or slighting her father's deepest convictions?

So far, the only answer she had found was not to marry at all. But to be forever excluded from life's most exquisite mysteries ... why, it was not to be considered.

Somewhere, sometime, she would find a solution, she decided as she returned to the east terrace, rustling fashionable green silk as she walked and looking much more like her mother's daughter.

"There!" Verity gave the waiting couple a smiling bob curtsy. "That did not take too long, did it?"

Maria Debenham, Viscountess of Strathmore, quizzed her niece carefully. "You clean up very well, dear," she allowed. "You should do it more often."

Verity murmured soothing civilities to her aunt and uncle while, in a detached corner of her mind, she considered the couple.

George Debenham, seventh Viscount of Strathmore, and his lady were the classic example of a suitable match. From families of like rank and like predilections, in thirty years of marriage they had even grown to resemble each other. Both were strong-featured, tall, and portly—but not too portly to be stylishly turned out. There was even a similarity in the way they held themselves, rigid of spine and head high. Verity occasionally wondered if the identical carriage had to do with similar childhood training or the tightness of the stays they both wore beneath their clothes.

"We are planning to take Laura to London next month," Lord Strathmore said after Verity had poured herself a glass of lemonade. "We count on taking you with us. This will take some forethought, Caroline, as we shan't be back until the following spring."

"London is a hotbed of iniquity," Verity said primly.

Aunt Maria frowned. "Whatever can you mean, child? London offers the finest amusements and the best society in the world. Do you not *want* to come?"

"Oh, yes, I should love to see the city. But . . . but not for so extended a visit. Father would never permit it."

"This Quakish posturing has got to stop, Caroline," Lord Strathmore rumbled as he rose to stand over her threateningly. "You know very well that I have your father's implicit consent in anything that concerns your future. That was decided a long time ago, thank heavens."

He folded his arms tightly and began to pace the flagstone, tapping his manicured fingers on the sleeve of his cutaway coat. After an ominous interval of silence, he came to rest, once more glowering down on Verity.

"You are going to be twenty-one." His voice was heavy with accusation.

Verity returned his gaze squarely for a moment, then lowered her eyes. "It happens to everyone, I'm told, Uncle George. Without exception."

He huffed and puffed at her flippancy, but she could not desist from provoking him.

"No, Uncle, I speak false," she amended. "There are exceptions, especially among the children of the poor whose conditions are such that they may never reach—"

"Stop it," he roared. "I will not have it!" Turning away in disgust, he appealed to Lady Strathmore. "Has it not been my life's work to see that my sister's misconduct is not visited upon the next generation? Maria, this wench is eluding me. If we leave her here with the Quaker much longer, she is quite capable of marrying one of them."

"Oh, not really, George," Aunt Maria said calmly. "She's a sly little fox. I'm quite sure she doesn't mean half of it."

Verity listened, fascinated. It was not the first time she had provoked them into speaking of her as if she were absent.

"Oh yes she does. Why else would she say it?" Uncle George complained. "It's bad enough he's not an Anglican, but must he persistently—" He broke off, exasperated, and turned on his heel to face his niece. "Your father's becoming notorious. Everyone in the county's heard tell of his wildness. First it was free medical care for the workers, then their families too. Now it's free school for their children. Whatever next, I wonder?" He clapped a hand over his eyes as though to shield them from his spectral vision of the future.

"He's just trying to make sure that there won't be anyone fit to be a worker in a few years. They'll all be lettered, by God! Then what's to become of us, eh?" He gave a deep sigh of mourning, and changed his tone from ominous to sepulchral. "What is to become of *any* of us, *including* your father?"

Verity lowered her head to hide her smile. Uncle George was merely letting off steam. Papa's methods were a constant annoyance. It was common knowledge that Josiah Cox shared his prosperity with his workers, and yet still fared far better than any other millowner in the shire. It was a phenomenon that defied explanation and irked Uncle George beyond all reason.

"He's made it too damn comfortable here for her," Uncle George fumed to his wife. "Look at the place!" He made a sweeping gesture encompassing the graceful brick facade of the house and the velvety lawns stretching out below the terrace.

In wifely obedience, Aunt Maria's eyes followed his outflung arms. She gave an approving nod at the formal gardens, then turned her head to survey the east wing of the house. "Well, it's hardly a Palladian manor, George. Not nearly so elegant as Strathmore House, actually. The reception rooms are almost dwarfish, I'd say. But then Cox doesn't hold with dancing, so I suppose they serve well enough."

"The ceilings are a bit low, of course," Uncle George conceded, "and there's no orangery, but dammit, the man's got flushing water closets. He's had an icehouse dug in the basement, and now they have iced drinks right through the summer months. In the winter he has every fire in the house going, stoves in the hallways and dressing rooms. Not a single draft anywhere. My God, he's even put in a fitted bath on the second floor." His voice was suddenly hushed, as if he had arrived at the final, unspeakable outrage. "I mean to say—a fixture!" He shook his head despairingly, a man betrayed. "She's never going to leave."

"And what if I don't?" Verity said.

With her husband purpling to the point of apoplexy, Aunt Maria was obliged to intervene. "My dear George, calm yourself! Why don't you sit down and simply explain it to the child in a straightforward manner? I'm sure she'll understand. She's quite bright, you know."

He did as Aunt Maria suggested, and after several deep breaths, he began bravely, in as reasonable a voice as he could summon. "As you know, Arabella's husband, the Honorable Nigel Morley, has succeeded in retaining his seat in the House through the past two elections."

Uncle George was referring to his oldest daughter and her husband. Verity could hardly see the relevance of the remark, but she nodded politely and, having no wish to provoke her uncle into a seizure, kept her mouth closed.

"Well," he continued, "that's just about all Nigel's succeeded in doing, retaining his seat. A member of the House for seven years, and he's still just a back-bencher. Now if you'd make a solid Tory marriage, Caroline, then perhaps he'd have a decent chance at advancement."

Verity's surprise was genuine. "Are you saying that my living here at Briarley is holding him back, Uncle?"

The corners of the viscount's mouth turned down glumly. "It certainly does him no good. Family counts, don't ye know, especially in the House of Commons. Look at Palmerston, for heaven's sake. Only two years in the House and he was named Secretary of War. You can be sure that *he* had no dissenters or Whiggish types in *his* family tree."

"But Father is not a Whig," Verity pointed out. "He despises politics."

"Hunh! You can't be a noisy, radical reformer like Cox and stay out of politics. It's a contradiction in terms."

There was some truth to that, she had to admit. Social reform had become a burning political issue, much to Papa's distaste. "I am sorry, Uncle George, but there it is," she said meekly enough. "I really cannot change what my father is." Nor would I wish to, she thought.

"No, no, no, of course you can't, child. But you could redeem the situation by marrying well and marrying promptly." The gentle light of reason softened the viscount's eyes. "After all, *he*'s not blood-related to the Strathmores, but you are. Once you're settled down away from Briarley, what your father does won't signify too much, because it will no longer be coupled to the Strathmore name. You've had three fellows offer for you, and any one of them would have done splendidly. You haven't been showing the right spirit, you know."

Verity's nose wrinkled at the memory of two of her suitors. The third she could not even remember very clearly. "But Uncle, they were exceeding silly fellows."

Uncle George threw up his hands. "I'm going for a stroll," he announced with admirable control. Shaking his head, he descended the twelve broad steps to the lawn, then headed in long strides across the smooth green expanse toward the coppice that separated the gardens from the paddock beyond them. He always found solace in the company of horses when his mind was troubled.

Verity and her aunt watched him go in respectful silence, then Aunt Maria stood up and shook out her fan with a little flourish, as though to dispel the stifling gloom her husband trailed behind him.

"My dear," Aunt Maria said brightly, "why don't you show me the herbaceous borders?"

Arm in arm, they descended the steps and took the fine gravel footpath to the right, where the lawns were formally divided into squares bordered by radiant beds of delphiniums, asters, dahlias, and lupins, all in bloom.

"You seem to regard the nobility as being quite without conscience, but I assure you, Caroline, nothing could be further from the truth. The Strathmores have always lived up to the dictum *noblesse oblige.*"

In meek silence, Verity followed her aunt, who made toward a bed of sweet william, then stooped to breathe in the fragrance of the crimson-flecked flowers. "Ah, I do so love the old-fashioned flowers," Aunt Maria murmured. "Did I tell you Laura has an admirer?" She moved on to a rose tree, and paused, lightly stroking the petals of a velvet purple specimen, large as a cabbage. "Yes, and she's not sixteen yet. Imagine that!

Of course, we don't know too much about him yet, but he's definitely a gentleman—a very fine regiment. And if we were to decide that he was best for her, I know she wouldn't give us a bit of trouble."

Verity refused to react to the unmistakable prodding, but she avoided her aunt's eyes.

"At any rate," Aunt Maria continued, "if you were to marry into the peerage, you would find yourself surrounded with good works to your heart's delight. You would see it for yourself if you visited us more often. Why, not a week goes by but someone isn't holding a charity function. We hold two winter dances at Strathmore House, and many of the garden parties have no other purpose than to raise funds for the poor."

She paused to cast an oblique look at her niece. "You did not invent compassion, you know," she added very gently.

"Oh, Aunt Maria, I never suggested that you don't—"

"I know, my dear. I know what you don't say." Aunt Maria tapped her lightly on the wrist. "And I have a very clear idea of what you're thinking sometimes."

They continued leisurely along the south side of the house, and Lady Strathmore's voice became intimate.

"Last June, I was elected Treasurer of the Board of the Foundling Hospital in Craddock. For the past three years—I don't believe you're aware of this—I have served as Secretary of the Committee to Provide Care and Shelter for Needy Married Mothers. I was very instrumental in forming that body, and there have been times when the position has been quite burdensome."

"I'm sure it has," Verity said. "And it does sound very worthy, but what about unmarried mothers? Are they not even more needy?"

"Caroline!" Aunt Maria let out an exhausted sigh. "You can be very, very trying. I know your passion for good works, dear, and of course it does you credit, but you must learn the limits. Everything has its place. For instance, there is never any need to make a spectacle of yourself as you did this afternoon. That was quite uncalled-for."

A torpid wasp droned toward Verity's hair, and Lady Strathmore flicked it away with her fan. "Oh, you're not entirely to blame, I suppose. I realize these things wouldn't have to be spelled out to you if your mother had lived. Yes, you have a good heart, but there is never any need for a gel of your station to get her hands dirty as you did today. Charity begins at home, remember, and you must be kind to your family first."

Verity paused for a moment, then decided to say what was on the tip of her tongue. "When you are collecting and labeling your mosses in the Lake District, do you not get your hands dirty?"

"That's different, my pet. Mossing is merely a hobby."

"Ah, so as long as there is no useful purpose to it, it is permissible to soil one's hands?"

Aunt Maria gripped Verity's arm sternly. "These silly equivocations just won't work anymore, Caroline. They were charming and amusing when you were a little girl, but it's high time you stopped all this Quakish nonsense. I won't have you being quaint. The world is what it is, and we have an order to preserve. Without social order there would be chaos."

Verity took her aunt's hand and squeezed it affectionately. She had behaved rather badly. "Oh, Aunt, I was only teasing, and I'm sorry if I vexed you. I really don't plan to disgrace you all. But there is one question I should like to clear up if I may. In this order of things . . ." She paused, deep in thought.

"Yes?" her aunt prompted.

"Precisely where does Quakish stand, in relation to, say, Popish?"

The stern lines of Lady Strathmore's mouth collapsed into a helpless gale of laughter, and they were obliged to stop their progress until she had recovered. Then she gripped Verity by the elbows and gave her a kiss on the cheek.

"You're a very wicked little scamp, and I'm glad your poor uncle is out of earshot. Yes, you can still make me laugh, my dear, but don't think for one moment that it will prevent me from doing my duty by you."

2

At dinner, roast suckling pig, partridge pies, salads, pastries, and ripe summer fruit disappeared slowly to the accompaniment of a succession of fine wines. By the time the syllabub was served, the mood at table was mellow. Lord Strathmore was very partial to this dish, particularly as it was prepared at Briarley, the clotted cream curdled with sharp cider and flavored with Mrs. Budgitt's blackberry preserves.

Mr. Cox, as he was wont to do, ate sparingly and drank no wine. Excess at table was not his habit, but he never imposed his simplicity of diet on the Strathmores. He had arrived home a scant hour before dinner and, much to the surprise of the Strathmores, in the company of a foreigner. It was Mr. Cox's custom to invite to Briarley such wholesale customers as had traveled long distances to do business with him. The poor accommodations at local hostelries were a discouraging prospect to the weary traveler, and he considered this gesture the least of courtesies. Thus, Verity had become acquainted with a variety of persons from the mercantile classes, ranging from London drapers to Portuguese trading mariners. But this evening's guest was neither.

Monsieur Etienne de Roncy was the only son of an aging French count whose family fortunes had been reversed during the Reign of Terror, but who had ingeniously rebuilt them by turning to foreign trade.

21

The young de Roncy traveled far and wide for his father, procuring merchandise to ship to France. After Bonaparte's defeat, he had lost no time in seeking out the superior woven goods from Cox Mills, which for almost four years, had supplied the shelves of a good many country drapers throughout France. This was not his first visit. In fact, his appearances in this part of Lancashire seemed a good deal more frequent than necessary.

Askance as she was at the thought of sitting down to dine with a tradesman, Aunt Maria was soon melted by de Roncy's charm. Verity expected as much. The Frenchman was well-bred, darkly handsome, and utterly fascinating. And there was, too, a far more romantic aspect to his travels than mere commerce. De Roncy was one of the aristocratic fraternity known as Les Chasseurs du Roi.

"It is a volunteer network, madame," he was explaining to Aunt Maria, reluctantly dragging his gaze away from Verity in order to respond to the Strathmores' interrogation.

"Our mission is to restore lost aristocrats to the bosoms of their families."

"Refugees from the Terror?" Lord Strathmore asked. "It's been more than twenty years. Surely those who escaped the guillotine have been restored to their rightful homes long since."

"But not the small children," de Roncy explained. "It breaks the heart how many of the little ones are lost beyond recall. Some would be heirs to great names and fortunes if they could but be found. King Louis's court is overrun with false claims. Some, to be sure, have survived and grown to maturity, perhaps with no notion of their lineage."

"Deplorable," Aunt Maria murmured.

"Deplorable indeed, madame," de Roncy replied, devoutly hoping that would exhaust the topic. "One does what one can."

But Lady Strathmore was not so easily dismissed.

"And what does one do with such a lost cause?" she asked. "Have you ever uncovered a lost scion?"

De Roncy gave a modest Gallic shrug. "Only two so far. A minor Valois of the Bordeaux branch who was left with monks in Flanders, and a de la Croix who was raised in the guardianship of a Scottish squire, although the latter discovery was only a partial success, a young woman whose twin brother had not survived his infancy."

"Incredible," Aunt Maria said, with cautious admiration. "I simply can't imagine how you would go about such a task."

"One leaves no stones unturned. One asks questions, studies family portraits, asks to see long-treasured possessions which sometimes bear a clue." He gave a barely perceptible sigh, then hastened to give Lady Strathmore satisfaction so that he could at last return his attention to Verity's flawless shoulders.

"If a child was entrusted to someone fleeing Paris, it was the custom of the parents to hang a ribbon around the child's neck, attaching a signet ring or some small trifle bearing the family name or coat of arms. Of course, such items were often sold or stolen. But there is always a slim chance, and while any possibility remains, it is a point of honor to pursue this mission whenever I can. Twenty-two of France's greatest families still have missing heirs they are not yet willing to count as lost. I always carry in my luggage the miniatures and colors of these families."

"You must show them to me this evening, monsieur," Aunt Maria ordered. "Perhaps a face will strike a chord, although I cannot recall any sons or daughters in this district who cannot be accounted for in the usual way. Except at the foundling hospital, of course, but one would hardly find the scions of the great French houses there. In any event, I shall look at them all very carefully."

De Roncy nodded gravely. "You will be doing France a great service, madame." He turned to Verity beside him, and gave an apologetic smile. "This must be tedious," he said. "You have heard it all before."

"No matter," she answered.

He bent his head until it was almost touching hers and lowered his voice. "It is an unexpected pleasure to find you still here in your father's house, mamselle."

Verity firmly suppressed the flutter under her ribs. The young man was, after all, a Roman Catholic, no matter how enchanting. She was not in need of further complications in her life.

"It is not a circumstance likely to last much longer, monsieur," Aunt Maria responded from across the table, much to Verity's astonishment. What incredible hearing her aunt had!

The Frenchman looked at Lady Strathmore for a moment, then returned his dark eyes to Verity's, his brows raised inquiringly.

"Quite right, monsieur," Aunt Maria continued. "As you might have guessed, Miss Cox is spoken for. It only remains for her to name the day before her suitor quite perishes from impatience."

"Indeed," he murmured, "how could it be otherwise?" His gaze was bordering on insolence now as it brushed Verity's bare shoulders and throat, and rose like a slow caress to her face.

She looked away, reddening uncomfortably at Aunt Maria's blatant falsehood, and de Roncy's advances.

"Verity," her father said from his seat at the head of the table, "would you be good enough to play for us? If so, we shall have our coffee in the music room."

"I should be delighted, Papa." She rose from the table with relief. "If you will all excuse me, I shall precede you and select some music while you finish your syllabub."

Midway to the door, she paused to give her father a long, loving look. He was a tall, spare man and plainly dressed. One might have judged him austere until one looked into his eyes, as golden brown as Verity's, and

in her view the softest, most compassionate eyes in
the world.

Of a sudden impulse, she went to him and clasped
her arms about his neck. "Oh, I do love you so, Papa,"
she whispered in his ear.

His dear, angular face softened with pleasure at the
sudden display. "Off with you then, my love," he said
gruffly.

De Roncy rose and looked at her longingly as she
made for the door. "Can I be of assistance, mamselle?
Your father keeps an excellent table, but I fear I can
eat no more."

"Please sit down, monsieur," Mr. Cox said, firm
but not unkind. "We are about to share the very fine
cognac you so graciously presented to me this afternoon.
And then we shall all repair to the music room."

The following day there was a clash of wills when
the family gathered in the morning room. The Strathmores were to leave within the hour and were insisting
that Verity gather a few basic necessaries together so
that she could leave with them to spend the next
month at Strathmore House, preparing her wardrobe
for the London season.

Verity dug in her toes. "I cannot possibly leave
until Mrs. Stodd has recovered her health," she said.
"Besides, there are household affairs to put in order before I leave Briarley for so long a time." She cast a silent
appeal toward her father, who gave a very slight nod.

"Mrs. Travers is the housekeeper," Uncle George
said. "Don't talk rubbish. You know very well that
your father's household runs as smoothly as one of his
infernal machines with its smoking chimneys. Is that
not so, Mr. Cox?"

"Oh," Verity cut in quickly, "I completely forgot.
The vicar and his wife are invited for tea this afternoon,
so I cannot possibly leave with you."

"The vicar of Denning?" Aunt Maria seemed surprised. "Coming here?"

Verity's mouth pursed modestly. "Of course, Aunt. Do you forget that I am a member of St. Dunstable's congregation?"

"Tish tosh!" Uncle George waved away the objection with a flick of the wrist. "Send them a nice note and postpone the tea."

"Until next year?" Verity said, appalled.

During this exchange, her father had reddened noticeably under his fine gray thatch of hair. He cleared his throat gently. "I believe that Verity can settle her affairs here given ten days or so," he said. "I shall send her off to you no later than Sunday after next. In the carriage and pair she should arrive at Strathmore House in time for supper." He nodded masterfully to the Strathmores. "We shall consider it settled then, and I shall be much obliged to you."

Lady Strathmore sighed and yielded, recognizing that her brother-in-law was taking one of his stands and there was nothing further to be done about it. "Oh, well," she muttered reluctantly, "I suppose ten days more or less will do no harm."

Monsieur de Roncy had discreetly accepted breakfast in his room. Mercifully, he was not a party to the scene. This was as close as they had come to a pitched family battle as far back as Verity could remember, but Papa seemed to have settled it now.

Verity and her father walked the departing couple to their waiting barouche. Just before she stepped inside, Aunt Maria embraced her niece, then turned to Josiah Cox.

"Just be sure to keep that French fellow from being alone with the child. He's impossibly charming, and he knows it. I saw where his eyes roved all evening." Her own eyes turned suspiciously up toward the third-floor windows where the guest rooms were situated.

"My daughter is a gentlewoman, Lady Strathmore," Mr. Cox replied with rather more asperity than he usually allowed himself. "In her twenty years, she has never been alone with any fellow to my knowledge,

French or otherwise. And while I breathe, she never will, unless and until it be her lawful husband."

"May the Lord hasten that day," Lord Strathmore uttered devoutly, and they were off.

As soon as the barouche had turned the first bend in the carriageway, Mr. Cox turned to his daughter with sad eyes. "Verity, you told a falsehood, did you not?"

"About the vicar?" She lowered her head sheepishly. "I am sorry, Papa, but they would not understand. You see, they really don't concern themselves with people like the Stodds, but it signifies to me."

"Yes, I know, my precious." He enfolded her in his arms and for a moment laid his cheek on the crown of her tawny hair. "God forgive me. I fathered a hybrid."

During the next few days, Etienne de Roncy did all he could to justify Lady Strathmore's suspicions. With the admirable ingenuity that accounted for his success in commerce, he made tireless attempts to be alone with Verity. But in Mr. Cox the Frenchman had met his match, and every move was checkmated with gentle but firm diplomacy, and by Monday morning, the houseguest was obliged to depart.

Barnaby was charged with driving de Roncy to Liverpool, where he was to catch a packet to Dublin. Once he was gone, Mr. Cox too set off in the gig for Manchester, where three of his five mills were situated.

A visit to Manchester meant that he would be away most of the week. Verity busied herself with her dairy chores and with preparations for her departure. By the middle of the week, Mrs. Stodd was in good health and Polly was restored to her post in the dairy shed. Sarah had readied her mistress for departure, and little remained to be done.

On Wednesday evening, an article in the *London Gazette* caught Verity's interest. Mr. Leigh Hunt was touring the mill country, and the following afternoon he was to speak publicly in Denning. She resolved to hear him speak.

"I don't know why tha's so all-fired set to this," Sarah complained, perched beside Verity as Barnaby drove them into the village.

Verity pressed her nose to the side glass as they rolled down the leafy lane. The foliage on the elms and maples was beginning to turn, and it occurred to her that she would miss the best of the autumn color this year; she would be in London before October.

"Well, of course I want to do this," she said absently. "Mr Hunt is a reformer and a fine orator. He is a great power for good in the land. He tries to correct injustice."

"Tha' own father does that well enough, but he don't go about the countryside rabble-rousing." The abigail shifted nervously in her seat. "What injustice?"

"You know right well, Sarah. Small children toiling when they should be learning their letters. Working hours so long that they crush a man's spirit; miserable wages that won't even feed his family."

Sarah adjusted her gray bonnet with an angry tug. "Just a lot of plether! Seems to me tha' father takes care of his people right well. Tha' don't hear them complaining, do tha'?"

Verity stared dreamily through the glass.

"Seems to me," Sarah said more loudly, "tha' father's a sight too good to them."

"Nonsense. Besides, Papa's the exception to the rule." Verity laughed. "You sound more and more like Uncle George every day, Sarah. I believe you're a true Strathmore under the skin."

"What's wrong with that?" Sarah muttered. "That's what tha's supposed to be, young lass." She lapsed into a huffy silence as the carriage emerged from the shade of the lane into the sunny main street of Denning.

Verity bid Barnaby pull up in front of St. Dunstable's Church, which looked out onto the flat grassy rectangle that was the Denning village green.

A cluster of people, some fifty perhaps, were gathered at the northeast corner of the green, just across the way from the Boar's Head. There was an air of quiet optimism and anticipation in the sunny afternoon scene.

Verity slid down the side glass and leaned out. They were not mill workers, these people. The natives of Denning were thoroughly country folk. Then she realized that the crowd was greater than the population of the village. Some had no doubt traveled quite a distance to hear Mr. Hunt. There were many women in the crowd, some with children, some with infants in their arms. Not mill workers, Verity decided, but surely not a one of them but had a parent, a daughter, a brother—someone dear to them who worked in a cotton mill.

A murmur arose from the crowd, and Verity noticed that a figure had emerged from the inn and had crossed the street to the green. It was a man of slight stature, dressed in dark city clothes. He seemed to disappear into the crowd, then emerge head and shoulders above them, and she realized they had erected a speaking platform for him.

"Ah, there he is, Sarah. Can you see? We shall never hear a word from here. Let's walk across the green and join the crowd."

"Not me, lass. Ah'll watch from the carriage, and tha'll do the same if tha've any sense in tha' head."

Verity shrugged, lifted her lavender sunbonnet from her lap, and put it on, tying it under her chin. "Just as you please, Sarah, but I'm going."

Verity opened her parasol as she hurried across the green, then halfway across she decided to close it again. Somehow, sunny as it was today, the lace-edged parasol seemed woefully out of place, almost offensive among these plain folk. She tucked it under her arm instead and quickened her pace, noticing that Mr. Hunt had begun to speak.

"Ma'am, ma'am! Please stay where you are," a voice rang out. The imperious command had come from somewhere just above her head.

Verity turned, looked up, then stopped in her tracks and gaped in surprise. A horseman, resplendent in a red-and-white uniform, was cantering right up to her. His cape streamed out behind him and his gold braid flashed in the sun. An enormous bay stallion reared up menacingly as the rider drew rein, but it halted a hairsbreadth from where she stood.

The horseman doffed a ferocious-looking fur cap adorned with a tall plume and nodded his head curtly. "Be so good as to return to your carriage immediately, madam."

Verity bristled at the arrogance in his voice. "What are you doing here?" she asked, trying to wither him.

His slight smile was positively patronizing as he replaced the ridiculous cap. "That, madam, is supposed to be my question to you. However, I am Patrick Tarkington of the Fifteenth Hussars, and my cornet is over there in case of trouble." He inclined his head toward the church.

Verity looked back at St. Dunstable's and to her astonishment made out a thin line of light cavalry, two abreast in the churchyard lane. It was just around the corner from where her phaeton stood.

"And your name, madam?" His manner was very crisp.

"My name, sir, is Miss Cox, and I have come to listen to Mr. Hunt, of course. I am not accustomed to being accosted and I mean to be detained not a moment longer."

She waited for him to remove himself, but he did not. He actually had the audacity to look amused. Her voice became icy.

"If you will be so good as to let me pass, perhaps I shall accomplish my purpose without further hindrance."

"I'm afraid that won't be possible," he said, not budging an inch.

"Whatever can you mean?"

"I have orders to disperse this meeting. We have

been informed that it is a conspiracy to insurrection," he explained, his voice becoming a shade less formal. "I am sorry, madam. You will have to leave."

"What utter balderdash! I can assure you there is no conspiracy about it. You would know that yourself if you read the newspapers. Mr. Hunt's intentions were clearly announced in the *London Gazette*." Verity congratulated herself on her presence of mind, but the stupid man seemed not to have registered a word.

"Be that as it may, Miss Cox, what signifies is the writ of the county magistrates. I have my orders to keep the peace."

Now it was Verity's turn to suppress a smile. This was quite preposterous! The derring-do uniform, the mounted cavalry at the ready, the suggestion of cloak-and-dagger plots—all because of an orderly little meeting on the village green in broad daylight.

"You can rest assured that I am a very lawful citizen and will in no wise disturb the peace or be party to an insurrection." She gave a stern bob curtsy which was intended to dismiss him like an unwanted suitor. "Now, if you will go about your business, I shall go about mine." As she waited for him to let her pass, she tried to stare him down, which was difficult since he was astride a horse that stood at least sixteen hands high. No matter, she thought. She would merely detour around the beast if its rider had no courtesy.

"Good day to you, Mr. Parkington," she said decisively, and turned away.

"The name is Tarkington, madam."

The mild statement was the very last thing she heard before she felt herself gripped by the waist and flying through the air. Her horizon tilted alarmingly, and all she could do was gasp as she realized that he had swooped down and picked her up bodily. As if she were a brown paper parcel, he tucked her under one arm and spurred his great beast across the grass. It was a brief but indescribable blur as they galumphed across the green, her arms and legs thumping against the hairy flanks of the bay, her vision bound by the cuff of one Hessian boot.

When he lowered her to her feet again, she was dizzy and dumbfounded. Never had she been treated to such an indignity.

The man bent forward in his saddle and steadied her with one hand, straightening her sunbonnet with the other.

"Is this your carriage, madam?" he asked politely.

Sarah's arm reached out from the open carriage door and hauled Verity inside, before she could say a word. Sarah was clucking like a laying hen, but Verity heard not a word. Her attention was riveted on the incredible hussar. He turned his head to Barnaby's perch, said something, then veered his great rearing horse around as if preparing for a cavalry charge. Still speechless, Verity watched him gallop back across the grass to the point where he had accosted her, swoop down to pick something up from the grass, then turn and head for the phaeton again without slackening speed.

It was her parasol. The carriage door hung open still, swinging on its hinges. He closed it firmly, as if he were fully in charge, and handed Verity her parasol through the window.

She snatched it from him and remarked breathlessly, "How dare you, sir!"

With infuriating courtesy, he doffed his silly cap once more. "My pleasure, madam," he murmured, as though nothing more than a simple courtesy had passed between them.

The man was not to be believed. His bay snorted and pawed the ground as if eager for more ridiculous exploits as the hussar called out to Barnaby, "Take the lady home, driver." And he was gone from sight before the carriage took off.

"Ah told tha' it weren't right," Sarah said in a frightened voice. "Now look what's gone and 'appened.

Ah doubt either side of the family would care to know about this 'owd'yado.''

"Hold your tongue," Verity exploded in an unprecedented burst of anger, and they passed the journey home in complete silence.

For the rest of the week, Verity confined her curiosity about current affairs to reading the *Manchester Clarion*. She could find no mention of the meeting in Denning, but there was an announcement of a second meeting. The undaunted Mr. Hunt would be appearing in St. Peter's Fields, it said, on Monday morning. St. Peter's Fields was in Manchester, and by Monday, Verity would be ensconced in Strathmore House. She sighed. She seemed destined not to hear the man speak.

She tried not to spoil her last day with her father by bringing up the subject of Mr. Hunt. It was the first time she had ever felt unable to discuss such things with Papa, and it vexed her that a ridiculous and boorish cavalryman had made the topic somehow improper, even at Briarley.

On Sunday she clung to her father in a farewell embrace, suddenly realizing how long their separation would be.

"I shall miss you terribly, Papa. Is this really what you want for me?" she asked.

"Is it what you want, my love?" He cupped her face in his hands, and his eyes were moist.

"I scarcely know. I think it is, and yet . . . I would not want to cross you for all the world."

He shook his head vigorously. "You are not crossing me, child. I gave my solemn promise to your mama—but, in the end, my wishes for you are simple. I just want you to be happy, down to your soul," he said fervently. "God knows, it won't be easy for you."

—3—

Verity's first few days at Strathmore House passed pleasantly enough. She had not breathed a word about the crude hussar in Denning, and neither had Sarah. Indeed, the entire affair had been successfully dismissed from her thoughts until a moment ago when Aunt Maria announced that they would be receiving some regimental officers that evening.

"I knew there was an ulterior motive to my coming here so beforetimes," she told Laura after Lady Strathmore left the room. "I could just as well have prepared my wardrobe at Briarley and seen a bit more of Papa before we went down to London."

Sitting in the middle of her cousin's pink bed quilt, Verity shed her slippers and tucked her feet under her. "Cassy Tate's been sewing for me forever. She knows my taste and she's very good. I couldn't fathom why your mama insisted on my staying here for a month and having Miss Hetty prepare my wardrobe. Now I begin to see."

Laura stood at the pier glass, a length of pale blue muslin draped over one shoulder. "What do you mean, ulterior motive?"

"Why, having the redcoats to dinner, of course." Verity frowned. "I didn't expect anything very grand until we were in London. Now it seems the season is to begin right here in the shire. I'm simply not prepared. Besides, I really don't care for the militia."

"Rubbish, Verity. You'll adore them. I'm just so plethered that Mama went and told you. It was going to be a delicious surprise. And it won't be so grand as all that. One of your poplins with lace over will do. Mama says in high summer, a good poplin is quite proper for unmarried girls, even on the most crucial occasion."

"Oh. In that case, I suppose I have something that will do," Verity said with reluctance. She sighed, remembering the intolerably bad manners of the one redcoat she had met, and cringed inwardly at the thought of an evening spent with a roomful of such ill-mannered brutes. Suddenly she remembered that Mr. Hunt had planned to speak in Manchester yesterday. Today's paper would surely carry a report.

"Do you think Uncle George has finished with the *Clarion*, Laura?"

Her cousin twisted away from the mirror. "Really, coz, you're positively addicted to news journals. I can't imagine why. They're so terribly dull, but if you must—" She broke off and sang out, "*Maaa-grit*," in two distinct tones that resembled nothing so much as a birdcall.

A plump young woman in frilled apron and cap responded to the call, emerging from a small chamber adjacent to the bedrom.

"Oh, there you are, Margaret. Please go down and fetch the *Clarion* for my cousin. If his lordship's finished with it."

So far, Verity had been enjoying her first week here, and it was largely thanks to Laura's company. In view of the extended season looming ahead, she was grateful that Laura would be her constant companion. Of her three cousins, the youngest was her favorite. Charles, married and settled in Leicester, was rather full of himself and very stuffy. Arabella, now married to Nigel Morley, was something of a shrew; ten years older than Laura, Arabella had always treated her younger sister rather badly, Verity thought. But Laura was a delight, full of laughter, lightness, and good humor. She was as slender as Verity, but a shade shorter, with snowy skin and dark, dark hair. Verity had always considered her a beauty.

"What do you think?" Laura asked, holding out two lengths of muslin.

"The dark blue. It brings out your eyes. The pale one's a bit washed-out-looking, don't you think?"

Laura nodded, then plumped down beside Verity. They were waiting for Miss Hetty Devine to return from her gig parked under the porte cochere. The vehicle was laden with samples of cottons, brocades, silks, and sarcenets. Verity had to admit, even if it seemed disloyal to Cassy Tate, that she had never seen such an opulent selection. The choice of colors was absolutely delectable. But then her eye caught her and Laura's reflection in the mirror. She looked at Laura, and they promptly collapsed with laughter.

They were dressed alike in a strange unbleached linen garment which was, except for certain missing appointments, a perfectly tailored dress. Instead of sleeves, it had thin camisole straps. It was cut in the latest style, very high-waisted, outrageously low of neckline, and just enough room in between to cover the bust.

It was Miss Hetty's custom to make what she termed "a cutter" for her ladies, before she cut into any actual dress yardage. The cutter was her prototype, a pattern to follow, except that it was completely sewn, finished, and fitted to perfection on the customer. Of course, the final articles would be modestly supplemented with sleeves of various shapes, lace inserts, overskirts, and all manner of ornamental gatherings, but here in the cutter was the basic line.

"The line, ladies, the line," Miss Hetty liked to say, "that is the secret of all proper costuming. The rest is mere frippery."

This was the second and final fitting of the cutter,

and now, at last, the girls would be able to choose colors and fabrics, and the details of styling.

"You've become quite the lady, Laura, complete with a proper bosom," Verity remarked, causing her cousin's eyes to drop to her neckline proudly.

"Is it too much, do you think?"

Verity laughed. "No, it's just right. And now you have a young man who's mad for you. I wish you would tell me his name, Laura. Why all the mystery?"

"Not a word," Laura said. "It's to be a surprise until tonight."

"Ah, he's one of those redcoats coming tonight. Is he handsome?"

Laura replied by placing a forefinger over pursed lips. Verity gave up, climbed off the bed, and took a turn before the pier glass.

"You and your surprises! You're quite as addicted to them as I am to the news of the day," she said, and bent to the colored muslins that lay heaped on the carpet. One by one, she held them up, testing the colors against her face. "Do you plan to encourage him? Perhaps accept his offer?"

"He hasn't offered for me yet," Laura said, "but I certainly wouldn't accept anyone before we go to London. What a fearful waste that would be! There might be someone much better there," she pointed out reasonably.

"Laura!" Verity draped a length of peach muslin around her shoulders and pirouetted. "What a thing to say! You are so—*ouch*! This cutter is scratchy."

"I'm so what?" When she received no answer save a smile, Laura scrambled across the bed and reached out to tweak Verity's hair. "What am I then?" she persisted. "A lady should finish her sentences."

"You are . . . practical. That's what you are. A practical imp."

Aunt Maria burst back into the room, followed by Miss Hetty and more of her samples.

"Put them on the bed, Hetty. My niece can look at

them while you finish my daughter's cutter. Let's get that over with—the waist still droops on the left, I believe." She turned to Laura.

"Stop lolling about, girl, and stand up for Miss Hetty."

Aunt Maria stood stout as a tree in her plum alpaca, the fingers of one hand drumming impatiently on the ecru lace at her throat, while the girls changed places.

Laura obediently took up her position again before the mirror, and Aunt Maria reached out and pinched her sharply on each cheek.

"Ooh, aah, ouch, Mama!"

"Pale as paper you are, child," her mother complained. "I shall be glad when you turn sixteen and it will be proper to use the rouge pot on you. I daresay you will, too. Be sure to pinch up before you come down tonight. You're a perfectly healthy gel, so there's no need to go about looking like a sickly creature."

She turned at the sound of Margaret, who had just reentered the bedroom, rustling the newspaper.

"Don't bring that filthy *Clarion* in here, Margaret," Aunt Maria stormed. "What are you doing with it?"

"I told her to, Mama. Verity wanted to read it."

Aunt Maria cast her niece an impatient glance. "No doubt she did, but not in here, she won't. That black newsprint rubs off on simply everything. I won't have it near the upholstery or your clothes." She had become a field marshal, directing her attention to every corner of the room.

"Pins, Margaret! More pins for Miss Hetty.

"And you are not to call your cousin by that Quakish name, Laura. I've told you before. She is Caroline Debenham Cox—and I want you both to remember that in London.

"If you *must* read it, child, you can do it later in the library, where it belongs. You don't have time to bother with that now. Good heavens, we have work to do.

"Heavens, Margaret, don't put it on the carpet!

We'll have ink stains from here to China. No, don't put it anywhere. Take it back to the library table.

"Straight, straight, child, or we'll have it drooping on the other side. You weren't born with one hip higher than the other, so please do not stand as if you were."

Verity sat amid a rainbow of silks and velvets, watching the activity come to a boil and wishing she could sneak out to the library and read the paper in peace. Well, there would be a quiet spell before they dressed for dinner. Meanwhile, she tried to avoid her aunt's attention and devoutly hoped her own cheeks were pink enough to escape pinching.

It was two hours before she was released from Miss Hetty. She slipped quickly into a blue wrapper and ran downstairs in search of the *Clarion*. The article was on page three:

MANCHESTER MILL RIOT AVERTED

Some 60,000 persons carrying banners gathered Monday in St. Peter's Fields to listen to the oration of Mr. Leigh Hunt of London. The meeting was dispersed after a troop of hussars was called to the scene. The unfortunate resistance of some participants led to more than fifty injuries, eleven of them fatal.

There was reason to believe that Mr. Hunt planned to incite the crowd to set fire to the homes of certain Manchester millowners following the meeting.

Mr. Hunt, who denied the allegation, was arrested at the scene. A week ago in Denning, a similar gathering was dispersed without incident or injury. On that occasion, Mr. Hunt was warned to cease all public appearances. He is now in Manchester gaol on charges of disturbing the peace and incitement to insurrection.

Verity threw the paper down angrily and pulled her wrapper tightly around her. Those dreadful hussars! Waves of disbelief, then shock washed over her as she stared down at the library table. Mr. Hunt could never have meant harm. She didn't believe a word of it. Why, Papa had spoken of him with open admiration. The two men had even corresponded.

"If tha' don't get a move on, Miss Verity, tha'll be 'aving a stone-cold bath," Sarah called from the doorway. She stood arms akimbo, looking very vexed with her mistress. "Margaret's 'alfway done with Miss Laura's 'air, and tha's not even started."

Silently, Verity followed Sarah back to her room, where a brass tub stood steaming.

Immersed in warm water, Verity smelled the rising fragrance of citronella and was comforted. But how she wished she were spending the evening with Papa, instead of a group of detestable redcoats. She didn't care how handpicked they were. They were monsters. After the bath, she wrapped herself in a towel, and sent Sarah over to Laura's room with a message. She had decided to beg off with a headache and stay in her room. If she couldn't be with Papa, at least she wouldn't spend the evening exchanging silly inanities with barbarians dressed as gentlemen.

Laura burst into her room just moments later. "But you can't, you can't, Verity!" She stood in her petticoats, her hair in shining ringlets, and her eyes tragically large. "Oh, dearest coz, it was all planned just for your pleasure. Please don't be ill now."

"It's nothing serious," Verity assured her. "I just don't feel up to company tonight."

"You should not have let your bath cool off so much. I knew it! You have caught a chill."

Verity shook her head vigorously, wishing Laura would not make such a to-do.

"No? Then it was too hot, and you've come over queer. I know how to cure that with smelling salts. Don't worry," she sang out, turning for the door. "You'll be right as rain in a jiffy."

"No!" Verity called out after the fleeing figure. "It

is not a physical condition. Please, Laura, don't fetch anything. It won't help."

Verity found herself suddenly telling all, starting with her mishap in Denning, and ending with the tragic account she had just read in the *Clarion*.

Laura's eyes brimmed with sympathetic tears, and she gave Verity a hug. "Oh, that's awful, just awful."

"So you do understand, Laura? I have no wish to socialize this evening. Particularly with redcoats."

"No, I don't understand. They were not to blame. They were only doing their duty," Laura said.

"But they killed unarmed people."

"I'm sure it was accidental. It was such a large, unruly crowd. Besides, none of the fellows you will meet tonight were responsible. They couldn't even be here if they had been in Manchester yesterday. Oh, I wish you wouldn't read the journals. I can't bear to see you so overset. You must rise above this. A diverting evening is just the thing to distract you."

"I don't want to be distracted. How can I eat and drink and make merry, when those poor innocent people . . ." Verity's voice trailed off, and she covered her face with her hands.

"Well, well, well, miss!" Laura exclaimed, echoing the tart Shrewsbury governess of her schoolroom days. "And if you don't eat, if you just loll about in your dressing gown all evening, moping and hungry, will it help those poor innocent people?"

Verity looked up in surprise at the sudden starch in her cousin's voice, and saw a stiff chin and a pursed mouth.

"Yes, quite right, cousin! Is it going to help one jot if Miss Cox chooses to ruin our evening and spend it feeling sorry for them? Will it heal any injuries? Or will Miss Cox simply be feeling sorry for herself?"

Laura turned stiffly to Sarah, who was mopping up moisture on the floor where the bathtub had stood. "Get her ready, Sarah. She is coming downstairs tonight."

*   *   *

Her cousin was not entirely at fault, Verity reflected, as she cast a final glance at the ormolu mirror and prepared to join the company. For all her flouncing, Laura sometimes displayed a wisdom beyond her years. Verity's sensibilities could help no one this evening, and perhaps they did amount to little more than self-indulgence. Despite her inclinations, Verity had yielded to her cousin's persuasions, and had consented to dress for the evening.

"Well? 'As tha' nowt to say, lass? Nay?" Sarah held out a delicate ivory fan with an expectant air, bringing Verity back to the pressing business at hand.

"You did beautifully, Sarah. Bless you," Verity said gratefully. And it was no more than the truth.

In less than thirty minutes, Verity was creditably turned out in her ivory poplin gown with overlace of palest apricot. There had been no time to heat curling irons, but Sarah had managed to coax little wisps at brow and temples into those unstudied Grecian love curls that were all the rage. The long, tawny mane was swept up into a silken coil threaded with a ribbon of apricot velvet, the same ribbon that trimmed her dress at neckline and waist. Her skin was glowing and fragrant from the bath, and a tiny gold locket adorned her bare throat.

Planting an appreciative kiss on Sarah's cheek, Verity hurried out into the hall. Thanks to Sarah, she would not after all be noticeably tardy, she thought, as she hurried along the gallery. Descending the staircase, she began to hear muffled voices and laughter, and steeled herself for the introductions.

The Misses Royce from neighboring Teverley Park had been invited to even the numbers, Verity had been told. They were maiden ladies in their middle years and would not impede Verity from having her choice of four "delicious young officers," as Laura had put it. Four vain, conscienceless peacocks, more like it, she thought, and gritted her teeth as she arrived at the bottom of the stairs.

A bewigged footman stood outside the large north drawing room, sentrylike, waiting for the late guest. Verity approached him, and with a movement of the head which managed to convey both respect and disapproval, he swung the doors wide for her.

Inside the drawing room, Lady Strathmore must have been anxiously watching the doors. "At last, Caroline," she said, looking relieved at her niece's arrival. "Mary and I had quite decided you had forgotten your way downstairs. I was on the point of dispatching a search party. Mary, I would like to present my niece, Miss Caroline Debenham Cox. Miss Mary Royce."

Verity found herself exchanging courtesies with a stout lady of pleasant countenance who was decidedly of middle years, just as Laura had promised. Miss Clarissa Royce, to whom she was next presented, was a taller, fiercer version of Miss Mary, and was busily engaged in advising Lord Strathmore on the breeding of collie dogs.

Clustered by the hearth, three stalwart young men in fashionable dress were amusing each other with boisterous anecdotes, but, unlike Miss Clarissa, they were positively eager to break off and be presented. Mr. Sloan Carshalton, Mr. James de Lyons, and Mr. William Bennington-Jones, Verity was informed.

Except that she had expected to see gaudy uniforms of some kind instead of civilian clothes, they were precisely as she had visualized—shallow, vacant-faced, and enormously preoccupied with their appearance. The fourth gentleman she took to be Laura's beau. At his present distance, he appeared to be cut from the same cloth, and was busily fawning over Laura at the far end of the room in a window recess.

"I understand you hail from Denning, Miss Cox. A pleasant enough spot I suppose, if one must be buried in the heart of the country."

This remark, offered by the blondest of the three young men, was for some reason received by the other two as a veritable jewel of wit and provoked a gale of laughter.

Verity groaned inwardly and attempted a smile at the same time. The evening was well and truly begun, and there was no turning back.

"Will you be gracing the London season? You will? Oh, top-hole, Miss Cox."

"The Fifteenth is quartered hard by St. James's. Our billeting here in the north country is ending soon, and we shall all be in town together."

"Then p'rhaps one can look forward to the pleasure of a dance or two at Almack's, durst one hope?"

Verity had not spent an evening with soldiers before, but the patter was achingly familiar. She recognized that she was already adrift in one of those passive conversations one could almost maintain while dozing off. Bored into a light trance, she vaguely heard Aunt Maria's stentorian voice bidding Laura to return to the fold and join the discussion.

Predictably, all other topics exhausted in three minutes, they were now mired in fox-hunting. She had made one feeble attempt to introduce the subject of Mr. Leigh Hunt, but not one of her three wits had ever heard of him. It was just as well, she decided. Aunt Maria would have been scandalized to overhear a discussion on anything so vital as the plight of the working classes. Succumbing to the apathy that often overcame her on such social occasions, Verity let chatter flow over her without complaint.

Mr. Carshalton (or was it Bennington-Jones?) was regaling her with a remorselessly detailed account of an exploit which had taken place in Surrey last year with an "absolute out-and-outer," indeed a "positive corker." She was unsure whether the repeated epithets referred to a horse, a hound, a fellow huntsman, or the unfortunate quarry. But it hardly seemed to matter, as long as she oohed and aahed and smiled in the right places. The object of the interminable story was clear enough: to put the raconteur in the best of lights as a witty, dashing, fearless fellow.

It was with great relief that she felt a tug on her hand and heard Laura's voice at her shoulder.

"Please, gentlemen," Laura said, cutting through the torrent of words, "may I be allowed to borrow my cousin for a tiny moment?"

Verity turned promptly to meet the fourth stalwart young fellow, thinking how indistinguishable they all were, like Mrs. Budgitt's cleverly cut gingerbread men. But the thought vanished when she met the gentleman's eyes. He was somewhat older than the others or at least appeared to betray signs of intelligence, and— *could she be mistaken?*—she had met him before.

"Mr. Patrick Tarkington," Laura said with a proprietary air. "My cousin and very dear companion, Miss Caroline Cox."

"A pleasure, Miss Pox," he whispered over her hand, with the merest ghost of a smile.

—4—

By the time the two cousins set out on their shopping trip the next morning, the heat of the day was making itself felt, but Verity was barely aware of it. In her pale green muslin with puffed sleeves, she drowsed on the banquette, lost in her thoughts.

Laura removed her yellow gauze cape and let the balmy air fan her arms as they rode toward Salford side by side in the open chaise. "You're quiet as a mouse," she remarked, and, when the observation was ignored, turned and noted the faraway look in Verity's eyes.

"Suddenly in love, coz? Smitten by a dashing hussar, perchance?" With her fan, she briskly rapped Verity's knees. "Aha, Cupid's revenge! It is your just deserts after railing so against the redcoats."

Verity rallied herself from the daydream. "Smitten? No, no. Not in the least." She raised one gloved hand in a sheepish little gesture. "Forgive me, Laura. I've been woolgathering."

"You certainly have."

"I slept poorly last night," Verity explained. "What was left of the night when we retired. I fear it was the heat."

She had indeed tossed restlessly in her bed after the long evening had ended, but it was not exactly on account of the weather. The acute discomfort she had felt upon recognizing Mr. Tarkington had been hard to dispel.

Scarcely an hour before joining the party in the drawing room, Verity had been recounting her Denning adventure to Laura, describing a certain dreadful hussar in the most disparaging, the most derisive of terms. And suddenly, the very same man stood before her, being daintily presented by her little cousin. *Laura's beau*! And oh, the insolence in his look of recognition! The appalling intimacy implied in the whispered allusion meant for her ears alone! *A pleasure, Miss Pox.*

Of a sudden, Verity had felt hopelessly compromised, and knew it was showing in the wave of quick warmth that surged from her throat and washed over her face. She could only hope that to the observers, it was as though they were indeed meeting for the first time. His straight-faced pun was the only sign he gave of recognition, after which she sensed a tacit agreement between them to ignore all reference to their prior encounter.

Instant complicity with the loathsome fellow! Once more she shuddered at the memory. There passed between them only the briefest exchange before Aunt Maria mercifully dispelled the moment by announcing that it was time for the gentlemen to escort the ladies in to supper.

Verity could only take comfort in the fact that although she had supplied Laura with a minute account of the Denning incident, she had by the merest chance omitted the name of the offending hussar. In the moment of telling, his name had escaped her. Now she blessed that lapse of memory. How crushed Laura would have been to hear that her very first beau was nothing but an overbearing, ignorant boor. She had come within a word of hurting this sweet child, perhaps losing her friendship forever.

Thoroughly discountenanced, Verity had spent the remainder of the evening allowing Mr. Bennington-Jones to monopolize her, and simulating the most animated interest in his stifling attentions.

Released at last and in her bed, she had firmly resolved never to speak or think ill of anyone again. Never!

"Well, if you are not yet smitten, it is quite clear to me who is," Laura persisted, determined to pursue the soirée and extract from it every last drop of amusing speculation.

Verity squeezed Laura's hand warmly. "Why, Mr. Tarkington is smitten, of course. He makes no bones about it. You have made a resounding conquest, little coz."

Laura giggled and became quite pink with pleasure. "Yes, I know, but you are perfectly aware that I was not alluding to Mr. Tarkington, you tease. You know very well I speak of Mr. Bennington-Jones, my dear. The handsome blond subaltern with the sky-blue eyes— which were turned on you from the moment you made your late entrance." Laura twinkled at her. "Would you have me believe you did not notice his ardent attentions? You scarcely froze him, Verity. It was evident that you weren't in the least averse to his society."

May I never encounter a worse bore, Verity prayed silently, and turned to look at the thrush-laden sycamores that lined the road. As she raised her eyes above the treetops to the shimmering sky, she felt a stab of guilt. She had just resolved not to think ill of anyone. Even Bennington-Jones could not be exempted from such a comprehensive vow. It would be difficult; she was not of the stuff of saints, she realized.

"Mr. Bennington-Jones is a ... pleasant enough fellow, Laura, but you are deceived if you think I was deliberately encouraging him. I was merely being courteous. Not that I find fault with him in any particular, understand," she added hastily, "not in the least. It is simply that ..." Verity faltered, her mind strangely misted with half-formed thoughts. "Surely there should be an indefinable something," she began again uncertainly, "a spark perhaps—er—an intimation of shared—of mutual—" She broke off once more, trying to organize her thoughts. An eddy of disturbing feelings and a vague sadness seemed to catch at her heart and tangle her words, and she almost gave up the attempt to express herself. "I suppose, when one meets the perfect partner, one will know it," she finished lamely.

Laura's smoky eyes became wide with interest. "Do you really believe in love at first sight, then? Do you not think it possible to fall in and out of love many times?"

Verity sighed. "I hardly know what I believe, Laura. Do you feel such a spark for Mr. Tarkington?"

"I know it feels splendid to have so attentive a gallant." Laura's head tilted in thought. "To have many attentive gallants would only increase the pleasure, I should imagine." She clapped her hands and laughed. "Oh, I am so looking forward to the season. I can hardly wait! As for Mr. Tarkington, if he is a foretaste of things to come, I shall enjoy myself hugely. He is terribly attractive, don't you think?"

"Terribly," Verity muttered, and realized it was no more than the truth. Bereft of the absurd uniform and set down in a civilized salon, Patrick Tarkington was indeed a man of most engaging looks. Pricked by the thought, she drew back from it and silently reminded herself of his behavior on the village green. He had very little besides good looks to recommend him.

"Shall we be in Salford soon?" Verity asked.

"Oh, very shortly."

On the vacant banquette facing the girls lay a small silk pouch filled with snippets of dress materials. Verity reached for the pouch and drew Laura into an intense discussion of bonnets.

Angeline Brent was one of the better Lancashire milliners. Her thriving Salford establishment was patronized by the gentry for miles around. She was not, of course, to be compared with the Bond Street milliners. Their more important headwear, calculated to turn heads when they drove through Hyde Park or down St. James's, would be purchased in London. Aunt Maria was timing their arrival in London seven days before the full bloom of the season for that very purpose. But Brent's was up to completing their traveling wardrobe, she'd decided, and having pressing matters to attend to, she had sent the girls off to the local milliner in the good hands of the head coachman, Hennessy.

At Brent's, the girls were confronted with such diversity of choice as would confound the most single-minded of women. After settling on the basic shape, they lingered for two hours over the alternative adornments. For with hats, Miss Hetty's rule of thumb was turned about. It was the trim alone that made the hat exceptional, while the basic line was preordained for the season. Accordingly, Miss Brent's shelves were filled with feathers, flowers, and fantasies of every conceivable color and texture.

By half past five, all decisions had been reached and the orders carefully inscribed in Miss Brent's order book. The girls were to return in a week to fetch their bonnets, and any last-minute changes would be effected in the shop while they waited.

On their homeward journey, they stopped at the Farmer's Pipe for refreshments. According to Laura, the inn was reputed for its table, but Verity found it less remarkable for its collations than for its patrons. It was obviously a favorite haunt of the militia, its walls adorned with all manner of regalia, mementos of battalions who had passed this way while billeted at the nearby cavalry barracks. In the dining room were displayed the insignia of several infantry regiments too. Mounted on the white lath walls and suspended from low beamed ceilings, rusted sabers jostled for space beside ancient muskets, Bonaparte tricornes, and the mounted head of a billy goat, all that remained of some bygone regimental mascot.

Judging from the flow of officers who stopped at their table to greet "my dear Miss Laura," Verity began to suspect that her cousin had made a serious study of the transient military population. She appeared at least to be on the most cordial terms with every swaggering dragoon in the shire.

Arriving home, they were informed that Lady Strathmore was waiting for them in her second-floor sitting room. Seated before a pot of green tea, Aunt Maria greeted them with a minute interrogation, demanding a detailed account of their purchases. Only when she was fully satisfied did she inform Laura that she had received a note. It was lying on Aunt Maria's marbled sideboard, and it was from Mr. Tarkington.

" 'My dear Miss Debenham,' " Laura read aloud. " 'What a delightful evening it was. I had hoped to enjoy the pleasure of your company at least once more before those fortunate Londoners laid eyes upon you, but alas, duty calls. We are ordered back to headquarters a week earlier than anticipated. My memories of last night will have to sustain me until such time as you arrive in London, and are disposed to see me once more—to which event I look forward with great impatience. Your devoted admirer, Patrick Tarkington.' "

Aunt Maria reached for the porcelain teapot, smiling with approval. "Very pretty sentiments. Are you sure you won't have any, gels? Mr. Tarkington has such dainty manners. I have every confidence that he will turn out to be very high-blooded indeed."

"I do hope the entire company is not packed off to London yet," Laura said fervently as they mounted the staircase to their third-floor chambers. "It will be exceeding dull here without the officers."

Laura need not have worried. The remaining days at Strathmore House went by at a gallop, enlivened by a dozen invitations. Boating picnics, farewell-to-summer garden parties, picnic breakfasts, redcoat suppers, and musicales, interspersed at frequent intervals with fussings and fittings conducted by Miss Hetty, all left little time to be dull. If Verity was less than capti-

vated by any of the eligibles who addressed her their
attentions, she was at least beguiled by the sheer
variety of the company. And now that Mr. Tarkington
was safely out of the shire, she was decidedly more at
ease.

On the Tuesday following the visit to Salford, Verity was disconcerted to receive a personal visit from
Mr. Bennington-Jones. He arrived gorgeously arrayed
in dress uniform—turned out, he explained, for the
Tuesday invitational in the officer's mess, where that
evening's guest of honor was to be a colonel of the
Grenadiers.

Satin sash and gold epaulettes notwithstanding, he
was as unremarkable as ever and even more long-
winded than she remembered. The household con-
trived to leave her to his tender mercies, Laura
adamantly refusing to leave her room, where she was
curled up with a vapid romance, and Aunt Maria
insisting that Verity preside over a pot of china tea
and a platter of cucumber sandwiches served in the
small west-wing salon.

There was nothing to be done. The butler withdrew
after depositing refreshments on the rosewood tea
table, and she was trapped. "This is a surprise, sir,"
she said, trying her best not to sound vexed. "I had
assumed your cornet was already on its way to London with Mr. Tarkington's."

Removing immaculate white gloves, Bennington-
Jones accepted a cup of tea from her. "No, not for
another week yet, Miss Debenham Cox. I don't quite
follow your meaning."

"Surely you know of the change in orders? Mr.
Tarkington's cornet was ordered back to St. James's
beforetimes. My cousin received a note to that effect
some days ago."

Holding out the sandwich platter, Verity briefly
wondered if the hussar was very slow-witted or if she
had misunderstood the content of Tarkington's little
billet-doux.

The sandwiches were cut in triangles not much bigger than a large coin, and as Bennington-Jones took just one, Verity had visions of being imprisoned all evening while he nibbled slowly through the tiny morsels.

"Tark is gone, certainly," he said, "but as far as I know, his cornet remains at Doncombe. I was not aware of any change of orders. I rather thought he had taken a personal leave." He nibbled mouselike on the tiny triangle and dismissed the subject. "But let us talk of you, ma'am. Are you too fearfully busy with preparations for the season, or could you take a brief drive into the country tomorrow afternoon? I hardly think this glorious weather will last much longer."

"I am afraid there is far too much still to be done," she answered, seizing gratefully on the excuse he had provided. "But how kind of you to ask."

"Ah, well," he sighed, "I feared as much. I know these things are a devilish onerous undertaking. But we shall all be reunited soon. In London, then. I shall certainly not take no for an answer there."

An interminable hour later, Bennington-Jones took his leave, casting a depressing pall over the prospect of the season. Verity was haunted by the thought of being repeatedly trapped so during their entire stay in London. But for the next fortnight at least, she was spared further visitations from the subaltern. By the day of departure, she had begun to catch Laura's fever of anticipation. The great adventure was about to begin.

The week of arduous coach travel bothered Verity not at all. Once they were south of Stoke, it was all new and beguiling territory to her. She was fascinated by the changing speech patterns and the difference in food preparation as they moved deeper into the Midlands and slowly approached the home counties, which stretched forty miles or so north of the capital.

She sat beside Laura and opposite Lord and Lady Strathmore. The long hours in the phaeton were colored alternately by bursts of animated conversation and extended silences, when the travelers dozed, read, or retrenched into private thoughts. They had brought along draughts and backgammon to while away the hours, and some playing cards.

Intermittently during the week-long journey, Verity's thoughts turned to her prospects for marriage, the *raison d'être* of these elaborate arrangements. Surely there would be a few alternatives to bores like the subaltern and boors like Tarkington, she assured herself. At times, she questioned the rightness of withholding from Laura what she knew of Tarkington's crass character. If he were to offer for Laura, she should of course be informed. But Verity judged her cousin to be entranced with the novelty of conquest, rather than with the man himself. She was so young, such an incorrigible flirt, and so delighted with everything at the moment. Verity had no wish to douse her pleasure from the start. Besides, it was clear from the social whirl in Lancashire that there would be other admirers clamoring for Laura's favor and quite possibly several bids for her hand. She was not only an irresistible charmer, she was the last marriageable Strathmore girl, and the Strathmore name stood for illustrious pedigree and a sizable fortune, to boot. With a little luck, the question of whether or not to reveal Tarkington's rudeness might never come up.

For their overnight stops, the Strathmores avoided the busier towns of Newcastle, Nottingham, and Coventry, wisely selecting a completely rural route and staying at inns in small country villages where the food was fresh, the service obsequious, and the night air sweet and peaceful.

The Wheatsheaf in Edgware was just such an establishment. After a sumptuous roast capon and an hour of whist, Verity and Laura retired to an airy room with dormer windows where they shared a huge bed for the night, as they had done twice before on their journey. But although the feather mattress was plump and clean, and the sheets were redolent of lavender, neither of them slept much for excitement.

On the morrow they would reach London.

—5—

Aunt Maria had described the house as belonging to the Earl of Cadogan. A widower of sixty-two, the earl was permanently retired to his country seat and offered his London house to let under the management of Covington, Penneyfeather, Estate Agents. The residence had been highly recommended for the season by a Strathmore cousin who had brought off a coup from the very same quarters—procuring not one, but two splendid matches for her twenty-six-year-old twin daughters. Who needed to know more? Aunt Maria had written off immediately to the Fleet Street agents to lay claim to 18 Sloane Terrace for the duration of the season.

Tucked behind Sloane Square just a mile from Hyde Park, number 18 was one of a row of tall, elegant Georgian town houses, such as graced Mayfair. But unlike Mayfair, the quiet neighborhood was well removed from the raucous hurly-burly of Shepherd Market. The family's early-morning slumbers would be undisturbed by the noise of street hawkers.

Covington, Penneyfeather had engaged the domestic staff one week prior to their arrival, following Aunt Maria's definitive instructions: ". . . so that the premises be thoroughly cleaned, aired, stocked with food and drink, and the beds made up against our arrival."

The butler, Grimshaw, had arrayed the entire staff

to greet them, lined up in order of rank from cook to stable boy. Aunt Maria inspected, approved, and asked for a thorough tour of the house.

The reception rooms were wide, high, and in good repair. Aunt Maria was less than enthusiastic about the furniture, which was somewhat older than the house, dating back to Queen Anne. The main salons, however, boasted several good pieces, and if the chaises and occasional tables were somewhat passé, the soft furnishings were faultless, as she pointed out in a running commentary to the girls who trailed behind her. Good Irish table linens, spotless sheets and towels, quality brocades at the windows, and upholstery newly refurbished in pleasing burgundies and blues.

It was one of Grimshaw's first duties upon their arrival to inform Miss Laura that a calling card had been left three days ago by a Mr. Tarkington.

"Ah, Laura," Verity teased, when they had at last closeted themselves in her bedroom, "your swain is truly breathless for your arrival. We shall find him pale and thin from pining for you these past weeks. Have you not missed him too?"

"About as much as you missed Bennington-Jones," Laura retorted, bouncing on Verity's bed.

Finally released from his close confinement with three females, Uncle George had vanished. He had sprung away sometime during their prolonged tour of the house with the alacrity of a furry creature sprung from a woodsman's trap.

"Your papa has gone to find his London cronies," Aunt Maria explained, joining the girls in Verity's room. "The diversion is well earned, and we won't see much of him for a se'nnight I daresay. And that is just as it should be, for we have much to do. We shall call on Lady Sefton immediately for our Almack's vouchers, and first thing tomorrow, we must address ourselves to the shopping."

As Sarah began to unpack Verity's trunks, Aunt Maria opened drawers, inspecting every corner for cobwebs. "We shall neither receive nor accept invitations before we are all complete," she announced, darting behind the drapes and examining the hems for lint. "We shall open the season with the first Wednesday assembly on King Street—only eight days hence if we count this one—and the forenoon is already gone!"

The hectic days dissolved into a collage for Verity, a pastiche of Regent Street arcades, smart Bond Street shops, and mazes of little alleys north of Piccadilly where the best glovers and hosiers were to be found. Thanks to Aunt Maria's frenzied pace, they were complete with silk stockings, gloves, fashionable boots, dancing slippers, elaborate bonnets, and fur pelisses by the time the Great Wednesday arrived.

To the girls' mutual surprise, Lady Strathmore insisted they rise early on Wednesday morning, and when they joined her over toast and Dundee marmalade, she looked rather solemn.

"There is one more task before you this morning," she told the girls reluctantly, "and then you may rest for the remainder of the day, until it is time to dress for the assembly." She cleared her throat and stared into her steaming coffee cup, as if she were at a loss how to begin.

"You have all the social graces, of course, but London being the pace-setter it is, you could not possibly have been prepared for the new rage. It is an Austrian dance popularized by the Tsar on his visit to London last season. I have it on the best authority that it is now *de rigueur* at Almack's."

Laura's sleepiness instantly yielded to wide-eyed alertness. "A new dance? However shall we learn it before tonight, Mama?"

"I have engaged the services of a dancing master for that very purpose. He is waiting below. The dance is, one might say, rather innovative, but fortunately very simple, he tells me. One lesson should suffice."

Aunt Maria was toying with her toast without eating it, as if she were uneasy.

"I can't say I care for the idea at all," she burst out after a moody silence. "But you cannot appear like graceless country bumpkins. Therefore we shall repair to the salon for instruction as soon as you have finished your chocolate." She heaved a sigh, as if her statement marked the end of an ordeal, and at last took a sip of coffee. "Meanwhile, gels, I shall admonish you on the subject of tonight's gathering." Her face became more cheerful.

"Almack's Assembly Rooms offer by far the most exclusive assembly in the civilized world."

"*Bien sur,*" Laura put in. "Presided over by the Lord High Mucky-Muck, Lady Sefton." She was treated to a stately frown from her mother intended to squelch further frivolity.

"Lady Sefton is one of several ladies of the highest rank in whose hands lies the privilege of admission, miss. It is not granted lightly," Aunt Maria continued in a tone colored by mild reproof.

"Of all the officers you have met in Lancashire, scarce one in a hundred will meet Almack's requirements. It goes without saying that while you are there, neither of you gels need have qualms about accepting any prospective dance partner or about being agreeable to any gentleman to whom you are presented. They will all be of impeccable birth and breeding, without exception. Do I make myself clear?"

"Yes, Mama," Laura said impatiently, pushing back her chair. "May we go down for our dance lesson now?"

"Furthermore," Aunt Maria continued, gesturing Laura to remain seated, "it would be most inappropriate for you to show the least partiality to any one man at the very beginning of the season. To encourage a proprietary manner in one fellow could severely discourage the rest, thereby narrowing your choice

unnecessarily. Besides which, it simply isn't done."
She gave a brief smile.

"I trust both of you will dance with as many partners as ask you, and on no account dance this new figure twice with the same man."

Laura drained her chocolate cup and dabbed her lips hastily with the serviette. "Why not?"

Verity saw her aunt's uneasiness return. "You'll see soon enough. The position one assumes is far more intimate than joined hands. Furthermore, one is, as it were, locked to the same partner, not just for one measure, but throughout the entire dance. This abomination is called the waltz."

Both girls had heard of the waltz's notoriety. It was still beyond the pale in the provinces, and they hadn't imagined finding themselves actually taking instruction. Verity carefully avoided Laura's glance, suspecting that if their eyes met under Aunt Maria's discomforted stare, they would both start to giggle.

Silk-liveried footmen took their wraps, and in the great foyer, Lady Sefton greeted them, introducing the Strathmore party to two more luminaries of King Street, Mrs. Drummond Burrell and the Princess Esterhazy, who was known to familiars as Countess Lieven, wife of the Russian ambassador. Verity decided that Almack's was indeed very grand.

The great ballroom was ringed by promenading spectators while the center was taken up by some thirty couples on the dance parquet, performing a fast reel. On slim fluted columns above their heads hung the musicians' balcony, adorned with scarlet quilted silk, a splendid aerie from which to overlook the main floor where the *haut monde*, aglitter in diamonds and silks, disported themselves in dance or quizzing under the gleam of crystal chandeliers.

Verity cringed inwardly now that the time had come to appear publicly in one of Miss Hetty's daring ball gowns. At the modiste's insistence, her décolletage was far lower than she had ever worn before. But eyeing the display of blatant bosoms all around her now, she was somewhat reassured. Her dress was peach blush (Miss Hetty's term) with a creamy border of Brussels lace at hem and neckline, which did far more to draw attention to the curves of her breasts than to veil them. She often wondered why that spot was still called a neckline, when in fact it was several critical inches below neck and throat. It was hard not to reach up with her long silk gloves and cover the naked expanse. Laura seemed to have no such difficulty. In her violet satin with lavender trim, she wore her bosom proudly and easily, and thought nothing of it.

Awed by the sheer number of aristocrats assembled, Verity began to wish she would spy just one familiar face, but the first one she spotted was scarcely a comfort. It was Mr. Bennington-Jones. Her heart sank at the idea of his name being the first inscribed on her dance card, but he was bearing down on her. There was no eluding him. Summoning as much courtesy as she could, she wrote his name against the cotillion, number seventeen on her program, consoling herself that since they had arrived during the progress of the fifth dance of the evening, there was hope at least that he would not be the very first man she danced with.

He was not. Having completed a circular tour of the room, they took their position beside Aunt Maria's chair, and began to accept a flurry of dance requests from elegant strangers whose demeanors ranged from the faintly cordial to the markedly condescending.

Lady Strathmore had been right; aside from Bennington-Jones, there was hardly a face she recognized from Lancashire. For Verity, the evening soon deteriorated into a weary procession of men whose names and faces were quickly forgotten. Laura's evening seemed to be taking much the same turn, with the important difference that her cousin was enjoying it all enormously.

Buck up, girl, Verity told herself as she was escorted back to Aunt Maria's rallying point after a fast waltz. You are mingling with *la crème de la crème*. But her latest partner had been an elderly marquis who had succeeded in mastering the clockwise steps, but not the reverse. He had made no conversation during the dance, and upon Verity's curtsy had mumbled, "Pleasure marm," with his eyes turned toward the supper room.

The bluest blood in all England did not make for the most scintillating company, and Verity's spirits began to evaporate. During a brief intermission in the music, fatigue overtook her and she sank down on Aunt Maria's vacant chair, watching the general flow of guests toward the refreshments.

"The mademoiselle appears to be in dire need of liquid refreshment," a voice purred. "May I escort you to the buffet table?"

With a rush of pleasure, she recognized the accent of Monsieur de Roncy and sprang to her feet, delighted. "What a pleasant surprise, monsieur."

An elegant sight in his gleaming burgundy velvet, the Frenchman kissed her hand, then slipped it through his arm and led her toward the open doors beneath the musicians' balcony.

"Ah, you are astonished to see me here, no? But we French have our connections too, mamselle. Countess Lieven is an Esterhazy by birth, and so too was my *grandmaman*."

"Oh, it was not that I doubted you could pass muster in this princely paradise, I assure you," she said happily. "I am merely surprised to see you still in England. I thought you had left our shores." Verity felt vitality seep back into her bones at the thought of a lively conversation.

"Tomorrow I leave for the coast to return to France. But tonight, by dint of traveling almost six days and nights from Ireland, I am just arrived in London." He grinned appealingly. "And famished. I cannot remember my last civilized meal."

As they entered the supper room, the music resumed and a trickle of guests began to leave the buffet table.

"Splendid," he said, squeezing Verity's arm and skirting the flow of departing guests. "We shall have the table almost to ourselves."

But the table was no great prize for a serious eater. It was laden, disappointingly, with thin slices of bread and butter, rather stale cake, and crystal pitchers of lemonade.

Verity looked at the miserable offering in dismay. "Poor monsieur! It is hardly a traveler's feast at the end of a journey."

He shrugged and gave a hearty chuckle. "*Le manger de l'haut monde*. No matter, some bread will suffice." Armed with glasses and a tiny plate of bread, they looked for a place to sit, but the chairs against the wall were all occupied.

Through the glass doors at the far end of the room, Verity noticed a balcony with a vacant cushioned banquette. They headed for it, but once through the doors it became clear why the balcony was deserted. It had rained during the day and the seat cushions were soaked. All other useful furniture had been removed owing to the recent downpour. The nook that beckoned so invitingly from inside the supper room was nothing but a wet, deserted shelf overlooking the quiet backyards of King Street. But they lingered, for the night was mild and sweet and it was quieter than inside.

Drink in one hand and plate in the other, de Roncy looked around for a place to settle. Verity saw that she had better hand-feed him his bread or he would starve for lack of a third hand.

Enchanted with this idea, he began to eat from her fingers, but after one bite his eye caught a flat section of the parapet where there was room to set down his glass and plate. "Ah, *ça suffit*," he said, declining the slice of bread in her gloved fingers.

"But you will perish, monsieur," she said lightly, offering the bread to his lips once more.

He caught her wrist, took the bread from her, and laid it back on the plate. "When I can feast my eyes on you, mamselle, I can no longer feel hunger . . . not hunger for bread, you understand." He smiled an amused smile, and the intimate expression in his eyes made his meaning clear enough.

A small tremor stole through Verity. After a stiflingly proper evening, de Roncy's boldness was like a breath of fresh air. As he relieved her of her lemonade glass, his eyes rested so tellingly on her bosom that she would have covered it reflexively with her hands had he not instantly captured them in his.

"*Verité.*" It was little more than a sigh. "Your name means truth, mamselle. I cannot therefore be less than truthful about my presence here tonight." His hands slid slowly to her shoulders, and the sudden candor that gleamed in his dark eyes caused her to catch her breath.

"And the truth is?" she prompted.

"I am here only because of you—to have one word alone with you." His casual flirtatiousness yielded to something more serious, infinitely more urgent. "Perhaps it will be my last chance to speak to you before you are married."

Verity remembered that he was still under the false impression, created by Aunt Maria, that she was spoken for. She was about to correct that falsehood when his forefinger touched her brow and tenderly traced her hairline, leaving a tingling in its wake that made her forget every word Aunt Maria had ever uttered.

"You must surely know that I adore you, Verity," he murmured.

Astonishment brought her somewhat to her senses and she groped for a diplomatic reply. "Adore me?

Come, monsieur, I am aware that you find me pleasing to look on, but—"

"Pleasing to look on!" His arms encircled her. "Do you not think I would have begged for your hand long before this if it were not for my church and my family?" His mouth hovered a mere finger's breadth from hers.

"But I *cannot*," she exclaimed, releasing herself from his embrace with a somewhat reluctant effort.

He let her go without protest. "No, you cannot, of course. And I cannot. But I want you to know that I shall never love another as I love you." Much as his expression was colored with the most poignant sentiment, Verity wondered if he weren't perhaps being a trifle theatrical.

Instinctively, she decided to laugh off the incident. "Nonsense, monsieur! You are the scion of an ancient family. Of course you will marry."

"Yes, of course." His reply was brittle, the tone so impatient that she scarcely knew what to make of it. "Could you love me?" he asked urgently.

It was outrageous. Had they not this very second agreed that marriage between them was out of the question? He caught her in his arms once more, and trapped in the small, persuasive circle, she was finding it increasingly difficult to remain detached and amused. *Could she love him?*

"The question is surely quite academic, monsieur."

"Far from it. The question is practical. I must know—I insist on knowing. You will doubtless be married within the year, and it is—"

"In that case, it is far better that you do not know." There was a treacherous shake in her voice.

He looked imploringly into her eyes. "Verity, I beg you to tell me. Do you not understand? Once you are married, we could at long last be lovers. I have dreamed of that moment. No! Do not look at me like that. I know very well that it is the same here as it is in France."

For a moment she was speechless as he pressed her even closer to his breast, intense and powerfully determined.

"Aristocrats have all the privileges save one. They cannot marry for love. Therefore, as you must surely know, it is quite acceptable—no, *necessary*—in the name of all that is reasonable and merciful—"

This time, when she tried to wrench away from him, he did not allow it.

"But I shall marry for love and for absolutely no other reason, I can assure you," she managed to say at last. By now, he held her so fast, she was obliged to tilt back her head in order to address his face.

His grip relaxed just a shade as he sighed. "You must marry as your aunt and uncle see fit, *ma chère*. Now I understand why you take so long about it. You are still looking for love where it is never found." He took her chin in his fingers and tenderly brought her face to his until she could feel his breath on her cheeks as he spoke. "Look no longer, I implore you," he whispered, and his lips came closer.

Just as she found her own lips about to meet his, the moment was shattered by a jarring voice.

"Oh, there you are, Miss Cox. Your aunt has been looking everywhere for you."

She started, blushing furiously, and de Roncy released her at once.

Patrick Tarkington leaned tall and lazy in the doorway, a not too amiable smile on his face. For a moment, she fancied a flash of intensity in his eyes, a suppressed fury that hardly matched the casualness of his words.

Verity's confusion froze her to the spot like a startled hare, trapped between hound and hunter with no escape. She was quite beyond mending the scene, incapable of any coherent explanation. For a long moment all she could do was stare, first at Tarkington, lazing in the doorway apparently waiting for her to stir herself, then at de Roncy, who was looking at the intruder with the most curious expression, almost as if he were appraising a painting.

"*Tiens, tiens,*" he muttered. "*Le nez tout à fait comme—peut-être je suis déçu. Mais le comportement, le menton . . .*"

The nose? The bearing? The chin? Why on earth was he gazing rapt into Tarkington's face and mumbling nonsense when he should be carefully retrieving the situation? Verity wondered. She was in desperate need of the Frenchman's delicate diplomacy at this moment, but he seemed utterly absorbed in his own speculations. There seemed little hope that he would address himself to the present impasse or make the least effort to restore her threatened propriety with some tactful excuse.

At last she rallied herself, and mumbling quite as unintelligibly as de Roncy, she bestirred herself, brushed past Tarkington, and fled back through the doors. Taking the arched antechamber in the supper room, she found her way to a quiet ladies' retreat. She was relieved to find the small sanctuary empty save for an attendant. Waving the woman away, Verity sank down on a chaise longue to compose her thoughts.

Frantic questions tumbled through her mind. How long had Tarkington been standing there before making his presence known? Exactly how much indiscretion had he overheard? And why had he glowered at her so—or had she merely imagined it? Could she dare hope that a man like Tarkington would be discreet? How long had Lady Strathmore missed her?

It was no use. She could think of numberless questions, but not one comforting answer. There was nothing to be gained now by tarrying in this boudoir, she decided. She must show herself to Aunt Maria before Tarkington did.

The orchestra struck up a bourrée as she emerged from her retreat. Not only Aunt Maria would be missing her now, but her partner for this promised dance. With head down and eyes glued to the intricate floral

design of the long carpet runner, she hurried through
the supper room toward the dance floor.

"No cause to hurry, Miss Cox. Your partner will
wait patiently for your arrival, no doubt." Tarkington
spoke lazily as he stood blocking her path to the main
room. Taking her hand, he pressed something into it.
Barely noticing, her fingers curled around a small
folded card.

"But my aunt—"

"Has not missed you for a moment," he cut in.

She looked up into his face, utterly bewildered.
Aunt Maria had dispatched him to fetch her, he'd
said. Had she misheard?

"That was a mere invention on my part, Miss Cox.
Quick thinking. I merely intended to rescue you from
a situation which could scarcely have been to your
liking."

Anger stirred in her bosom. The insufferable, self-
righteous meddler! How dare he set himself up as the
guardian of her propriety?

"Sir, you are not in a position to decide what is and
what is not to my liking. I shall thank you not to
meddle in my affairs in future."

"A thousand apologies, ma'am." He gave a broad
grin. "I see that I was mistaken. It was all quite to
your liking, then. In that case, it seems I have deprived you of a kiss. A simple enough matter to mend,
if you . . . Ah! I see Sir James Doughty approaching.
No doubt in search of his elusive partner for the
bourrée." He bowed. "Until number thirty, then," he
murmured, and stepped aside to make way for the
dignified gentleman who was about to claim her for
the dance already in progress.

Until number thirty? But there was no time to
puzzle. Tarkington was gone, and the imposing silver-
haired gentleman who reminded her of Uncle George
was offering an imperious arm to lead her into the
dance.

Mechanically, she went through the motions of the

Gallic jig. The name of her partner she had promptly forgotten—indeed, he might as well have been faceless. As she dipped and paced, bobbed and chasséed in perfect rhythm, her mind darted back over the jumbled events of the last half hour.

Verity was aware of the routinely unfaithful marriages of the stylish set, of course, but in Lancashire, such topics were never discussed in front of her. Scandals were something one associated with the less reputable gossip journals, current novels of a certain type which she never read, and, of course, with the court of the Prince Regent. Gossip circulated more freely in London salons, but still, in her own personal experience, the concept of adultery lacked all reality. It existed, like the gibbet at Tyburn, as a recognized fact, but quite outside her own imaginable future. Certainly she had never before actually entertained an open invitation to adultery, so flagrant, so calculated . . . and yet so unexpectedly disarming. *And from Etienne de Roncy, of all people, who had been a frequent guest at Briarley!*

But what most shocked her was her own reaction. She had actually found herself responding shamelessly to his advances. If it had not been for the interruption, she would have allowed his kiss. It would have constituted an implicit consent to his indecent proposal, no less.

She cast an anxious eye down the line of dancers and was relieved to see that the Frenchman was nowhere in sight. Yes, she had to confess it, the unexpected urgency of her own response had caught her completely off guard, and would have found her wantonly encouraging the Frenchman's ardor, had it not been for that odious Tarkington.

Silently she cursed the hussar, knowing that she should more properly thank him; he had saved her from being compromised. But he had also prevented her from receiving her first kiss, she thought wistfully. How thoroughly detestable he was! Such a hateful habit he had, too, of appearing out of nowhere with apparently no other purpose than to embarrass her. By his own admission, he had not after all been sent by Lady Strathmore to find her. A mere invention, he'd confessed. He had no stake whatever in her morals, her propriety, or her marriageability. Why, in heaven's name, was he stalking her like a chaperon?

And then the meaning of his parting remark dawned— he was referring to her dance program. Number thirty was still open. But he had never requested a dance from her. Suddenly she remembered the card still clasped between her fingers. He had pressed it into her hands when he stopped her progress in the supper room.

Of course! In the heat of the moment, she must have dropped it on the balcony without noticing. Tarkington had retrieved it as, a month ago, he had retrieved her parasol under equally frightful circumstances. The man was a walking, stalking plague. What unspeakable gall! He had actually read her dance card and had taken the liberty of writing in his own name against the one dance still free before returning it to her.

She nodded distractedly to Laura as she twirled past partnered by a jovial, ruddy-faced young man. Number thirty was the dance after this. She had quite deliberately kept it free, because it was another waltz. Having drawn the three most uninspired gentlemen in the gathering for the previous waltzes, she had meant to wait for a more personable partner with whom to share the last one of the evening.

She cringed. So the last waltz was to be spent in the hussar's arms. And to add insult to injury, she would have to be civil. She must ensure his discretion, or she was undone!

By the time she was returned to a beaming Lady Strathmore, Verity was seething with resentment.

"I hope you are as pleased with the evening as I am,

child." Aunt Maria positively glowed. "It is going along splendidly, is it not?"

"Splendidly," Verity replied, fanning herself vigorously to cool her inflamed cheeks.

Laura arrived, dismissing with a curtsy the florid fellow who deposited her at Lord Strathmore's side. Verity's young cousin seemed to bubble over with glee.

"Oh, Verity," she whispered, "such fun! I've enough stories to keep us up all night when we get home. I've been too busy dancing to catch up with you before. And it seems you've been busy too." She launched into a string of names and descriptions of her dance partners. "And have you noticed? Mr. Tarkington is here. I've danced with him, and—"

"And now your cousin will dance with him," a voice whispered just above Verity's right shoulder. Tarkington had stolen up silently again, almost startling her out of her wits. He nodded genially to Lady Strathmore, then bowed to Verity as Laura skittered away, claimed by a tall dandy in rose velvet.

He was forever stealing up on her, Verity observed. He had cat feet, she was convinced of it. She closed her fan with an eloquent click and her eyes blazed with suppressed anger as she slid into his arms for the waltz. Instinctively, her own arms became rigid, as if to hold him at bay.

Tarkington held her lightly and guided her across the polished floor. After a few moments, he cleared his throat. "Your arms should be bent at the elbow, Miss Cox. Not quite so stiff."

How dare he! She could not disagree, of course. The relaxed position was required by the style of the dance; she had learned that from the dancing master only that morning. In order not to draw undue attention to herself, she was obliged to bend her arms, which had the effect of bringing her closer to her partner. Her fury came to a boil.

"You *stole* this dance from me," she exploded.

He threw back his head and laughed. "Why, so I did, Miss Cox. You conveniently allowed me to steal it. You are something of a dropper, ma'am."

"A what?"

"You drop things," he explained gently. "A parasol here, a dance program there." He arched one eyebrow, then with a slight pressure at her waist, brought her unpardonably close.

She struggled with conflicting voices; one which told her, against all reason, that she was quite content to be held thus, the other protesting that this was an outrage. Outrage won, and she strained away, forcing her head back as far as she could to avoid having her brow graze his chin.

Apparently unaware of her inner turmoil, Tarkington went on in a cordial vein. "And when you drop things, it appears to be my role to retrieve for you. What will it be next, one wonders? A handkerchief perhaps?"

At the insulting setdown, Verity was tempted to pull away and desert him in the midst of the dancers. But she dared not forget that she was at his mercy. How mortifying! One word from him about that scene with de Roncy could, if not totally ruin her, at least cause a great deal of distress. He was well aware of the fact and taking advantage of it in the most exasperating way. She resigned herself to see the dance through to the bitter end.

Her teeth gritted behind her smile, she allowed him to sweep her around and around the polished floor. After a few moments he fell silent, apparently deciding he had provoked her enough, and as the dance progressed her anger relented enough for her to consider him objectively.

If one could set aside his outrageous behavior at Denning, he was, to be quite fair, a man of considerable charm and wit. His intrusion on the balcony might have been occasioned by a genuine concern for her. Had she indeed needed rescuing? Quite possibly, if de Roncy's ardor had gone completely out of bounds.

The Frenchman had taken her completely by surprise, and she was deplorably unschooled in how to handle such encounters. Since de Roncy's intentions were quite openly dishonorable, there was no resorting to the excuse of harmless flirtation. The fury she had directed against Tarkington should more accurately have been aimed at de Roncy for his blackguard's assumption, and at herself for her own mindless response.

This evening she seemed to be given to mindless responses, she thought, suddenly aware that for the past few minutes she had been unconsciously enjoying the pressure of Tarkington's hand at her waist, supporting her as she leaned back into the circles they were describing as they wove deftly past other twirling couples. Instantly she stiffened, reminding herself that they were in no sense of the word a couple, except for the brief space of this waltz. Tarkington's cap was set at Laura, not herself. And besides, one could never set aside his outrageous behavior at Denning. It was all part and parcel of the man, a hussar and a barbarian.

Only during the last bars of the waltz did he break the silence between them. "I seem to have caused you the most acute distress," he said with genuine remorse. "If my person is displeasing to you, I apologize."

With a strange reluctance she heard the musicians waft into the closing chords. Tarkington searched her face gravely and waited for her reply, but she could think of nothing à propos to say.

"I shall not be so bold as to dance with you again," he murmured, releasing her and bowing.

She rose from her curtsy with a cold glance. "That will be more than satisfactory."

— 6 —

Lady Strathmore was more than pleased with the season's opening. Miss Hetty's pains over the gowns had been gratifyingly justified; both girls were a credit to her, their attire always *dernier cri* without ever being shockingly *avant-garde*, and their respective looks contrasted interestingly enough to bring attention to both of them. They would, she decided, make their indelible mark on the *ton*.

Following the eventful Wednesday evening, Verity found herself plunged into a relentless round of theater parties, salon crushes, routs, receptions, teas, and every other conceivable social event that provided a setting for the marriage stakes. Any excuse for a gathering was acceptable as long as it enabled eligible males to be presented. The resourcefulness of noble dowagers in their matchmaking activities never ceased to amaze her.

As the weeks wore on, Tarkington's behavior was so unimpeachable that Verity's fear that he might betray her indiscretion began to fade away completely, and alas, along with it faded the spice and novelty of the London season.

Although the month of October went by at a dizzying pace, and although Laura seemed tireless and bubbling over with vivacity, Verity began to find it all a trifle wearying. Nothing occurred that could compare with the excitement and eventfulness of her first evening at Almack's, and now that the dangerous de Roncy had departed the scene, doubtless finding greener pastures in the Paris salons, Verity found a certain tedium, an undeniable silliness, in the repeated social exercises.

Worse still, Bennington-Jones had become a pest. Near her wit's end to discourage him, Verity was often driven to feigning keen interest in the most indifferent of men in order to avoid the leechy subaltern's attentions. It was to no avail. He would stalk her at salons and balls, and he called on her with growing frequency. Much to her vexation, he appeared to be on the list of every hostess in London.

Not so, Tarkington. He never appeared at Almack's again, and although he seemed to have the most serious intentions toward Laura, his appearances among the *haut monde* were curiously sporadic. He kept himself fresh in Laura's mind, however, by plying her with bonbons, posies, and graceful little notes when he was obliged to absent himself from town for a few days. Regardless of the unexplained demands on his time, his constancy to the object of his affections was unquestionable; he meant business.

If Laura was at first flattered by his attentions, time did nothing to increase her regard for him. There seemed to be an inexhaustible supply of young eligibles in the capital, and as they presented themselves to Laura and fell under her elfin charm, she promptly lost her heart to one after another in such rapid succession that it was quite clear she was by no means ready to commit herself to a partner ... at least, not for more than two or three days at a stretch.

It must surely be clear to Tarkington, too, Verity frequently reflected, but his determination did not flag. In spite of discouraging appearances, he persisted in plying Laura with the most assiduous attentions until his course could not fail to become clear to Lady Strathmore. Privately, Verity was very irked by it; it showed either blindness on Tarkington's part, or slow-wittedness, or a positively mulish stubbornness.

"We must try to get better bearings on the man," Lady Strathmore would say each time Tarkington made his presence felt.

Why bother? Verity would wonder, when it was so clear Laura would have none of him. But there was something intriguing about the man that piqued Verity's curiosity too, and she found herself speculating about his yet unknown family background almost as much as her aunt.

On a crisp morning early in November, the cousins set out for a carriage ride in the park escorted by Tarkington and Bennington-Jones. The two hussars were an unlikely tandem, since they were far from intimates, but the occasion had come about through Verity's reluctance to spend time alone with the inescapable subaltern. Several times she had evaded his pressing invitations to an outing on grounds of propriety, finally declaring that her aunt would never permit her to ride with him unless Laura accompanied them. When he produced Tarkington as an escort for Laura, prevailing on the latter to agree, Verity had run out of excuses.

Warmly wrapped in an emerald cape, she took her place beside Laura in the landau, remarking as she did so on her young cousin's unusual pallor that morning.

"Are you feeling quite well, coz?" she murmured, recalling that Laura had not been quite as effervescent as usual the previous evening.

"I am a trifle weary," Laura confessed, "and if it were not for the Clements' tea this afternoon, I declare I'd return to my bed after this ride and sleep away the rest of the day."

"That would be most sensible, Miss Debenham," Tarkington said, leaning forward from the facing seat. "Allow me." He extended a hand toward Laura's face and very gently raised her eyelids. "You should sleep every afternoon while you are in London, and look to your diet."

"My diet?" Laura reared away from him, very irked at his forwardness.

"Yes, your diet," he said solemnly. "Do you eat liver and spinach and kale?"

Laura's face contorted with outraged disgust. "*Of course not.*"

"You should. But if you find it too distasteful, you should at least be able to tolerate blackberries and port wine and artichokes."

Verity stared at him in astonishment. His sudden change of manner was quite unaccountable. It was not merely his solicitude for Laura, but a certain curious formality that reminded her of a physician prescribing for a patient. It was nothing like his usual detached, slightly amused style.

"What impudence," Laura muttered under her breath to Verity, as Tarkington leaned back in his seat beside Bennington-Jones. "He really has become impossible."

Verity could not but agree. His manner was quite uncalled for. He seemed to be studying Laura with a clinical detachment, as if she were no more than a specimen of some kind.

"A girl's resources are not unlimited, Miss Debenham," he drawled from his corner seat, "even at your age. I do suggest you fortify your blood with a better diet if you wish to enjoy the season to advantage. You are far too pale."

"What are you blethering about, Tark?" Bennington-Jones asked impatiently. "Miss Debenham's snowy skin is flawless."

"Indeed," Tarkington agreed, "but her pallor should be looked to." He seemed to address the words directly to Verity, and there was an earnest message in his eyes. "There is a world of difference between a fine white skin and a total absence of natural color."

Seriously concerned now, Verity resolved to take the matter up with Laura in private.

"Horse feathers!" Bennington-Jones retorted. "How would you know of such things, Tark? You're just a cavalryman, not a medico."

"Quite. Just common sense," Tarkington replied, dismissing the subject and leaving the floor clear for the subaltern, who could be relied upon to launch into an unremitting stream of inanities. Not long after his discourse had begun, Verity's eyes became glazed and her thoughts wandered, exploring the question of Laura's health.

Laura had turned sixteen a month past and was now in the habit of applying rouge to her face. This morning, having overslept, she was hard put to be ready when the gentlemen arrived. Evidently she had rushed Margaret through a hasty toilette and had forgotten the rouge. Without it, her fatigue was only too obvious.

For once, Bennington-Jones's mindless verbosity was a blessing, freeing the others to subside into their own thoughts and pay him no mind. Several times, Verity caught Tarkington's eyes upon her with a certain intimate speculation in them that eventually obliged her to look away. His behavior was so unaccountable, she reflected, that he was himself a prime topic for speculation. Finding herself disconcerted by the frequency with which her eyes met his, she turned her head to the side glass and fixed her gaze more neutrally on the equestrians using Rotten Row and the barouches and curricles of the passersby.

After returning to Sloane Terrace, the men took their leave, and before Verity could approach Laura on the topic of her pallor, the girl slipped away to her room to change for luncheon.

"Where is the little minx?" Uncle George demanded a half hour later, staring morosely at the dining-room door as his oxtail soup cooled.

Verity was wondering too. Her cousin had had ample time to change her clothes, and it was unlike her to be late for luncheon. They had all been waiting nearly ten minutes.

"If you will excuse me from the table, Uncle," Verity said, "I shall go up myself and see."

Laura lay curled up on top of the coverlet, white as a sheet. "You tell Mama I do not care to come down," she said in a small voice. She was still in her carriage clothes, apparently too apathetic to call Margaret and get herself changed.

"I shall have something nice and hot sent up, then," Verity announced cheerfully. "What would you like?"

"Only to sleep." Laura closed her eyes.

"Just as you like," Verity said and tugged the bell pull for Margaret.

"Go in to Miss Laura and help her to bed," Verity told the abigail. "She is unwell."

"I have no wish to alarm you," Verity told Lord and Lady Strathmore when she rejoined them in the dining room, "but I fear Laura has need of a physician. She seems very weak today, and she will not be coming down. Margaret is presently putting her to bed."

That afternoon, the family gathered in Lady Strathmore's small sitting room, waiting for Dr. Vetch to finish his examination of the patient. He was taking an interminably long time.

Uncle George had brought on a fit of sneezing by one dip too many into the snuffbox. He couldn't abide waiting and in his impatience had taken pinch after pinch absentmindedly.

Aunt Maria sat on a chaise before the coal fire, while Verity paced the room, stopping every now and then to stare down from the window that gave on to Sloane Terrace.

The sound of hooves pulling up at the front door drew her back to the window once more. The landau was regrettably familiar, and just as she feared, it was the blond head of Bennington-Jones she looked down upon as he stepped out of the vehicle. *Not again!* Had she not just suffered through the morning with him?

Twice in one day was too much by far. Verity groaned softly to herself.

"It's getting devilish dark in here," Uncle George growled. "Why are the lamps not lit?"

"It's barely three o'clock," Aunt Maria answered shortly.

"Three o'clock or no, it is dark and dingy in here."

Grimshaw entered the room before the bell had sounded. He was carrying a calling card on his salver, but before he could open his mouth, Verity forestalled him.

"I am not at home to Mr. Bennington-Jones, Grimshaw," she said quickly.

"Ah, he's returned?" Aunt Maria looked up. "That's not necessary, Caroline. The world doesn't stop turning because Laura is mildly indisposed; you may leave us and see the subaltern in the library. Send him our compliments, and I'll have a tray sent in."

"Certainly not! He had your compliments only this morning, Aunt. It is more than enough. Besides, I want to hear what Dr. Vetch has to say."

Aunt Maria paused for a moment, then nodded a grudging consent. "Light the lamps before you go, Grimshaw," she told the butler, dismissing him.

"Certainly, m'lady," he murmured, slightly aggrieved that Lady Strathmore should so far forget herself as to require the chief steward of the house to perform a mere parlormaid's chore. After he lit the lamps, he withdrew quickly, his head at a curiously stiff angle.

Uncle George reached for his snuffbox again and glanced at the gold clock on the mantel. "He's taking an infernal long time, that doctor. Are you sure Margaret is with her?"

Aunt Maria gave her husband a withering glance. "Of course. Lady Sefton assures me he is very reliable and thorough," she said icily. "Vetch is her personal physician in London."

They were an exceptionally healthy clan as a rule,

Verity reflected. None of them was in the least accustomed to physicians in the house, and in their mutual
anxiety for Laura, they were all becoming rather testy.
By the time Grimshaw showed Dr. Vetch into the
sitting room, their respective forebodings had become
quite sinister. They sat with bated breath awaiting
his verdict.

"Nothing too grave, I'm glad to say," Dr. Vetch
began, while he wrote something on a slip of paper.
"The child is somewhat overtaxing herself. I see this
time and time again during the season. Her blood
needs fortifying; it's just a slight case of anemia."

Vetch was a small spry man in his sixties, but with
the weighty authority of a much larger person. Seated
at the gateleg table, he paused to write once more. "I
am prescribing a powder to be taken four times daily.
Three teaspoons mixed into her beef tea, or orgeat,
whatever she prefers to drink."

Removing his gold-rimmed spectacles, he peered at
Lady Strathmore. "I suggest you have a word with
cook, m'lady," he added. "Calf liver and spinach and
blackberries for the child daily. If you run out of
blackberry preserves, then blackberry wine will serve.
She won't like it. They never do. If they did, they'd
never get so debilitated in the first place. But you
must insist. She will have her strength back in a few
days, but keep up the diet."

After a few more admonitions, the doctor took his
leave, arranging to return in five days for another
visit.

Vastly relieved that it was nothing worse, Aunt
Maria strove to follow the physician's instructions to
the letter. Laura was to remain in bed for two complete days.

Laura was the most impatient of patients, fussing
and fuming at her grilled liver, heaping deprecations
upon Mr. Tarkington's head, and bemoaning her lot.
Uncle George stalked out of her room quite purple

after a five-minute visit, and by the end of the first
day, Aunt Maria had a fearful headache. Even good-
natured little Margaret began to roll her eyes in des-
peration at the thought of attending her suddenly
vitriolic mistress.

Verity alone had managed to sit at Laura's bedside
without succumbing to extreme exasperation.

"I've no intention of missing the Sotheby dinner
tonight," Laura said at noon on the second day.
"Valentine Prendergast is to be there, and that settles
it." Propped against pillows, Laura stared at the food
on her tray as if at any moment it might crawl right
off the plate.

Verity recalled Mr. Prendergast as Laura's man of
the moment, a stalwart grenadier officer she had met
the previous week. "We shall all be forgoing the Sotheby
dinner. You can't get up until tomorrow, and there's
nothing to be done," she said firmly. "Now do eat,
Laura."

"I shall probably never see Valentine again!" It was
such a tragic last-curtain of a statement that Verity
was unable to hide her smile.

"I daresay the young man's constancy will at least
outlive yours, coz."

Laura slammed down her fork. "How can you say
that! Valentine Prendergast is the light of my life."
She let out a heartfelt sigh. "He says my eyes are the
color of a storm at sea."

"There'll be a storm right here if you don't start
eating this minute!" Verity picked up Laura's fork
and tasted a morsel from her plate. "I think Mrs.
Johns is brilliant. It's quite delicious. She's sautéed it
with shallots and simmered it in red wine. It doesn't
taste a bit liverish this time. And look at that beautiful soufflé she's baked to go with it. All puffy and
golden—at least, it was very puffy when Margaret
brought it to you."

"And crammed with spinach!" Laura fixed her eyes
on the ceiling and wailed. "Oh, that awful Patrick

Tarkington! He's entirely to blame for this. Why did he have to stick his nose into my affairs? How dare he?"

"You can hardly blame him for your anemia, coz. He merely spoke up. And rightly so. He didn't cause your indisposition, he merely remarked upon it out of concern for you. You're being most unreasonable." It felt odd to be defending Tarkington, Verity thought, but fair was fair.

"I'm not in the least unreasonable," Laura insisted. "Tarkington is the archfiend of my misfortunes, dreadful man. Was he not the very first to mention spinach and—*ugh*!—liver?"

"Yes, come to think of it, he was."

While Laura subsided into a fit of silent pouts and grimaces, Verity wondered at the accuracy of Tarkington's amateur diagnosis. Was he perhaps a physician's son? Hardly the background of an officer. They were invariably much better connected, the sons of the leisured classes. Still, it was strange how his suggestions so neatly matched the doctor's. And quite sound advice, evidently. After one day of rest and prescribed diet, Laura's energy was already on the rise, albeit at fearful cost to the family. Today, Verity even observed a hint of natural color returning to her cousin's cheeks.

Aunt Maria marched in on them wearing her bulldog expression. "Eat!" she barked, pointing a threatening finger at Laura's untouched tray, then turned to her niece, seated at the bedside. "Is she acting up again?"

"Lydia Languish," Verity murmured, casting her eyes heavenward, but the severity of her aunt's expression was not softened by amusement.

"Grimshaw tells me Mr. Bennington-Jones called twice this morning, and you refused to see him. Why were you not at home to him? That makes three times in a row."

Verity released an explosive little sigh. "Oh, Aunt,

he calls far too often. I fear a little of the gentleman goes a very long way."

Aunt Maria drew herself up and folded her arms. "Be that as it may, we are not here simply to amuse ourselves, whatever you may think—and whatever my daughter may think," she added after pausing to round on Laura, who was poking viciously at the calf's liver with her knife and fork.

"Ha! There's little danger of my *amusing* myself *here*," shrilled Laura from her bank of pillows.

Ignoring the remark, Aunt Maria's eyes swiveled back to her niece, and Verity knew she was about to be harangued.

"It would be different if there were other prospects for you, Caroline. Oh, there could be, of course, but you seem bent on discouraging them all. You simply don't show the interest you should. You're a lively enough creature at home, and amusing, heaven knows. But among the gentleman, you've been showing as much vivacity as a dead frog. Men are not entirely without sensibility, you know. They do catch these overtones."

Stooping to pick up a novel Laura had thrown to the floor, Aunt Maria began to pace about the disorderly room, accompanying her steps to a brisk *crack, crack*, as she thwacked the slim volume resoundingly against her open palm.

"Mr. Bennington-Jones seems to be the only prospect who is not entirely daunted by your coldness. And I for one have every intention of encouraging him mightily."

"*Oh, Aunt!*" Verity protested with a sinking heart.

"Don't 'oh, Aunt' me! I hope you're going to be a sensible gel about this and not cause me an attack of the vapors. Besides"—here a smile broke through the severe Strathmore mien—"as it happens, he's a splendid choice for you. You couldn't do better."

As Verity drew breath to protest, her aunt cut her off by rounding on Laura.

"Eat that up immediately, or you shall remain in bed for the rest of the week and I will have Vetch put the leeches on you!"

Laura at last began to eat, her complaints lowering to a subdued mutter.

Verity set herself to bustling about the room, picking up backgammon pieces from the carpet, in the hopes of avoiding further discussion of the subaltern, but Aunt Maria was not so easily distracted from her purpose.

"I have it from Lady Sefton that his widowed mother lately remarried. The man is Lord Tickberry, a trusted counselor of the Prince Regent," she confided to Verity, taking her arm and promenading her past the foot of Laura's bed. "Tickberry holds considerable sway with the Prime Minister, of course. With such a father-in-law for you, Nigel's career would be quite made."

No doubt, Verity thought, allowing herself to be led back and forth down the length of the room from bay window to chiffonier. But there wasn't the faintest possibility of her succumbing to such expediencies—certainly not when they would involve a lifetime sentence with blond, bland Bennington-Jones. She was about to point this out in no uncertain terms when she suddenly thought better of it. Perhaps it was wisdom not to scotch Aunt Maria's schemes too quickly. The lady could make the remainder of the season especially tedious for her if she felt she was being deliberately thwarted.

"I've looked up the Tickberrys in *Collins' Peerage*," she was saying. "Everything Lady Sefton told me is there in black and white. A sterling family, the Tickberrys."

Leaving a silent Verity positively wilting on the window seat, Lady Strathmore returned to the bed and smoothed down Laura's coverlet. "I just wish as much could be said of your faithful admirer. Oh, do finish up, child, and stop pushing it around the plate."

"Which admirer, Mama?" Laura looked up eagerly,

showing keener interest in the conversation than in the congealing mess on her tray.

"Why, Mr. Tarkington, of course. It's obvious he'll pop the question before the season closes, and I was so hoping to be ready to deal with it. But I can't find his family tree listed anywhere. It's not in *Collins'*, nor do I see it in *Hawley's*. Not even a one-line mention of a Tarkington. Lady Sefton seems to know nothing of the family." She gave a sigh of exasperation. "Oh, I do wish he would just out with it and offer for you, instead of forever hovering about paying court in this leisurely way. Then of course we could sit down with him in a civilized manner and ask him straight out exactly who his parents are."

Her head began to shake slowly in hopeless mystification. "The man seems well-bred enough, and very charming, of course. But when two reputable directories make absolutely no mention of him, I simply don't know what to make of it. . . . Caroline," she called out, turning to her niece, "what does your nice subaltern know of him? They're regimental colleagues, after all."

Verity cringed at the pointed personal pronoun. "Mr. T and Mr. B-J are not close friends, Aunt," she said neutrally. "The subject has never come up."

"In any case," Laura put in, "I personally don't care for Mr. Tarkington in the least." She pushed away her luncheon tray. "He's an odious man, so it really doesn't signify in the least who his family is, Mama."

"Of course it does! Caring for him is neither here nor there, child," she pointed out, waving away Laura's remark with a flick of her wrist. "The point is, he's making his intentions clear, and I simply must know whether we should consider his suit or eliminate him as a possible."

"Eliminate him by all means," Laura demanded.

"It's very trying," Aunt Maria persisted, ignoring her daughter's remark. "I don't think the printers are at all conscientious when they compile these genealogies. I can't truly believe he's a nobody. It doesn't make sense." She stopped to push Laura's tray back under her nose, then stared at her daughter in surprise.

"Eliminate him, did you say? You were enchanted with him just recently. What happened? Has he grown horns since then?"

"Oh, Mama, that was ages ago, ancient history! I've grown fearfully tired of his attentions. He's no fun at all. A positive sobersides."

"And you're nothing but a crosspatch today."

"Be that as it may," Laura said, unconsciously aping her mother, "for the rest of the season, I should just like to flit."

"Yes, I'm sure you would—like a silly little butterfly. I fear Caroline has not been the example I'd hoped she would be for you. I thought that she at least would take this venture more seriously. Giddiness at sixteen one can understand—there will be other seasons."

Verity caught another dire Strathmore look.

"But as for you, Caroline, I trust you haven't forgotten that you will be twenty-one next spring. There's very little excuse for this attitude, less with each passing year. I expect a far more responsible attitude from now on."

"I mean to try, Aunt," Verity uttered fervently. "Truly I do."

Faced with the threat of Bennington-Jones, she did indeed mean to set about finding an acceptable alternative. It wasn't as though she found the thought of spinsterhood all that attractive, it was just that so far, no one had really engaged her feelings.

She cast about in her mind, trying to remember all the men who had paid her any attention; save for a few widowers of declining years and health, none of them seemed very distinguishable from Bennington-Jones. What made him especially intolerable, she decided, was that he was less easily put off. Perseverance, she told herself firmly, was an admirable quality in a man, a sterling virtue. Bennington-Jones had perseverance in abundance. It didn't help a bit.

She had not, of course, included Patrick Tarkington in her mental explorations. Although her feelings toward him had softened in inverse proportions to Laura's growing distaste, he was still her cousin's faithful suitor, undeclared, but also undeniable. The circumstance irked her a little. Laura was much too young for him to begin with, as well as being disinclined. How could a self-respecting man abide such disdain from such a little coquette? It was beyond reason, particularly as she suspected that she herself was capable of stirring more genuine response in his breast than Laura was. Outwardly courting Laura, he was nonetheless forever casting his glances in her own direction, glances of a most intimate nature, as if they were in mute collusion. Perhaps it was merely meant to remind her of her rash behavior with de Roncy, but she fancied it meant a good deal more than that.

It was a tiresome puzzle with no answer and she tried to dismiss it from her mind, but it returned to her thoughts later that day when Grimshaw entered Laura's sickroom, accompanied by Lady Strathmore.

"Mr. Tarkington has come to see you," Lady Strathmore announced, tugging on the bell cord to summon Margaret.

"I can't possibly see him in bed," Laura said.

"Yes you can. You have your mama and your cousin in the room, and you're perfectly decent. Margaret will fetch a fresh wrapper, and mend your hair."

"I'm supposed to be taking a rest, Mama."

"But you just refused," Lady Strathmore reminded her. "Only a few moments ago you declared you've had enough sleep for a week and you wanted to get dressed and go riding."

"That was ten minutes ago, Mama! I'm quite exhausted now, and I'm ill. I will not be put upon in this way. I want you all to leave me."

Lady Strathmore gave a fitful sigh and motioned Verity out of the room. "Come, Caroline. We shall leave the ungrateful wretch to her own devices. She's fit company for no one."

On the upper landing, Verity found herself dispatched to receive Mr. Tarkington in the downstairs drawing room. She was to offer him Laura's regrets, and thank him for the posy of violets which Laura had regrettably failed to notice on Grimshaw's salver.

"Have him tarry awhile, and I shall join you presently when I have completed my regrets notes for the Sotheby dinner," she told her niece.

"Good day, Mr. Tarkington," Verity said, joining the visitor where he stood rigid on the exact center of the drawing-room carpet. "I'm afraid my cousin is feeling poorly and cannot receive today."

His face became momentarily grave. "Nothing serious, I hope?"

"No, just a trifling indisposition that requires some bed rest. I'm quite sure she will be receiving again by next week."

Tarkington nodded and clasped his hands behind his back.

"She does so appreciate your violets, sir. She asked me to thank you." Verity found his gaze disturbing, as if he had detected her lie. She glanced away. "Won't you sit down? My aunt will be down in a moment."

He shook his head and murmured, "Thank you," then cleared his throat awkwardly. "And you, Miss Cox? You've been quite well, I trust?"

"Quite well, thank you. And you, Mr. Tarkington?"

He inclined his head and impaled her with a second intense look while he inquired after the health of her aunt and uncle in a tone that suggested his very life hung upon her answers.

A vague panic seized her, even while she observed that their discourse had sunk to the innocuous level of a beginner's class in French conversation, and there was therefore no need to panic. She looked imploringly at the seating arrangement by the hearth, where stood two sofas separated by a low table, certain that if she could get him to sit, it would somehow break the distressing tension she suffered.

"Won't you please, *please*, make yourself comfortable?" she begged, motioning to the sofas and leading him toward them.

He obeyed. But seated primly across the table from him, she discovered the maneuver had brought no relief.

"My aunt has ordered a tray of refresh—"

"I find it impossible to make myself comfortable in your presence, Miss Cox."

Verity folded her hands in her lap. "If that is in the nature of a 'gallant' remark, I find it uncalled for," she told him with a sternness she did not feel at all, "and in view of the circumstances, unworthy of you."

He leaned forward, his fine dark brows knitted in apparent perplexity. "Circumstances, Miss Cox? What circumstances?"

"Why the fact that we are presently unchaperoned, for one—and the fact that you have made your intentions unfailingly clear toward my cousin, Laura Debenham."

The smile on his lips seemed a trifle cool. "Were you this admirably proper while you diverted a French nobleman on a certain King Street balcony? Equally unchaperoned, I might add, until my timely arrival."

So, at last, he meant to use it against her, she thought, reddening at his words.

"Oh, forgive me," he added remorsefully. "I had not meant to refer to it or take advantage in any way ... it is merely ..."

Words seemed to fail him for a moment, but having nothing further to say, Verity merely waited for him to continue.

"I've not been able to forget the pretty scene these past weeks, much as I've tried. . . . The thought that I should have deprived you of a much desired kiss has bothered me greatly. I have put myself in your debt, Miss Cox, and fear I will not rest until I have honorably discharged that debt."

"You owe me nothing, Mr. Tarkington," she said, by now blushing to the roots of her hair. "There is no way you can undo your deliberate intrusion on a private *tête-à-tête*, so please dismiss it from your mind."

He rose swiftly, casting a brief glance at the door, then pulled Verity to her feet. "Will you not accept my most abject apologies—and my kiss in lieu of the Frenchman's?"

"Really, Mr. Tarkington!"

"Surely a lady of stalwart English birth would hesitate to suggest that English currency cannot hold its own against a French embrace?"

The tremor in her breast did not betray itself in her voice. "Unhand me immediately, sir!"

Paling slightly, Tarkington subsided to his opposing side of the table only moments before Lady Strathmore burst into the room.

7

Disturbing as Verity found it, Mr. Tarkington's untoward dalliance was left entirely unresolved, and in the days that followed, he was to behave as though it had never taken place at all.

Despite her unconscionable behavior, Laura was duly allowed to rise on the third day, and pronounced much recovered. However, Dr. Vetch urged that she continue to rest every afternoon for the rest of the season. For a week or so, she did. But by the end of November, she was completely restored, and the nap meant missing a great many tea invitations, as she repeatedly complained. After a great deal of importuning, a compromise was reached; Laura would rest on a salon chaise for two hours after luncheon, but be allowed to receive visitors during the second hour, provided she was up to it.

She was always up to it. The large second-floor drawing room became a noted salon, with Laura holding court to an increasing number of eager young men each afternoon.

Mr. Tarkington, briefly absent from the scene during the first few days of Laura's recovering, sent her more violets and a note. When he next called, it was to find her surrounded by admirers, and he seemed somewhat put out at the scene.

"How long has this been going on?" he asked Verity.

"All week," she replied, expecting some allusion to

their last meeting, at the very least an apology for his behavior on that occasion.

"I should like to take Miss Debenham for a carriage ride some afternoon. The crisp air will do her good. Will she come?"

"I couldn't say." Verity found his attitude infuriating. "It is up to her, provided her physician approves, and Lord and Lady Strathmore consent."

"I see."

His intentions had apparently not cooled in the slightest, but as he listened to Verity, it was almost as if he were pondering the conditional clauses of a will.

Each time he visited thereafter, Verity noticed that he was always impatient, as if he had serious business to discuss with Laura and no time for this giddy nonsense that was taking place about her chaise.

Laura, of course, was in her element and hardly noticed his presence at all.

For a suitor, Verity could not help remarking, he was very dispassionate toward the object of his desires, although invariably polite and solicitous for her health. But when he looked at Verity—and she caught him frequently . . . no. She really had to be imagining it. He had been merely trifling with her like any dandy on that afternoon when he had come so perilously close to kissing her. It had meant absolutely nothing except that he was diverting himself.

Although both of them thereafter studiously avoided reference to his lapse in behavior, Verity was quite unable to resist constant speculation. He never behaved toward Laura with such impulsiveness. Indeed, he comported himself with the utmost sobriety in her presence. Had her rashness with de Roncy given Tarkington the idea that she was far more susceptible to male advances, and therefore fair game? Oh, surely not, but . . . ?

She became filled with a sense of irony. The only fellow who afforded her any mental stimulation was

not only thoroughly untrustworthy, but someone whose
attentions were directed elsewhere.

Lady Strathmore invariably presided over Laura's
afternoon *levées*, and she fully expected Verity's presence too. After two solid weeks of it, Verity longed to
take off for a brisk walk, but it became impossible.
Laura would certainly not have missed her, but
Bennington-Jones had quickly grasped at these daily
opportunities to attach himself. Trapping Verity in
the far corner of the room by a window seat, he would
daily talk her to death. There was an ever-changing
list of visitors, save for two constants: Bennington-
Jones and Tarkington.

A pattern quickly developed in the blue-and-bur-
gundy drawing room. Tarkington would appear regularly at half past three with the air of one bound by
duty to call on a rich and ailing relative. By that time,
there would already be a cluster of young men around
Laura's chaise. Often he would have no opportunity
to approach, or give her more than a brief nod. His
presence was always registered by a calling card, often accompanied by a posy or some other small token.
Rarely would he penetrate the cluster of men around
Laura's chaise and attempt to present his gift to her
himself. Instead he would hand it to Grimshaw as he
entered the room, then for the remainder of his stay
he would stand on the edge of the group, always a
little apart.

Hopelessly trapped at the window seat, Verity would
watch him obliquely. When she caught him unawares,
he would often be glowering at her. He would recover
himself with a brief nod if their eyes met, and offer a
cool smile.

While the subaltern droned on vacuously about nothing at all, Verity would find herself hoping that
Tarkington would intrude on the incessant monologue,
giving her the tiniest chance to escape, or at least a
respite. He had not shown the least hesitation in doing
precisely that when she had been alone with de

Roncy. Why would he not do the same now? What an impossible, infuriating fellow he was!

But at least he would not bore her. She could think of a dozen burning questions to ask him. Why had he left Lancashire before his regiment? Why did he absent himself from London so often? How had he come by such precise knowledge of anemia? Why did he no longer present himself at Almack's? She had once had the opportunity to question him, and had found his behavior so disconcerting that she had let it slip through her fingers. Now, he provided no opportunities for the least exchange.

The round of evening events resumed its pace, and the season went busily on. As Christmas approached, Verity was assailed by a longing for home. Although the London streets grew bright with garlands and holly boughs, although shop windows delighted the eye with seasonal baubles, and Regent Street glittered with hundreds of gaily painted novelties, her thoughts turned increasingly to Briarley. This would be her first Christmas away from Father. He missed her sorely. All his letters were redolent of bygone seasons and cherished memories. Winter came earlier to Lancashire. Nostalgically, Verity wondered if the first snows had not already come, dusting the lawns of Briarley with a light, evanescent sparkle.

Laura's irrepressible delight in all things had returned in full measure. She would chide Verity good-naturedly for her glum silences and try to tease her out of them. After a week, she gave up the attempt and took to her bosom a more congenial companion.

Clarissa Clement, youngest of Lady Clement's brood, was a mischievous slip of a girl with bouncing ginger ringlets and a ready laugh. She was closer to Laura in age and temperament, and best of all, she was conveniently quartered for the season in a terrace house just across the street and the strip of gardens from 18 Sloane Terrace.

Laura and Clarissa took to impromptu visits during

the morning or late afternoon, one or the other darting swiftly across the gardens and startling the passing horses with a lightning flash of bright petticoats as they dodged the carriages on the street. If she was free, Clarissa would join the two-o'clock visitors and pick up the slack. Verity was happy for Laura, and grateful for the occasional solitude this new friendship provided. Fond as she was of her young cousin, she had begun to tire of her remorseless enthusiasms.

The bosom companions were closeted in Laura's room late one afternoon when Mr. Cox's letter arrived. It was as though he had read her thoughts, Verity observed delightedly as she read the welcome news.

"At all events," he wrote in the careful, spidery hand, "we shall be together for Christmastide. I have decided that my banking affairs in Threadneedle Street would be better expedited in person than by the post, and the length of the journey weighs but little in the scale against the great joy of seeing my dear child at this time. I have written to your aunt to expect me no later than Christmas Eve, for a stay of five days."

Verity's heart soared, and she hurried up to Laura to share her news.

Laura was curled on the bed in her petticoats, Clarissa beside her. Both of them were pink from high spirits and, as Verity could hear when she reached the landing, a spell of the giggles. Some hilarious event had apparently diverted Laura from the serious business of dressing for the evening.

"Tell her, do," Clarissa gasped as Verity entered, poking a finger at the open book that lay between them on the quilt.

Laura gave her cousin an oblique look. "I don't know, Clarrie, she's such a sobersides lately." Raising herself to her knees and wobbling in the cushiony softness of the feather mattress, she gazed up at Verity. "Are you in better spirits today, coz, or are you still in the gray glums?"

"I'm in the best of all possible spirits, my dears,"

Verity answered, bounding onto the bed with a joyous leap that set them all jouncing. "Father is coming down to spend Christmas with us."

Laura hugged her cousin with genuine delight. "Oh, thank heavens, Verity! Now we can all get back to the proper business of enjoying ourselves. Clarrie and I have decided to spend tomorrow morning in Oxford Street shopping for presents. Mama said we could take the phaeton. You will come, won't you?"

"I would be chahmed, honored, preeveeleged and al-to-gethah deelaahted, Miss Dahbenham," Verity drawled in an unmistakable parody of Frawleigh Montague, Laura's latest.

Hilarity exploded once more, then Clarissa rolled over on the quilt until she almost went over the edge, gasping, "Tell her, tell her!"

Laura hauled Clarrisa back to safety, feet first, then pounced for the slim volume. "Clarrie was at the booksellers in Drury Lane this morning in search of a gift for her sister—who is a *heavy reader*," she added, as if the odd circumstance required a careful explanation.

Verity reached for the book, but Laura held it out of her grasp. "No, I'll read it to you. It is a collection of poems by Lord Byron, including this 'Hymn to the Waltz.' " She cleared her throat.

"Endearing Waltz!—to thy more melting tune
Bow Irish jig and ancient rigadoon.
Scotch reels, avaunt! and country-dance, forego
Your future claims to each fantastic toe!
Waltz—Waltz alone—both legs and arms demands,
Liberal of feet and lavish of her hands;
Hands which may freely range in public sight
Where ne'er before—but—pray 'put out the light,'
Methinks the glare of yonder chandelier
Shines much too far—or I am much too near;
And true though strange, Waltz whispers this
    remark,
'My slippery steps are safest in the dark!' "

Verity shrugged. "It's little more than doggerel. Not at all comparable with his finer poems."

"I told you so, Clarrie!" Laura turned to her cousin. "You're quite impossible, you know. And furthermore, you have no appreciation of the arts." Hastily, she turned some pages. "The point is, you goose, it is dated 1813, just five years ago. At that time, the shocking Lord Byron found it all terribly *risqué*, and here we are dancing it at Almack's every Wednesday at Mama's insistence. Listen!

"Seductive Waltz!—though on thy native shore
Even Werter's self proclaim'd thee half a whore—

"To think of it! Imagine Mama's discomfort that first morning when she hired a dancing master for us. I do wonder if she's ever read this."

"I doubt it," Verity said, climbing off the bed. "And if I were you, Laura, I'd not show it to her. It might bring on the vapors."

Back in her own bedroom, Verity glanced into the pier glass before she rang for Sarah, and noticed the rich glow on her cheeks. Laughter, good news . . . and another warmth that was less explainable. She was thinking of the waltz she had danced just once with Patrick Tarkington, and their very brief exchange today, at Laura's reception. For once, he had approached her more or less cordially.

"You won't be confined to the bay window today, Miss Cox. Bennington-Jones is required to attend the colonel," he had said, still standing on the edge of the cluster surrounding Laura, and making no attempt to penetrate it.

"Ha!" Verity was openly delighted to learn of her reprieve. "I have often wondered if His Majesty's officers had aught else to do but attend the ladies and ride to hounds."

His laugh was genuine. "As it happens, there is precious little to do in times of peace, ma'am. No doubt the good fellow would be here at his drawing-room post were he not at this moment signing his captain's papers."

"He is to be promoted? Bravo! What sterling virtue, what act of heroism, is being thus rewarded, Mr. Tarkington?"

He tried to assume a grave expression, but experienced some difficulty with the corners of his mouth. "Why, the virtue of being well-heeled, Miss Cox. The promotion cost him something upward of six hundred pounds."

She should have known, of course, but she hadn't been thinking entirely logically. "Oh, a purchased commission. I see."

"Don't despise it. There are few paths to a captaincy save gold." He paused, examining her with a streak of avid curiosity, and perhaps something more than that. "Does your admirer disappoint you, Miss Cox?"

"Sir, nothing in Mr. Bennington-Jones could disappoint me!" She had not meant to be quite so emphatic, but her implication was unmistakable.

He drew breath quietly and let a silence mount between them as he regarded her beneath knitted brows. "I rather thought you held him in very high esteem, Miss Cox. You entertain such constant attentions from him."

"Not by choice, I assure you." Again, it came out forcefully, as if she were intent on making herself very clear.

The pinpoints of pure flame that briefly lit his dark gray eyes faded so quickly that Verity questioned whether she had seen them at all.

"We all have our exigencies, ma'am." He bowed very stiffly, and wandered off to the punch table to pay his respects to Lady Strathmore. Verity was left restless and dissatisfied, and strangely moved. It was such a brief, perfunctory exchange, but so enigmatic. What on earth could he mean?

We all have our exigencies, ma'am. She stared into the mirror and recalled every word of their conversation, looking for a possible clue to his meaning. He was a most infuriating fellow.

Mr. Cox arrived on Christmas Eve, and having concluded his business affairs the previous day, declared himself completely at Verity's disposal. Her day passed in utter contentment. After three months in London, she was struck anew by the simplicity of his gray alpaca suit and black cravat. After all the silks and ruffles of the city dandies, to see him was to be home in gentle Briarley once more, all other considerations brushed aside.

After a quiet family luncheon, Verity excused herself from Laura's salon—a gala affair that day—and spent the entire afternoon in her father's carriage, pointing out to him the splendid new shops of Regent Street, the palaces along Piccadilly, and the newly landscaped gardens in St. James's. If all went as planned, when she returned to Briarley in the spring, she would be betrothed, marking the end of their harmonious life together. She did not like to dwell on the thought, but it lent a poignancy to their hours together which neither needed to put into words.

They returned to Sloane Terrace to find the family gathered before a roaring fire and taking tea.

Mr. Cox took the wingback chair and Verity pulled up a footstool, where she sat sipping her tea and leaning against her father's knees.

As Lady Strathmore savored her favorite oolong brew, she admired her niece's peach-perfect throat glowing smoothly above her dark green bodice. Her cheeks were deeply rosed from the brisk weather, and in the fading light her eyes shone, reflecting the leaping yellow flames in the grate. What man could resist? she thought. If only the girl could summon such animation at the assemblies, where it counted. "I'm delighted you've had this chance to spend time with your papa, Caroline," she said, smiling.

"I have him to myself for four whole days yet," Verity murmured contentedly.

"But you must not forget this is the festive season." Lady Strathmore became uneasy. "Like it or not, we do have rather more social engagements than usual this week. There is the Harrington luncheon tomorrow—preceded, of course, by the morning visit to the de Lyons for a champagne toast—and, let me see ..." Eyes on the ceiling, as if it were encoded there, she continued, ticking off on her fingers a calendar of events so remorseless that Verity protested.

"No, Aunt. I will not fritter these days away on the usual folderol. You know that Father could never be persuaded to attend any of these, and he is to start for home on Wednesday. I should hardly see anything of him." She set down her cup and hugged her father's knee fiercely. "I shall beg off until Thursday, and have Father all to myself."

Aunt Maria rattled her own cup and saucer in retaliation as she set it firmly down. "*Beg off?*" she exclaimed, sending a silent appeal to Uncle George, who continued to stare annoyingly into the glowing coals as he chewed on a muffin. "You can't beg off. It's out of the question!"

"I shall call him Pettigrew," Laura murmured. Sublimely oblivious of the impasse, she sat fondling a fluffy Pekinese pup who left a trail of shed hair on her deep rose skirts. The pup was Clarrie's Christmas gift.

"I told you not to hold it on your lap, child. Put it back in its basket this instant. You'll ruin your gown." Aunt Maria returned to Verity, her indignation now in full bloom.

"Have you lost your senses, Caroline? You can't simply beg off. These are social obligations. You would not, you could not, possibly submit me to the humili—"

"And she will not," Mr. Cox cut in, sharp as a

whipcrack, and pressed down firmly on Verity's shoulder as she tried to rise. "She will fulfill her obligations to the letter, like the responsible, conscientious daughter she is."

Her mouth open to protest, Verity tried to rise once more, but her father's voice continued authoritatively, as did the pressure on her shoulder.

"Verity has always been a credit to me, and she will be equally a credit to you. I can assure you of that."

As his grip on her relaxed, she swung around to face him indignantly. "Papa, would you rob me of the pleasure of a few precious days for the sake of a parade of utterly silly and insignificant—"

"Silly they may appear to you, child. Insignificant they are not. I'll not let you break faith with your good aunt."

As the good aunt nodded her vigorous approval, Mr. Cox's expression gave way to a humorous smile.

"Rather, I shall break with custom and accompany you on this round of pleasure."

Verity was stunned. Did her father actually mean to submit himself to the indignity of a salon crush, the idle chatter of the assembly rooms, the malicious gossip and simpering of the Mayfair receptions and suppers? She knew it would cost him dear in tedium, in patronizing stares and unintelligible conversation. The discomfort of it! The complete alienation! And yet he would consider for her sake attending those events which epitomized everything he despised. Overwhelmed at this magnanimous gesture, Verity fell into his arms sobbing.

"There, there, child," he murmured, patting her back. "Don't make so much of it. It's only four days. Any Lancashire man worth his salt can survive that."

Lady Strathmore too was overwhelmed, and not a little appalled. It was the last thing she had expected. Caroline's father was a social misfortune at all times, but it was easily overcome in his absence. To have the dour, disapproving, impossibly clad fellow actually visible! It would be all over London in one evening. She let her mind dart frantically over the coming engagements, attempting to picture the scene. Caroline might well become a social pariah after four days of it . . . possibly dragging the entire Strathmore clan down with her. Dismayed, she stared at her niece, who was positively sobbing with ecstatic joy. There had to be a graceful solution to the problem, she thought, trying to stay calm.

"There is a Mr. Benjamin Fotheringay from Chancery Lane here, m'lord," Grimshaw announced. "He says he has been summoned for this hour."

Lady Strathmore had been too absorbed to hear the butler's knock. Well, at least this gave her a brief spell to prevaricate, before she pronounced the last word on the subject.

"We have some business to attend to, if you will excuse us, Mr. Cox," she said. "George?"

Lord Strathmore roused himself from his fireside reveries and the couple withdrew.

Laura soon excused herself too and, cradling her puppy in its basket, left to dress for the evening.

Verity rose, replenished her father's cup, then stood by the hearth, savoring his company.

From his chair, Mr. Cox studied his daughter curiously. "I have rarely seen you so affected," he said.

"I was overcome, Papa. The magnitude of your sacrifice was just—"

He gave a hearty laugh. "You make far too much of it, child. Sacrifice indeed! It is no more than pure selfish gratification. Do you not think I want to see with my own eyes the kind of man to whom I shall be entrusting your future happiness? Your aunt is a good woman in her way, but I trust my own judgment better. I hope to be reassured when—" He broke off and studied her expression. "Who is he?" he asked.

"Who is who, Papa?"

Private amusement tugged at his lips. "Why, the

object of your affections, of course. There is someone, is there not?"

"No one, I'm afraid. Aunt Maria is quite put out with me for not responding more willingly to . . ." Her upper lashes swept modestly down over her cheeks. "Oh, there are those who dance their silly attendance on me for a space, but not a one whom I would dream of taking seriously, in all conscience."

"Are you sure?" Mr. Cox was oddly insistent.

Verity sighed. "I know it's tiresome of me, Papa. I am reminded of it daily these past weeks, but here we are three whole months into the season, and still there is not one living soul whose company I could be persuaded to accept in trade for yours."

"I see. And you are quite certain about this?" His look was so keen, it was almost as though he suspected she was holding something back from him.

Verity was puzzled. Surely he knew she was always candid with him? "Do you doubt me, Papa?"

He laughed for some reason, and reached across the console table to take her hand. "No. I simply remember being your age. I knew a great love, and I would wish no less for you. Just for a moment, I thought perhaps you had found it. I sensed a certain . . ." He shrugged lightheartedly. "No matter. No need to press the point."

That night, before they left for the midnight service at the Brompton Oratory, the family exchanged gifts. The large flat parcel Papa had brought was revealed to be a breathtaking watercolor. He had commissioned the work from a fine north-country artist, and chosen the scene with infinite thought. It was the view from Verity's bedroom window at Briarley—the east lawns, the delphiniums at their height, the rolling sweep to the coppice in the distance. Briarley in its late-summer glory. It spoke keenly of her father's love; no matter how widely they might be separated, she could carry her childhood with her always. Once again, and quite uncharacteristically, Verity burst into a flood of tears.

Mr. Cox comforted her in his arms, and over her shoulder, smiled an enigmatic smile.

Lady Strathmore's apprehension notwihstanding, Mr. Cox's visit passed smoothly enough. Finding no graceful way of avoiding the possible debacle of a Quaker let loose in London society, she merely decided to hold her head high and carry the whole affair off with panache.

Mr. Cox owned no cherry satin waistcoats or creamy nankeens, but his shirts were finest lawn and his suits, if somber, were very finely tailored. What he lacked in glitter he made up in quiet grace and good humor. There was, of course, no way one could guess from his manner or his appearance that he was a rich and powerful man, but discreetly, Lady Strathmore bruited about that he was a moneyed recluse, slightly touched in the head since the death of his wife, but quite wealthy enough to afford the eccentricity of remaining in mourning clothes for twenty years.

Laura's three o'clocks resumed on Boxing Day, and Verity circulated the drawing room on her father's arm, presenting him to the gathering and whispering an occasional commentary.

"That was Laura's most serious prospect so far, though Laura ignores him. Mr. Tarkington's suit dates back to Lancashire," she whispered behind her fan, after a brief introduction.

For once, she was able to avoid an hour's captivity by Bennington-Jones. She presented him briefly to Mr. Cox, then quickly moved on with the magnificent excuse that she had many more introductions to perform.

"The bane of my life," Verity explained *sotto voce*, when the new captain was safely out of earshot. "He pins me to that window every afternoon with a vapid monologue of foxhounds and Prinny's court, and the banal doings of the officers' mess. A positive prig. Shallow, self-absorbed, and utterly insensible."

On Wednesday morning, Verity spent a quiet hour

in Mr. Cox's room before he departed. Together, they shared a few humorous moments over some of the more outrageous dandies he had become acquainted with during his visit. But there was no malice in his laughter.

"Try to see them as individual souls, Verity," he urged. "I know how silly and shallow some may seem to you, but remember, *en masse* their faults are magnified. The general artificiality of the occasion tends to color their behavior," he said generously. "Be gracious and forgiving, and never forget, it is the way of the world to marry. They mean no real harm."

For a while they sipped hot chocolate in silence, and Mr. Cox was lost in thought, frowning slightly. "The tall quiet man, the hussar who pays court to Laura . . . what was his name?"

"Tarkington."

"Yes, Tarkington. The fellow disturbs me."

"A most odious fellow," Verity said hastily.

"Why odious?"

Under her father's studied gaze, Verity found herself chattering. "A dozen reasons, Papa! He is arrogant, boorish, surly, forward. He has none of the social graces, don't you agree?"

"I can't say that I do," Mr. Cox said slowly. "We conversed a little over port at that supper in St. James's. He is quite knowledgeable for an officer. A cordial enough fellow, I should think, as far as the social graces go."

"Then why does he disturb you?"

"I just don't like the way he looks at you, girl. Far too impassioned. It's not seemly if he intends to pay such serious court to your cousin. Not seemly at all." He shook his head. "It grieves me all the more because I took a liking to the fellow, but a man who pays court to one lady and casts his eye elsewhere even before his marriage vows are uttered is either a born womanizer or a fortune hunter. I'm surprised your vigilant aunt hasn't caught it."

Verity felt an alarming lurch under her ribs, as if some vital organ had torn loose from its mooring. She set down her chocolate cup very carefully, afraid she might spill it and betray emotions she could not begin to explain or justify.

"Aunt Maria is much too busy trying to trace his connections. It appears they are elusive." There was a tiny shake to her voice, and she hoped he hadn't noticed.

"Well, I trust you will never put expediency before the dictates of your heart, my dear. You won't, will you? No matter how the Strathmores press?"

She shook her head vigorously.

"Good." He looked reluctantly at the heavy-caped greatcoat that lay waiting on the clothespress. It was time to go, and he opened his arms for a farewell hug.

"When in doubt, my dear, remember that your mother and I knew true happiness, and all the world was against our marriage. It was not conventional, not desirable, not acceptable, not proper, not advisable, not expedient." He laid a kiss on her brow. "And never would I have traded our two short years of bliss for a lifetime of social convenience." He slipped quickly into his greatcoat, smiling broadly.

"Social convenience is a poor excuse for a marriage. Let your Aunt Maria look to her peerage books, but you look to your heart. Never forget it, and never tell your aunt I said it."

"Oh, I won't, Papa. I promise."

8

The year 1820 arrived with a light flurry of snow that muted the sounds of hoof and carriage wheel for the space of the night's festivities, and was melted by daybreak. The new year brought little outward change at 18 Sloane Terrace.

That Laura had made no resolution to abstain from fickle attachments was abundantly clear. Her sun had set on Frawleigh Montague in late December, only to rise anew on young Sir Roger de Vere over the holidays. De Vere was eclipsed on Boxing Day by the advent of Lieutenant Esme Quire, an officer whose brief ascendancy ended when poetic-looking Geoffrey Chipping-Sodbury kissed Laura's hand at the Clements' *bal masqué* on Twelfth Night. The girl was incorrigible, and through it all Mr. Tarkington continued to exercise his cold courtship, apparently unmoved by jealousy.

Verity could hardly fault her cousin for ignoring such peremptory attentions as Tarkington offered. And ignore them Laura did with a vengeance. He must surely have long since known that his suit was a lost cause. He might be many things, Verity reflected, but he was not obtuse. What then could he be up to? she wondered, despite her own New Year's resolution to refrain from dwelling on the subject.

After her father's frank observations, Verity could no longer pretend that the fervor in Tarkington's frequent glances was merely her imagination. But they still exchanged no more than passing civilities, his words never reflecting the mysterious message in his eyes, and never alluding to the kiss he had once offered.

She stoutly refused to believe he was a womanizer; he was always the perfect gentleman in his comportment to females. She never saw him leer, never heard an innuendo, never observed his dance partners subjected to any uncalled-for intimacy. And he kept the promise he had made after their first waltz together, never inviting Verity to dance again.

Her observations of him had become minute and obsessive, she realized, but it at least afforded some relief from the remorseless tedium of Bennington-Jones. Since the latter's promotion to captain, he had become more pompous and predatory than ever. She must find her amusements where she may.

At night, she took to reading some of Laura's romances, to lull her to sleep, although the family rarely returned home of an evening before the small hours. But good, bad, or indifferent, the novellas never held her attention. After a mere page or two, her mind would wander back to its favorite subject.

If he were not a womanizer, then could he really be a fortune hunter, as Papa feared? The possibility had occurred to her even before Papa's visit. There were in circulation lurid tales of young cads who staked their patrimonies to buy their colors, then used the bait of a fine regiment and a dashing uniform to lure an unsuspecting heiress. It would certainly account for Tarkington's detached yet persistent pursuit of Laura. His bored persistence would be quite understandable if it were not his affections that were engaged, but only his purse.

And then of course there was the enigma of his origins. Your average hussar had a pedigree that read like an open book, but nary a soul knew aught of Tarkington, as Aunt Maria was always pointing out. If he were indeed a nobody, an out-and-out fortune hunter, he certainly seemed much more substantial

than the flighty young peacocks who flashed their
swords and sported their ceremonial scarlets, or
preened themselves in the most foppish civilian garb.
Verity had seen Tarkington in scarlet regalia just
once, in Denning (and what a splendid sight he was
in them, she now had to admit!). But for the most
part his demeanor was serious, most unlike that of his
fellow hussars, and his clothes, although they had a
certain panache, were somewhat understated compared to his colleagues'. Frequently he appeared in
the same clothes. With the other eligibles, there was
always a new satin waistcoat and a different cutaway
on every occasion. It might very well be that he was
short of funds.

And why did he disappear so often? He seemed to
have far more pressing duties than your typical man
about town. If his business was truly fortune hunting,
the pursuit certainly did not hold his undivided attention as one would expect.

Verity would exhaust herself nightly with such im-
ponderables until she slept, and she would wake so
drowsy that she took to drinking black Ceylon tea at
breakfast to rouse herself.

On a rainy January morning, she sat half dozing
over her breakfast. Laura looked charming and tou-
sled in her pink velvet peignoir, dabbing away her
faint chocolate mustache. Aunt Maria, the only one at
table dressed for the day, wore her raspberry alpaca
morning dress with ecru lace. Uncle George's place
was empty as usual, since he always took coffee in his
room. The three of them were recovering from Lady
Sefton's very long supper party the previous night,
and rousing themselves for the plans ahead.

Laura turned to look through the window at the
slanted downpour. "I do pray it clears up before we
go. How long has it been coming down, Mama? I can't
wear my cashmere cape if it continues this way."

Aunt Maria had already finished breakfast. She
looked as if she had been up for hours. Her fingers

drummed impatiently on the linen cloth. "It won't shrink if you take an umbrella," she remarked absently.

"But I don't have one that wouldn't clash with the ice-blue. Yellow or rose or green. They would all look simply crass."

"Take my black one, then," Aunt Maria said, but her mind for some reason was intent on the table crumbs. She began picking them up one by one and placing them in a neat pile on her bread plate.

Laura had got up a party of six for today. The two cousins and Clarrie were to visit the British Museum with Geoffrey Chipping-Sodbury, Mr. Carshalton, and, inevitably, Bennington-Jones. Verity had wanted very much to see the Elgin Marbles, but at the moment, she wanted only to go back to bed.

Laura was about to protest the idea of a black umbrella when Grimshaw entered the breakfast room to announce Mr. Fotheringay, at which Aunt Maria became very brisk.

"Show him into the library, Grimshaw, and ask Lord Strathmore to join us. He should still be in his sitting room."

As Grimshaw withdrew, Aunt Maria picked up the lorgnette that hung by a velvet ribbon on her bosom and peered through it at the pelting rain outside.

"On second thoughts, Laura, wear your reverse seal cloak with the hood up. You won't be back for hours, and you'll get drenched just going up the portico steps at the museum. They are quite unsheltered."

Rising to go, she turned to Verity. "You have a hooded fur too, do you not, Caroline? Good, the red fox, then. Buck up and dress, girls. The gentlemen will be here to fetch you soon."

Mounting the stairs to her room, Verity wondered where she had heard the name Fotheringay before.

In her bedroom, Sarah had the little oil burner going. The curling irons rested in their twin cradles, heating in the blue flame. Verity grimaced at the sight and flopped down on the bed. She did not feel like a big to-do over her hair today. "No curls this morning, Sarah. They'll only fizz out in the rain."

"Tha's not going to *walk* in it, lass! Tha'll be stepping right into the gentlemen's carriage," Sarah retorted, and continued setting out the curling rags, pin combs, and ribbons on the dresser top.

"Ah'll wager Miss Laura's goin' to be all ribbons and curlicues. Tha'll look proper dowdy." Approaching the bed, the abigail held out her hand with a coaxing smile. "Come on then, Miss Verity. That nice young captain's to be there. Tha' can't go plain."

Verity rolled over with a groan and buried her face in the pillow. "That nice young captain is forever there! My nemesis! My *bête noire!*" She attacked her pillow with vicious little jabs of her fists. "One of these days," she muttered, "I shall be downright rude to him. '*Avaunt!*' I shall cry. '*Never darken my doorstep again, for I cannot abide the sight nor the sound of you, nice Captain Bennington-Jones!*'"

Sarah listened skeptically. "Tha'd never do that and tha' knows it."

With a sigh, Verity rose from the bed reluctantly. "I'm afraid you're right, Sarah. I'd never have the courage."

She allowed Sarah to dress her in an elegant rose velour gown, but dug in her toes about the curling irons. Sarah was finishing a very simple coiffure with little grunts of disapproval when Aunt Maria entered the bedroom. Holding still while Sarah affixed the pin combs, Verity watched her aunt's approach in the mirror.

"Whatever ails you, Aunt? You look thunderous. Is something amiss?"

"Nothing, nothing." Aunt Maria clutched a slim roll of parchment, which she tapped nervously against her left palm. "I merely want a word with you before you leave. Finish her off, Sarah, then leave us."

The last comb in place, Sarah fetched the fox cloak from the clothespress and held it out for Verity.

"Just lay it on the bed and fetch her gloves," Aunt Maria ordered impatiently. "I shall help her on with it."

Sarah meekly complied, then left the room at full speed.

Aunt Maria had been unusually preoccupied of late, Verity observed, deciding to humor her. Arms held out, Verity stood and daintily pirouetted for her aunt's inspection. "Will I do? Or do you agree with Sarah that I'm coiffed 'a sight too plain by far'?"

Ignoring her niece, Aunt Maria frowned and tucked in her chin, creating a second one in the plump folds of her neck. "What hour will you be back, do you suppose, Caroline?"

"Do you not want us back for Laura's two-o'clock rest? I assumed we would lunch early to be back in time."

"No." Aunt Maria shook her head emphatically. "It's quite *farouche* to take lunch before two. I suggest you take your time at the museum, and not repair to Bond Street any earlier than two."

Verity was intrigued at the unexpected suggestion. For weeks, the household had bent its usual routine, lunching promptly at half past noon, in order to accommodate Laura's afternoon rest. When had it suddenly become "quite *farouche*" to take lunch before two?

"No rest for Laura today, then, Aunt?" she asked ingenuously. "No three-o'clock at home?" It occurred to Verity that her aunt wanted Laura away from the house at that time, and she would dearly have loved to know why.

"It's the theater tonight," Aunt Maria murmured distractedly. "The curtain at Drury Lane doesn't rise until half past eight o'clock. And I daresay if we missed the first act, it wouldn't really signify. We all know Oliver Goldsmith. Laura can rest in her room when you return at, say . . . fiveish."

"*Fiveish!*" Verity's eyes grew wide. This was a drastic change of plan.

"At any rate, no earlier than half past four," Aunt Maria decided. "Can you see to it that Laura doesn't gobble? It's not at all healthy to rush through a large meal."

During the season, luncheon had become anything but a large meal. The rich banqueting fare of the evenings had shrunk the midday meal's proportions to a mere light collation, a cup of broth or a cucumber salad perhaps. More substance might be offered at a host's table, but one no longer took it in view of the sumptuous evening ahead. Large meal indeed! Verity was hard put to give a serious answer.

"I shall make sure she doesn't gobble, Aunt. In fact, with Mr. Chipping-Sodbury in the party, it should be no effort at all to have Laura linger over the table for hours."

Aunt Maria looked relieved. "I should be much obliged, my dear."

The visit to the British Museum had been prompted not by the glories of Greece, but by the arrival of the new Paris exhibit: "Memories of the Revolution." The exhibit was not the first of its kind, but the first to be socially acceptable.

A Swiss woman, Marie Tussaud, had already exploited the lurid taste of Londoners by setting up, some eighteen years ago, a waxworks recreation of the Reign of Terror. The grisly display had always been shunned by English aristocrats out of respect for their noble French cousins. But now, twenty-six years had dimmed the shock of the revolution; the Corsican jack-in-the-box was well and truly exiled on remote St. Helena these four years past, having been trounced once and for all time at Waterloo. And a reassuring Bourbon now occupied the French throne. The once fearful relics of the bloodbath had at last become respectable curiosities. Madame Tussaud's display might still be considered off limits to the genteel, but the British Museum was not.

No lurid wax models here, the newspapers announced, but the genuine artifacts of that tragic episode, of the most profound and moving historical interest.

Despite the claims of the *Times* and the *Tatler*, Verity found it all decidedly lurid. A white satin gown in a glass case dated January 21, 1793, Marie-Antoinette's dress worn to the guillotine; a rusted blade that supposedly parted Louis XVI from his head; a penned document recording his last words on the scaffold. Louis's last cravat, cream silk and sporting a dark, granular stain on the neckpiece; a group of highly idealized portraits of the royal family; the prie-dieu upon which the queen offered her last prayers; the wig worn by the executioner.

The exhibit room was stuffy and overcrowded. It gave Verity the shivers, and she longed to leave it for more uplifting subjects. The Acropolis frieze was here under the same roof, she reflected, if only they would finish. But the others insisted on lingering over every last snuffbox and lugubrious inscription.

When they were at last ready to leave, Bennington-Jones declared that they must all see the Talley-Ho corner next. No cozy corner this, but an enormous enclosure crammed with trophies and etchings and indifferent paintings of famous fox hunts. It was the last straw. Losing patience, Verity slipped away from her party and made her way alone to the halls of the Greek marbles.

She was feasting her eyes on Diana the Huntress when a cough at her side drew her glance. She turned, expecting to find the others had at last caught up with her, but it was none other than Etienne de Roncy who took her hand and bent over it.

"Exquisite, is she not?" he said, inclining his head toward the marble goddess flanked by two Ionic colonnades. "But if the sculptor had only had you for a model, Miss Cox, ah, what wonders he could have left for posterity!''

As always, he was a feast for the feminine gaze, his brown eyes as velvet as his voice, his snuff-colored nankeens taut under his chocolate cutaway. Diverted as she was to be so suddenly confronted by this vision of masculine grace, Verity was forearmed. She was not about to be seduced into the attractive Frenchman's arms a second time. His charm was not altogether irresistible if one had strength of purpose.

''Monsieur de Roncy,'' she said pleasantly, removing her hand from his. ''In London again so soon? Quite amazing how our paths cross so fortuitously, is it not?''

''I must confess, mamselle, it is not by chance that we meet. I have just come from Sloane Terrace. I was apprised by a manservant of your whereabouts this morning.''

''And you followed me here?''

''I confess. I wish only a moment with you, but my mission is most urgent.''

Guessing his mission to be identical to the one which had brought him to Almack's—planned adultery, not to put too fine a point on it—Verity did not hesitate to nip it in the bud. ''You must fulfill your mission elsewhere. I am here with my cousin—a party of six, in fact—and I must rejoin them on the lower floor before they count me lost. Enjoy your sojourn in London, monsieur,'' she added primly, then gave him a deep curtsy and turned away.

''You misunderstand, mamselle,'' he called, striding after her. ''I come to you on the business of Les Chasseurs du Roi.''

Verity slowed her steps and allowed him to walk beside her through the exhibit, albeit a trifle suspiciously.

De Roncy thrust a sheet of paper into her hand. ''It is a drawing,'' he explained unnecessarily. ''I beg you to examine it.''

It was an odd design one might expect to see on a

signet ring or possibly mounted above a family motto: two griffins above a gauntleted hand clutching a serpent. If he had ever shown it to her before during one of his visits to Briarley, she did not recall it. The device signified nothing to her.

She smiled, knowing that de Roncy was devious enough, outrageous enough, to use his royal mandate as a pretext to press his advances. It was all very flattering, but she was hardly deceived by it. "Monsieur, you are well aware that I am no expert in the insignia of the French nobility. My aunt, on the other hand, is a veritable human encyclopedia of the aristocrats of Europe. She would be charmed to give you every assistance in your rescue mission."

"I made every attempt to see Lady Strathmore this morning, mamselle," he said, his pursed lips offering the most earnest protestations of innocence misunderstood. "She was busily engaged and could not see me."

"Then perhaps some other time, when she is free, she will be able to assist you." Verity gazed distractedly at a fragment of frieze depicting a discus thrower. What an incorrigible, elegant rogue he was, she thought, very much doubting he had made the least attempt to see Aunt Maria that morning.

Gently, he pressed her elbow. "Perhaps on this occasion you can be of some assistance. What do you know, for example, of the man whose name is Patrick Tarkington?"

Verity stiffened as though she had been offered an indignity. What fiendish tactic did he have in mind now? Had de Roncy always known Mr. Tarkington by name? Or had he merely made it his business to identify the intruder who had thwarted his planned seduction? At least she knew now that she had been quite correct in her assumption. De Roncy had no genuine rescue mission in mind this morning, he was merely using all the ingenuity at his disposal to disarm her.

"I know very little of Mr. Tarkington," she said archly, "save that he is a serious contender for my cousin's hand. What possible interest can you have in the fellow?"

He shrugged. "None, except that unlike his fellow officers, his lineage escapes us. Curious, no? The resources of Les Chasseurs are considerable, mamselle. Of all the officers in the southern English regiments, only two are of unverifiable descent, a colonel of some six and fifty years, and Patrick Tarkington."

"It therefore follows, as day follows night I suppose, that he is the long-lost son of some great French house?" Verity did not bother to disguise her laugh. "Is that what you believe?"

"I believe nothing, mamselle," de Roncy said, somewhat impatiently. "A certain case has been brought to my attention, and I merely do my duty. In 1792 a French infant was brought to England by his wet nurse following the imprisonment of his parents in the Bastille. That the woman arrived safely in Folkestone with her charge has been attested to by eyewitnesses, including the master of the sailing vessel in which she crossed the Channel. As instructed, she was en route to Sussex to place the child in the guardianship of his maternal relatives when all trace of her was lost. It does not mean that the *enfant* was lost. He could have been fostered by a kindly family; he could have been stolen by gypsies. There are several possibilities."

Verity narrowed her eyes. "And he could have perished along with his nurse, monsieur. Surely your task is hopeless."

De Roncy shrugged. "Remote, to be sure, but not hopeless. Tarkington appears at least to be of the right age, and if he should have still in his possession the signet ring his parents hung by a cord around his neck—"

"And if the signet ring bore the very same device depicted in your ink drawing . . . ? Really, monsieur, you do not deceive me in the least. I declare, for inventiveness you rival Sir Walter Scott!"

"Who, mamselle?" De Roncy raked a hand through his unruly chestnut curls in desperate confusion.

"He is the author of dashing historical adventures, full of swashbuckling heroes, coincidences, damsels in distress, and secret devices. Last year I read his *Ivanhoe*, and I highly recommend you read it. Although from your preposterous suggestions, I believe you already have!"

Unfamiliar with the English author as he was, de Roncy still felt the brunt of her sarcasm. "Perhaps I have earned your disdain," he said humbly, "but in Mr. Tarkington, I fancied that I detected what could possibly be a family likeness—"

"You fancy many things, monsieur," Verity said, beginning to tire of this transparent game. She clearly remembered that first assembly at Almack's, de Roncy's indecent proposals when they were alone on the balcony—alone at least until Tarkington's appearance. The balcony had been dim and shadowy, and the two men were total strangers to each other. It was unlikely that de Roncy had caught more than the most fleeting glimpse. Tarkington had been standing with the light behind him. Now the rogue was implying that he had in the heat of that moment just *happened* to notice a family resemblance. And to whom, pray? Some person whom de Roncy had assuredly never laid eyes on.

"Mamselle," he pleaded in a small voice, "the infant's parents were guillotined, but there remains a relative who is determined at any cost to pursue—"

"I have told you that my aunt would be delighted to assist you," she cut in. "And she is a far likelier target for your questions."

Catching sight of Laura and Clarrie in the archway and the rest of their party trailing behind, Verity bid the Frenchman a short adieu and hastened toward them, dismissing the whole ridiculous tale from her thoughts.

Reunited with her companions of the morning, she now found herself propelled through the display of priceless antiquities at top speed with no time to admire, because Clarrie and Laura had by now had quite enough, because Bennington-Jones was devilish hungry, and because Chipping-Sodbury—who at this juncture would have gladly hurled himself from the second-floor balcony to accommodate Laura—declared that he had seen it all before anyway, and didn't mind a bit.

For Verity, the entire purpose of the visit was spoiled, but when she ventured a mild protest, she received a gratuitous threat from the captain.

"I shall be happy to bring you back here alone for a much longer visit," he declared, and Verity said no more.

Laura was delighted to learn that there was no need to rush home, and as Verity had predicted, she was more than content to linger over the luncheon table, bathing in the adoring light of Mr. Chipping-Sodbury's eyes. For Verity, the afternoon dragged endlessly. Poor Mr. Carshalton did his best to hold up his end of the conversation, but he was no match for Bennington-Jones. By the time they reached home, Verity's head ached mightily, and her teeth too. They had been clenched for so long.

Laura glanced at the clock on the hall table. "Almost five—can you believe it, coz! How time does fly in good company!"

Time, Verity decided, was not restricted to measurement by clocks after all.

—9—

She had given Etienne de Roncy short shrift, Verity thought, mounting the stairs to her bedroom. No shorter than he deserved, of course, for he was an outrageous fellow and not as attractive as she'd once thought. It was rather an intriguing idea that Mr. Tarkington might have exalted connections on the continent. But it was, of course, all a hum, she reminded herself, just another fancy French excuse to trap her into a corner. At least she knew that her dangerous susceptibility to de Roncy's charm was gone for good. Nothing had stirred in her upon seeing him again. He was simply a family friend. If so many family histories had indeed been checked by Les Chasseurs du Roi, it was a trifle curious that Tarkington's had not been verified. Perhaps Lady Strathmore had cause to—

As she entered her bedroom, her train of thought was broken by Sarah, who looked fairly swept into the boughs with apprehension. At the sight of her mistress, the abigail's hand flew to her breast in a gesture of utter relief. "Lord be praised," she breathed. "Ah thowt for sure Jack Tibbit 'ad got the both of tha's!"

"Jack Tibbit? Hardly!" Verity laughed as the abigail pounced to remove her damp fox fur with exaggerated haste. "Good Lord, Sarah! Whatever ails you? If we all came safely through the week-long journey from Lancashire, we're scarce likely to be attacked by

121

highwaymen in broad daylight a mere five minutes from Oxford Circus."

"Tha' should 'a' bin 'ome hours past," Sarah scolded.

"But surely my aunt told you? No? How unlike her!" Verity sat down at the dresser and smoothed back the wisps of hair at her temples that always curled mutinously in damp weather. Over her shoulder, she noticed the very genuine agitation in Sarah's reflected face. "I *am* sorry you were worried, Sarah, dear. My aunt did not expect us back before half past four."

"She said nowt about that to me." Sarah stood hovering behind her, frowning into the glass and twisting her hands nervously. "At three sharp, she rang for me and Margaret. Said we was to send the both of tha's down to her in the sitting room the moment tha' came back."

Verity twisted around to face her, wondering at the distress in Sarah's voice.

"All het up, she were. Ah thowt it were just because tha' was late. Eee! Such a to-do all afternoon! Front door bell ringing off the rope from half past two on. Grimshaw never even served tea, just stayed by front door telling the callers Miss Laura weren't 'ome. Ah never seen the likes! Tha'd best go straight down this minute with Miss Laura. Waitin' there *simmering*, m'lady is, for nigh three hours, and like to burst."

Sarah was known to overstate, but this time she had not. When the girls entered the sitting room, they both recognized immediately that Aunt Maria had indeed been distraught and had already resorted to the usual measures to aid her recovery.

Dosed up, and more or less composed now, she lay stretched out on a chaise, a gray astrakhan pulled up to her chin. The telling arrangement on the little wine table beside her chaise underlined the extremity of the situation: a tea tray, a brandy decanter, an opium bottle with a tiny spoon, and a small vial of smelling salts.

Laura ran forward and knelt by the chaise. "Oh, Mama, what is it? Terribly bad news?"

"It could have been disaster, but it has been safely averted." Lady Strathmore's words floated out slowly as she stifled a light yawn. "Don't distress yourself, gels," she drawled. "It is merely imperative that you are told immediately. Please sit there where I can see you. My neck is stiff."

Quickly, they perched on the edge of the sofa facing her chaise, all attention.

"Patrick Tarkington is forever banned from this house and this family," Lady Strathmore began, her voice oddly lacking the dire emphasis one would expect to accompany such a dire pronouncement. Opium, Verity surmised, had kindly removed much of the sting of the calamity by now.

"Laura," the dreamlike voice continued, "you are forbidden to speak to him or see him again."

"Very well, Mama," she replied cheerfully. "But what if I should see him at some gathering?"

"Highly unlikely after I've finished with him, but should that misfortune occur, you are simply to cut him dead—you too, of course, Caroline."

Verity rose to warm her hands at the fire, finding the room suddenly quite chilly.

"Is that all, Mama?" Laura's disappointed tone suggested that she had been summoned to view a reenactment of the fire of London and had witnessed nothing more eventful than a sputtering candle.

"Yes, that is all." Lady Strathmore closed her eyes. "And now I really must rest for an hour. It's all been quite exhausting." She dismissed them both from her presence with a languid arm.

Hand on the doorknob, Verity turned back to the chaise. "Are we not to know why, Aunt?"

Lady Strathmore put a hand to her brow in a gesture of utter weariness. "He is simply not acceptable in our circle, and that is all there is to it."

"There's a good deal more to it than that, I'll

warrant," Verity whispered to her cousin as they mounted the staircase to their rooms.

But Laura disposed of the entire topic with an indifferent little shrug. "Mr. Chipping-Sodbury won't be at the theater tonight, so I shan't see him until tomorrow afternoon. I do wish we had something planned for the morning."

On the landing, Verity caught her cousin by the elbows. "Are you not the least bit curious to know why?" she asked Laura.

"Why what?"

"For heaven's sake, Laura! A faithful admirer for six whole months is suddenly banned from the house without explanation, and you have no curiosity at all?" Verity was quite put out by her nonchalance.

"It's obvious! He's just not very well connected, that's all. Why should I be interested, Verity? You *know* he's become very tiresome to me, so it doesn't signify." Laura paused outside her room and beckoned to Verity. "Now do come in and have some tea with me. I want you to help me choose my gown for this evening. Did you know we're to be seated directly opposite the Royal Box tonight? I wonder if the Prince will attend?"

"I'll come by later perhaps," Verity said, her tone rather clipped. "You're supposed to be resting now," and with a sharp sigh of exasperation, she marched past Laura and down the hallway to her own quarters, where Sarah was still hovering about between dressing chamber and bedroom, endlessly busy.

"You can go, Sarah. I should like some tea and biscuits at seven o'clock. We'll be supping after the play, so I shan't dine. And I would like to rest quietly until then," Verity added pointedly.

Sarah helped her out of the rose velour and brought her yellow chamber wrap, after which she continued to flutter about the room, fussing with the glove stretcher and the brown kid gloves, which were soaked from the day's rain. When she had at last done with the business of stretching each finger taut over the holder, she drew out the feather duster resting in her apron pocket and made a great business of going over the gleaming marquetry of the dresser top.

From the bed, Verity followed Sarah's movements, wondering how long she would keep it up. "Very well, Sarah," she finally relented, "if you must know, there isn't much to tell. The situation concerns Laura more than myself. Mr. Tarkington has been banned from the house. That's all."

Sarah immediately pocketed the duster. "That nice hussar? Miss Laura's suitor?"

"Miss Laura's *ertswhile* suitor," Verity amended, then pulled up the coverlet, turned on her side, and closed her eyes. "Now please, Sarah. No more hovering. I must get some rest before tonight."

But she was far from drowsy, and as soon as Sarah left the room, Verity rose from the bed and paced her chamber for more than an hour, searching in her mind for some plausible explanation—any explanation other than the obvious one she had toyed with for weeks, that Mr. Tarkington had been uncovered as a cheap fortune hunter. Her mind refused to accept it, insisting that there must be some other explanation. There was of course, de Roncy's suggestion, but no, that was clutching at straws. That had been no more than a ruse, a bid for her attention. Now she would never be able to put it to rest, she feared, unless she could extract the real substance from her aunt.

That evening at Drury Lane, they were to share the Rothermeres' box and attend with them the intimate supper party that followed the performance of *She Stoops to Conquer*.

The Rothermere party consisted of Lady Rothermere, her handsome eldest son, Lord Richard, and his guest, Sir Nicholas Gresham, apparently an old school friend. The Rothermeres had only that week arrived in London, owing to their attachment to a freezing Scottish castle in East Lothian, a minor and dilapidated family property where, inexplicably, they all insisted on spending every Christmas and New Year's holiday.

Lord Richard sported bronze curling locks and wide blue eyes. Before the evening had much progressed, Verity suspected that Chipping-Sodbury was in imminent danger of losing his foothold in Laura's affections. The latter had already lasted an entire fortnight, so a change of heart was not entirely unexpected.

At supper in a cozy private room at Blackley's in the Strand, Lord Richard gazed steadily at Laura from beneath slender dark brows. Had she remarked upon leaving the theater what a perfectly splendid evening it was? So bright with stars! A pity they had driven to Blackley's in separate vehicles.

Laura had indeed remarked the stars. She blushed adorably. "I do believe the rain has left us for a spell, Lord Richard. Tomorrow morning promises to be splendid and crisp."

Promptly engaged for a morning ride, Laura was no longer at loose ends on the morrow. The good Lord Richard was to come by Sloane Terrace with Sir Nicholas, and take the cousins along the embankment and through Green Park. The mad Scot, McGraw, was to make another balloon attempt, weather permitting. There was a good chance they would be treated to the spectacle of the balloonist soaring over the treetops.

But Laura's predictions for the morning weather failed miserably.

"Mama," she wailed, her nose pressed against the breakfast-room window the following morning, "it's even worse than yesterday! Oh, just look at the filthy weather."

Aunt Maria, much restored this morning, raised her head from her plate of kippers. "Oh well, there's no point going out in that flood."

"But they'll be arriving soon. Lord Richard and his friend. What are we to do—send them away? I couldn't face another dull morning." Laura buried her face in her hands. "It's bad enough to be confined to the house every afternoon, as it is."

"It won't be dull, dear," her mother promised. "No, of course you shan't send them away. There's a splendid fire going in the library. Ask them to stay, by all means. Perhaps you and Caroline should get up a game of shake piquet. That should make the morning fly. And see if you can't prevail upon the gentlemen to stay for luncheon."

Laura returned to the table much relieved, and planted a kiss on her mother's cheek. "Oh, it's a marvelous idea, is it not, coz?"

Shake piquet bore little resemblance to its simpler cousin, piquet. The game required four players, thirty playing cards, three dice, and—to Verity's mind at least—a disproportionate degree of concentration in order to follow its convoluted rules. She was partnered with Sir Nicholas, a plump and jolly enough fellow, whose manner turned at once deadly earnest as soon as the cards were dealt.

"Shame, Miss Cox," he declared testily, when their hands were revealed at the end of the third set. "You called me fours—it should have been *twos*. Twos, Miss Cox! Pray look at your cards."

Verity was embarrassed. It was her third *faux pas*, and she feared it was becoming painfully obvious that she was either half-witted or hadn't the least interest in the game or the players.

As Sir Nicholas began to deal the beginning of the fourth set, Grimshaw announced Miss Clement and Laura cordially invited her to join them.

"Hallo, Clarrie. Do stay and watch for a while. Lord Richard Bonning, Sir Nicholas Gresham—my dear friend, Clarissa Clement. Pull up a chair, Clarrie, and have some lemonade and biscuits."

"Oh, shake piquet," Clarrie exclaimed, taking a seat by Laura's shoulder. "I adore it. I'll watch you play just for a moment. Whose winning?"

"They are," Verity confessed. "I'm afraid I've let

Sir Nicholas down dreadfully. Would you like to take over my hand, Clarrie?"

"Heavens, no." Clarrie nibbled on a shortbread. "I wouldn't dream of spoiling your fun, Caroline. I merely dropped by for a moment. We have nothing afoot at home until luncheon, and it was dreadful dull."

"You would be doing me a service," Verity said, and leaped out of her chair. "Truly, it would give me pleasure to pass you this hand, Clarrie." She glanced across the table. "And the pleasure would be shared by my good partner, I'm sure."

Before anyone could protest, she pulled the chair back from the gaming table, took Clarrie by the shoulders, and marched her over to it. "I shall do far less mischief if I am sent to my room to catch up with my letters," she insisted. "Pray excuse me, ladies and gentlemen. And pleasant sport until luncheon."

Closing the library door on all of them, Verity gave a sigh of relief. Clarrie would be a willing partner in the vexing game, and Sir Nicholas would be delighted.

Verity made for the private boudoir that adjoined her bedchamber, picked up a volume of verse, and curled up in a chair. But her curiosity about Mr. Tarkington made her restless. The subject had given her no peace since yesterday. Even the stage performance had barely registered.

Drat the man! So feverish had she become on the subject that the entire evening had been wasted upon her and she had made a perfect donkey of herself at the gaming table this morning. Everything so far had been wasted on her, she reflected, and the season was slipping by. It was absurd. She must pull herself out of this. The questions surrounding Mr. Tarkington were no concern of hers. And even if he were, as she fancied, inclined to have a *tendre* for her, it no longer mattered because Aunt Maria had pronounced him to be beyond the pale.

After wrestling with herself strenuously for twenty minutes, she decided to take the bull by the horns and put her weary mind to rest on the subject, once and for all.

Wearing her pince-nez, Aunt Maria sat at her escritoire, at work on what appeared to be a vast undertaking. A tall pile of notepaper stood to one side of the writing surface, each sheet densely covered with line after line of her small, elegant script. She was in the process of writing yet another letter and so absorbed in the task that she did not look up when Verity entered the sitting room after knocking thrice without response.

Stopping midway between the door and the curved niche of the bay window where her aunt sat working, Verity cleared her throat tentatively. "Invitations, Aunt? A dinner party? Supper? When is it to be?"

The only sound that greeted her questions was the soft, industrious scratching of sharp pen on fine linen paper.

"Perhaps I could help you address the envelopes?"

Coming to the bottom of the sheet, Aunt Maria dipped her pen into the inkwell, described a florid signature, dusted it with a sprinkling of powder from her pewter shaker, then at last looked up.

"What is it, Caroline?" She peered over the pince-nez, a trifle distracted. "Shouldn't you be with Laura entertaining those nice boys in the library? What are you doing up here?"

Verity approached and dropped into the damask chair by the escritoire facing her aunt. "I'm a dreadful cardplayer—particularly that game—too many rules. Sir Nicholas was becoming quite put out with me. I gave my hand over to Clarrie when she came in."

"The Clement girl here again? Well, it wasn't necessary to give up your place to her." Taking a fresh fold of notepaper, she reached for her pen.

"No, but it was most desirable, I assure you," Verity said, watching her aunt covering the linen sheet at great speed, and trying to catch the gist of the message upside down. "May I help you address those? I should be happy to. It will take you hours, and I have a great longing to do something useful for a change."

"If you're that anxious, I suppose it would be a help, dear." She reached below the rosewood surface and drew out a small leather volume from her drawer. "This is my London list. I shall need an envelope addressed for everyone in there who has a daughter in town for the season. You know them all by now. Ask if you're not sure."

Verity riffled through the pages of the address book, judging there would be at least fifty names. It should give her ample time to coax some information out of her aunt. On a console table under the window stood a box of envelopes fresh from the printers.

Aunt Maria rose and stood flexing her back as if she had sat far too long. "There are extra pens and sealing wax in the top drawer. I'm ready for a pot of coffee, I think. This is very tedious work. So many of them!" She went to the hearth and pulled the bell cord. "Would you like some coffee, Caroline?"

"Yes, please." For a while she watched her aunt walk about the room, easing her stiff legs while she waited for Grimshaw to answer the bell. "Is it invitations, Aunt?"

"Heavens no! It's Tarkington."

"Oh." Verity drew in a sharp breath. Aunt Maria lifted the top sheet from the pile, and glanced at it as she resumed her stroll back and forth over the Aubusson carpet.

"The fellow's deathknell is what it is. Of course, it's no less than merest duty to inform other unsuspecting parents whose gels may fall into his clutches."

"His clutches, Aunt?"

"Don't be so dull, child." Aunt Maria looked up at her niece impatiently. "You can't have forgotten already. I told you all about it yesterday when you came back from the British Museum."

"Not quite all. You merely said he was banned. Not a word about why. May one know?"

Aunt Maria removed her pince-nez and rubbed at the red indentations on her nose. "But I'm sure I told you all there is to know. Every word of it."

"Scarcely, Aunt." Verity took a handful of envelopes from the console table and set them down on the edge of the escritoire. "You were very distraught yesterday, and ... well, dosed up at the time. You merely said we were to cut him dead, and then you dismissed us from the room. I thought perhaps you wished us to know nothing more."

Astonishment transfigured Lady Strathmore's long features. "Gracious, Caroline, of *course* you should know!"

At the moment of truth, Grimshaw appeared. A veritable clairvoyant, he had anticipated Lady Strathmore's request by some ten minutes and already bore a steaming coffee tray with a platter of Mrs. Johns's excellent shortbread. "I thought m'lady might be ready for some refreshment," he murmured, placing it on a gateleg table behind the hearthside sofa.

"Quite right, Grimshaw. You're a positive marvel. I only wish I could take you home to Strathmore Hall with me. Bring another cup for my niece, will you?"

As the butler withdrew, she poured some coffee and took her cup to the sofa. "Now, where were we? Oh yes, you wanted me to repeat everything I told you yesterday, you tiresome child—I *did* tell you, didn't I?"

"No, Aunt. I can promise, you did nothing of the sort."

"Well, it's all quite cut and dried. I began to have my suspicions about the fellow some time ago, and just before Christmas I set Ben Fotheringay onto it. Nigel's solicitor. He's a very thorough man. *Do stop fidgeting, Caroline, and sit down!*"

Aunt Maria paused, and when her niece was seated across the fireplace from her, she continued.

"Fotheringay visited Tarkington's commanding officer straight after the holidays and explained my

concerns. The colonel was most obliging. He produced
the sworn statement Tarkington had made at the time
of his commissioning, and let Fotheringay copy it all
down. It was a complete family tree—and all false."
She glowered into her coffee, swirling it around with
her spoon.

"I could have told just by looking at at. All good
titles, and not a single one of them known to me.
Highly unlikely. Of course I checked in my *Collins'*,
but it was obvious something foul was afoot. Not one
of them was listed, needless to say."

Aunt Maria sipped her coffee with relish. It was
evident the topic was no longer very distressing. In
fact, all danger safely averted, she was rather enjoying it.

"Naturally, one does not doubt the word of a gentleman without facing him with it, so I summoned
Tarkington here yesterday to explain himself."

"That is why you wanted us out of the house,"
Verity murmured dully.

"Of course. It could have become quite ugly. I
charged him with lying about his parentage and simply demanded to know the truth." She shook her head
in remembered wonderment. "The audacity of the
man is not to be believed!"

Verity fancied that it was a look of reluctant admiration she saw.

"He replied cool as you please that he had not so
much *lied* about his family as simply *invented* it, con-
fessing freely that he had no parents whatsoever, living or dead. A foundling, of all things!"

"Good God!" Verity paled, not fully aware of the
expletive she had just used for the very first time.

Aunt Maria nodded in grave agreement, equally
unaware of the unprecedented vulgarity. "Yes, an out-
and-out impostor. Now you know why I was taken so
ill, my dear. It was so very much worse than I expected.
And imagine it taking me six whole months to un-

cover!" She sighed. "He was very convincing, of course, but I blame myself entirely for being so lax about it."

"No, you mustn't, Aunt," Verity answered mechanically. "He was so plausible."

"And so bright!" Verity watched her aunt gaily pour a second cup from the coffee pot. "He actually won an Eton scholarship, mind you. Then an endowment to study medicine at Oxford." Again, a wide-eyed look of reluctant admiration. "Such a perfect air of gentility. Such refinement. No wonder I was taken in! But the fact of it is, he came by none of it honestly. His birth is uncertificated, and his only known parents were the domestics at St. Agatha's Foundling Hospice in Greenwich."

Aunt Maria bent her head as if she herself were touched by the limitless shame of it all. "*Not even a known mother!*" she breathed. "All that breeding and polish and education, and all a fraud—simply acquired through brains and hard work, the bounder!"

Verity was suddenly bitterly sorry she'd asked, even regretting her offer to stay and help with the addresses. She had absolutely no desire to hear a word more.

When Grimshaw returned with a second coffee tray, Verity poured herself a cup and let it cool while she made a start on the addresses.

"And that's not the half of it," Aunt Maria went on, thoroughly warmed to the subject now. "When his studies were near complete, he took up gaming and bought himself the cornetcy in the Fifteenth Hussars with the winnings. The *Fifteenth*, imagine—under the pretense of being a gentleman."

Verity's hand shook as she began to address the pale violet envelopes, until she could barely manage to write at all. She changed pens twice, complaining they weren't sharp; she mixed up two addresses, misspelled a street name, and left ink blots all over. After she was obliged to tear up her fifth envelope, Aunt Maria completely lost patience with her and shooed her out of the room before she could do any more damage.

Behind the closed doors of her own room, Verity prowled aimlessly, one of Sarah's nursery adages returning to taunt her.

Curiosity killed the cat!

Now you know all and you should be quite satisfied, she told herself. You should be thoroughly cured of this ridiculous obsession with the man. You found him odious when you first laid eyes upon him in Denning, and you were absolutely right. There's no more mystery; nothing further to intrigue you. He is simply a nobody who spun himself a lineage out of thin air, and that's that.

Only it wasn't. The pesky creature was more in her thoughts than ever. She reviewed the information now in her possession. It was pathetically sparse. No, it wasn't. It was altogether too much!

He was clever, and that was something she admired. He had studied to be a physician, apparently. Ah, that was why he had so effortlessly diagnosed Laura's anemia. To have been drawn to the gentle healing arts suggested a compassionate man, a true sense of values. How could she help but warm to that? If he had continued thus, he would have become a self-made man—not so different from Papa ... anathema to the Strathmores, of course, but not to her.

Oh, why must she dwell on it? He had thrown it all away in the end for the gaming hells, so that he could become a fortune hunter. He was exactly what Aunt Maria said he was, a bounder and a cad.

With a fatally dull feeling in the pit of her stomach, she turned to the writing table and decided to pour it all out in a letter to Papa. Papa was so wise about people. Would he enjoy learning that he had been absolutely correct about Tarkington? she wondered.

The stark letter completed, Verity felt no better. She decided to ask for a tray instead of going down to luncheon. The Strathmores would be less than pleased about that, what with Lord Richard and Sir Nicholas as table guests today. Now *there* were two men whose listings in *Collins'* were doubtless long and distinguished. Ah well! She had already fallen so far short of Aunt Maria's expectations, it hardly signified any more, she thought as she summoned Sarah.

Happily for Verity, Aunt Maria was far too discreet and too preoccupied with her hostess duties at luncheon to make a great to-do about Verity's defection. She was temporarily left in peace to eat her cold veal collops from a tray in her boudoir. She wasn't hungry anyway. The reprisals would come after the guests had departed, at which time Aunt Maria would no doubt launch her heavy artillery, Verity reflected.

She looked at the envelope she had addressed to Papa at Briarley, and it occurred to her that she might postpone her aunt's harangue still further if she slipped out to post the letter herself, instead of having the coachman take it for her.

There was a runner service in Shepherd Market, she recalled. Letters left with the service before six in the evening were taken that same day to the London collection at Lombard Street Post Office. Shepherd Market was just a half hour's walk from the house, and the idea of a brisk solitary walk was appealing, now that the rain seemed to have abated for the day.

Slipping into her blue melton cape, Verity tiptoed down the stairs and past the closed doors of the dining room where the family and guests were still at table. Out on Sloane Terrace, it was wetter than it had looked from her window, but it was quite delicious to be out alone for once and she was not in the least deterred. Raising her hood, she headed toward Sloane Street, staying close to the iron railing of the terrace houses on the inner side of the pavement to avoid the muddy splash from passing carriages.

Within a few paces from the corner, a hackney skidded to an abrupt halt alongside her, splashing the gutter puddle so violently that the spray spattered her cape.

"Miss Cox! Miss Cox!" a voice called from the hackney window. As she turned, the carriage door opened and a tall figure, head bent to clear the low doorframe, stepped down to the street. Approaching her, he straightened to his full height.

It was Patrick Tarkington.

He bowed, then stood bareheaded before her, smiling absurdly, and apparently undisturbed by the raindrops already glistening in his dark hair and coursing down his face.

Instinctively, Verity tightened her hood around her face. What unspeakable nerve, she thought. On his way to Laura's two-o'clock as if nothing at all had happened yesterday. It was hardly credible.

"Mr. Tarkington, I'm sure you know that you may not call on us. Laura is forbidden to see you again, so it will do you no good to try. I strongly suggest you redirect your hackney away from here."

He seemed unabashed, eyeing her with all the calm assurance of a born aristocrat. *Damn* that Frenchman, she thought. Damn him for putting such fanciful fairy tales into my head, and all for his own nefarious purposes. This man is no French aristocrat. He's nothing but a bounder.

"It was not my intent to call on Laura. I was coming to see you, Miss Cox."

She looked up stunned, her hood sliding back to bare her tawny head to the rain, and did her best to set him down with dignity. "I too am forbidden to see you." She was quite shocked at the sound of her voice. In spite of every effort, her composure had fled, her heart pumping wildly, and her voice came out squeaking like a country mouse. It served her right, she thought. "Cut him dead," Aunt Maria had directed. If only she had done as bidden, she would not have been required to open her mouth.

He gave a disarming grin that did nothing to calm

her. His gray eyes were soft as rain mist under the wet lashes, and, *yes*, they were laughing at her as he reached out and replaced her backsliding hood over the crown of her head.

"Mr. Tarkington, I am *forbidden to see you*," she repeated with more emphasis, which only emerged as more squeak.

"Then *close your eyes*." He was still sporting a wide grin. "And I shall offer you shelter from the gathering rain, and—*ah!*—a whole afternoon off from Captain Bennington-Jones." Gesturing toward the waiting cab, he offered her his arm, unbelievably debonair.

She pressed back against the iron railing, rendered speechless.

"Oh come, Miss Cox," he said, passing a hand lightly over his wet head. "My darkest secrets are plumbed. I am unmasked. A cad." His caped shoulders moved in an insouciant shrug. "And now that you are forewarned that I am thoroughly reprehensible, you are forearmed. What possible harm can there be in it?"

He knew very well, but she could not trust her voice to point it out to him. Instead, she tried to stare him down.

His face sobered for a moment, the magnificent eyes so candid, so utterly unguarded, that he looked almost vulnerable. And in that moment, she was convinced he was indeed incapable of harming her. But still . . . a closed hackney, alone with this man? It was unthinkable.

He read her thought, for his expression clouded, then all seriousness vanished in an infectious smile of amusement. "Dear lady," he murmured in gentle reproof, "*that* much of a cad I am *not!*"

She felt a light but irresistible touch at her elbow. "Come. We shall both be soaked to the skin soon." And all at once she was out of the rain, seated cozily beside him in the hackney, and rolling right past 18 Sloane Terrace again, bound in the other direction to heaven knew where.

He had called out directions to the cabby before following her into the hackney, but she had paid no attention to them. She was far too busy trying to recover her wits.

Between the treacherous mouse in her voice box and the pressure at her ribs that made breathing so difficult, she had no inclination to speak whatsoever. In fact, she dreaded the moment when he might initiate a conversation.

Apparently sensible to her predicament, Mr. Tarkington remained obligingly silent until they traveled up Park Lane and were rolling along the Edgware Road toward the rural district north of the city.

Oddly, as the distance from Sloane Terrace lengthened, so did Verity's breathing capacity, and after a long quiet spell she recovered enough to venture a question.

"You were coming to see me?"

He nodded.

"You seriously expected to be admitted to the house?"

"I am a resourceful man." He gave her a droll oblique glance.

"Yes, of course," she said with a trace of asperity. How could she forget who he was? A man who had surely perpetrated far worse outrages than gaining uninvited entrance to a private house. Resourceful, he called it. She supposed it was, after a fashion.

"However did you manage Almack's?" she found herself asking.

"Exactly as I managed the Fifteenth Hussars." He chuckled, and for a moment his eyes left hers to glance through the side glass. "Except that the ladies of King Street are far more efficient than my colonel. Lady Sefton found me out after the first assembly and canceled my voucher."

"Impossible! My aunt is her dear friend. Lady Sefton swore to her that she had no knowledge of you at all. I can't believe she would have deliberately withheld such information."

"Ah, I was quite safe on that score. The Almack's committee would never admit to a mistake. They have a reputation for infallibility, my dear, and they mean to keep it."

"*Ah!*" How fiendishly clever he was, Verity reflected. "But the colonel of your regiment? Did he never suspect anything false in your statement?"

Tarkington leaned back in the corner and half turned to face her. "As long as one appears to be a gentleman, one is always trustworthy until proven otherwise, Miss Cox." He folded his arms and the grin came out again, delicious, boyish, and totally disarming. "Besides, *hors de combat*, the militia is noted as the least competent of all His Majesty's institutions."

"And, of course, Mr. Tarkington, you would never hesitate to take advantage of the incompetent."

"*Touché*, Miss Cox." He bowed his head with exaggerated gravity.

Verity turned her eyes to the side glass to hide her smile from him and was obliged to remind herself that she was conversing with a total blackguard. It was becoming harder to remember by the minute. There were market gardens on either side of the road now, she noticed. They were passing small dairy holdings, chicken farms, and neat patchwork quilts of vegetables on Verity's side. The rain had stopped.

Drawing down the glass, she looked out, enjoying the wet country smells.

"And what exactly was it you intended to see me about?" she asked presently.

"Oh, nothing in particular," he murmured lazily, and made a vague hand gesture. "Just a civilized farewell, I suppose you'd call it."

"*A civilized farewell*? Is that what we're having?" Try as she might, she couldn't stop warming to the man. Trapped beside him in this tiny intimate bubble of enclosed space, shift and lean as she might, she could not remove herself from his person by more than a hand's breadth. Heavens! It was bad enough that she was here. She certainly had no business enjoying it!

"I am taking you to visit some friends of mine, if you have no objections," he said.

If she had no objections, indeed! Verity couldn't help grinning to herself as she thought of the rush there would be on the sal volatile, if Aunt Maria could see her now.

"They are plain, unpretentious people," he went on. "They live in a very ordinary three-room house in Somertown. Nothing grand. But I love them dearly, and I can at least promise you a more interesting afternoon than Bennington-Jones at the window seat."

This time she laughed openly. Perhaps it was his own lack of pretensions that made him so engaging, she reflected, then amended the thought immediately. *Don't be absurd. The man is a fortune hunter. An impostor. If that isn't pretension, what is?*

Somertown was an unfashionable three miles north of London, and the house of Mr. Tarkington's friends was indeed ordinary—not much bigger than a gardener's cottage. But it was cleanly whitewashed, with a thatch roof in good repair, and the front window was bright with pyracanthus, laden with orange berries. In the summer, Verity was sure there would be geraniums in the window box.

In something approaching a trance, Verity walked into the cottage on Tarkington's arm and was presented to a round-faced young countrywoman who was comely and clean. Dora Reese, she learned.

Mrs. Reese gave Tarkington a bright smile and a bear hug. Then, much to Verity's amazement, she herself was treated to the same welcome.

"Lovely, Pat! You brought a lady friend with you. Come and sit down. Did you have your dinner yet? I've lots of boiled ham left, and there's a lovely artichoke in the back ready for pulling."

They sat around a scrubbed deal table that dominated one side of the room and settled for a simple cup of tea. A kettle stood simmering on the hob. It was, Verity sensed, a house where visitors were always welcome.

Their hostess produced half a sponge cake layered with raspberry preserves and without asking cut them both a large wedge. Verity was dismayed at the size of her portion, but then she tasted it.

"It's just left over from dinner," Mrs. Reese apologized, "but it's fresh baked this morning. We had a good berry crop last year. I think you'll like it."

"It's more than fresh, Mrs. Reese, it's absolutely delicious," Verity murmured, savoring every mouthwatering morsel.

"Just call me Dora, miss," Mrs. Reese said, blushing at the compliment.

"Very well. My name is Verity."

"Verity?" Tarkington said in loud surprise.

Dora shushed him fiercely. "You'll wake the baby! Stop that hollering, Pat." She turned to the teapot and poured them a strong brew. "It's a beautiful name, Miss Cox, but I couldn't use it. I wouldn't feel right. You're a lady. We're just country folk here."

The observation sat less than comfortably with Verity. It was not quite just, somehow, but she made no comment. Instead, she watched the enchanting little creature who was cautiously approaching from the other side of the chimney breast. It was a tousle-haired boy, barefoot and dressed in a blue nightshirt. He came a shade closer, rubbing his eyes with his fists, then turned tail and disappeared the moment he caught Verity's eye.

"There, you see?" Dora rounded on a remarkably subdued Tarkington and glared. "He's only been down half an hour."

"Come back, Robbie," Tarkington called out. "It's all right. Just a very nice lady I want you to meet."

"He'll never come in his nightshirt! And he won't go back to sleep neither, now he knows you're here," Dora scolded as she rose from the table and went after the child.

Beside her at the table, Tarkington fidgeted in his chair and stared intently into his cup. "I've just broken the Reese Commandment," he said. "Thou shalt not wake the baby. When Robbie is ready to take a wife, I swear he will still be 'the baby' to Dora.

"Jack Reese rents an acre or two not far from here," he went on, suddenly speaking very fast. "He's a market gardener, Jack. He raises vegetables—turnips, swedes, cabbages, and the like—and sells them to the Somertown greengrocers. On some days he takes them into Covent Garden. If he's there today, you won't get to meet him."

He continued to chatter in a most uncharacteristic manner, offering redundant details about Jack Reese, as though Verity didn't know precisely what a market gardener was, and he refused to stop until Dora returned with the child.

Dressed in a pressed white shirt and little nankeens, Robbie appeared to be about three years or more. He said nothing for a while, and Verity attributed his timidity to the presence of two city-dressed visitors. But after a few minutes, the child steeled himself to edge past Verity's chair and flung himself eagerly into Tarkington's outstretched arms.

Tarkington held out the small wooden box which

Verity had noticed lying on the facing seat of the hackney during their journey. The box, she now discovered, was the repository of twelve tin soldiers, mounted hussars. The child's delight was a sight to see, but nothing compared to his sheer exultation at being allowed to remain on Tarkington's knee.

"Do put him down while you finish your tea, at least," Dora complained, as the toy soldiers began to invade the kitchen table, conquering more and more territory. Dora held out a cup of milk to the boy, trying to coax him away, but he shook his head. Astride Tarkington's knee, he was absorbed in commanding his platoon.

"You're gonna spoil him to death, Pat."

"Nonsense. Robbie and I are just fine like this, aren't we?"

Indeed, Verity observed, Mr. Tarkington seemed to derive as much pleasure in the reunion as Robbie, whose affection for the man was overwhelming.

After tea, the table was cleared off, and Robbie fetched a division of grenadiers and a small French army from the back room. A brief but fierce battle was joined, and it was Tarkington who finally surrendered his troops to the British commander.

When they rose to leave, Robbie clung to Tarkington in a warm embrace, chattering incessantly by now. Dora finally plucked the child off Tarkington's shoulder and held him firmly on her hip. Tarkington seemed to melt at that moment, and insisted on taking Robbie off for a few private words. And while they took their protracted farewells, man to man, Dora showed Verity her vegetable garden.

It was a patch no bigger than the front hall at 18 Sloane Terrace, enclosed with a low picket fence at the back of the cottage. But it was dense with fat white cabbages, pale winter lettuce, and dark green kale. Verity followed Dora along the line of hard-packed dirt between the rows, and watched her bend now and then to pull a weed.

"Jack'll be right sorry he missed you," Dora said as they returned to the house. "He won't be back till after six. Well, next time, p'raps," she added with a smile.

"Yes, next time," Verity echoed, knowing very well there would be no next time. That she had ridden here alone with Tarkington and stayed for tea defied rational explanation, and she did not attempt it. It was an episode removed from ordinary time and experience. A fairy tale.

But it was real enough to have touched her profoundly, she realized, as the hackney bore them away from the village. She had seen a different Patrick Tarkington in the little house. Was it the real one? she wondered. Now that he was placed for all time outside her social circle, she would never have the chance to know for certain. But she knew surely that she would never despise him again. It would always be beyond her now to think unkindly of him.

The skies had cleared to unveil the setting sun. As they rode homeward, the little farms and the cattle were bathed in red-gold light. By now, she was sufficiently at ease with her traveling companion to enjoy the sight.

She leaned against the backrest as the hackney took off, feeling unaccountably happy and sad at the same time, watching the pastoral landscape slip past the side glass. There would be a positive uproar when she got home, but the thought failed to alarm her.

"Verity, eh?" Tarkington said, at last breaking the companionable silence between them. "If you felt impelled to be incognito this afternoon, you might at least have chosen a more likely name."

"But it *is* my name. I was christened Caroline Verity. It is only the Strathmores who insist on Caroline. Not even my cousin calls me that when we're alone." Verity suddenly recalled that the letter she had written to Papa that day, and that she had been on her way to post, still lay in her reticule. Ah, well, tomorrow would serve well enough.

"And you, Mr. Tarkington," she said. "Your friends called you Pat and even Paddy. I find that equally unlikely."

"No, no. I'm often called Pat, but no one has ever called me Paddy."

Verity stared at him, puzzled. "But the boy called you Paddy all afternoon! In fact, I wondered Dora made no attempt to correct him. It's most disrespectful of the child."

As she spoke, his expression changed to a solemn white mask, and when he replied he sounded excessively stiff.

"The boy was calling me Pappy, Miss Cox. His speech is still a babble when he is excited, or you would not have misheard him. Pappy. Babyish perhaps, but not disrespectful—and not inaccurate. Forgive me. I thought you had guessed."

The meaning of his words seemed to reach her slowly, as though they had come from a great distance. "You actually had the audacity to take me to your— *your nest*? To meet your mistress and your lovechild?" All traces of warmth drained away from her face. "*I see.*"

"No, you do not see," he said, his voice suddenly strident. "Dora is a loyal wife to Jack. She has never been my mistress. The couple simply foster my son, since I can scarcely bring him up in an officer's rooms."

"I stand corrected, sir," she said, suddenly all ice. How dare he reprimand her! "I take it then that you are widowed."

"No, dammit, I'm not widowed. I've never been married."

"So you *do* admit to having a mistress somewhere." The cordiality between them had evaporated.

"I have neither mistress nor wife, Miss Cox," he shouted, "nor son, to be completely accurate—"

"Nor any capacity for the truth," she cut in, match-

ing his volume. She would not listen to another word.
Lies, lies, and more lies. "Liar!" she exploded. "You
offer nothing but falsehood to all who are unfortunate
enough to cross your path. Do you take me for a
witless idiot?" She was so furious by now that she
would have cheerfully jumped out of the hackney and
walked home, if she had only known the way.

Tarkington groaned softly and covered his eyes.
"Would you please calm yourself and allow me to tell
you what I have been *trying to summon the courage to
tell you all afternoon*? I swear I have never lied to you,
not today, not ever."

"Your whole life is a falsehood," she retorted.

"*Yes*," he bellowed at the very top of his lungs, "but
for God's sake let me tell you *why*!"

Verity's reaction was to drop her voice to a hissing
whisper. "Don't ever shout at me," she said slowly.
"My hearing is keen, and since I am perforce confined
to this hackney until we reach Sloane Terrace, you
are unhappily at liberty to spin as many lies as you
can invent. Have at it, if you must. But don't expect
me to believe a word of it."

"Oh, very well, I don't." His long sigh seemed to
emerge from the very depths of frustration. "But at
all events, you shall hear it, and whether you believe
me or not, it is the simple truth."

"Hah! Lie number one."

His hands became clenched fists. He opened his
mouth on an angry retort, then clamped it shut again.
Closing his eyes, he took several deep, noisy breaths,
finding it difficult to quell his anger. But at last, in a
wooden voice, he began to speak.

"I had studied five years at Oxford, and was almost
ready to stand before the medical examiners at the
time," he began. . . .

He was four and twenty, and his life had not been
easy. His endowment paid only the cost of his tuition.
For room and board and books he had to fend for

himself, and because his studying was of necessity relegated to the small hours, he was also obliged to burn extravagant quantities of midnight oil, which his landlady did not supply.

He served ale in a Fogg Street tavern, he chopped wood, swept rubbish, hauled coal, and ran errands. Whatever menial jobs were offered, he took to eke out his living.

Such circumstances had not, of course, allowed for dalliance with the ladies. He had little expertise in gallantry until he met Phyllida St. Regis. She was a lady of fair, ethereal beauty who mysteriously appeared in one of the small residences that lay above the grassy banks of the Cherwell, in one of the better neighborhoods of Oxford.

The house lay on Tarkington's coal route, and twice a week he found himself delivering fuel to Lilly, the housekeeper. On one fateful occasion, it was Miss St. Regis herself who answered his knock on the tradesmen's door.

The next morning, recognizing the very same young man on the High Street, Miss St. Regis accosted him, apparently curious to know what he was doing clean, dressed like a student, and visiting a bookseller. Was he a student, or was he a coalman? The lady being exceptionally gracious and friendly, an acquaintance was struck, and very soon thereafter, Tarkington's circumstances took a turn for the better.

He could scarce believe his good fortune. Miss St. Regis was not only beautiful and kind, but a lady of considerable independent means. Out of the goodness of her heart, she offered to improve the young medical student's lot. At her urging, he forsook his cold, ill-lit garret for a splendid study with a river view, and abandoned his menial tasks to bend all his attention to his lectures and books and cadavers. His lovely benefactress not only provided room and board and a stipend for his supplies. She also initiated him into the exquisite art of love.

In less than a week, she had confided to him the most intimate secrets of her life. She was one of London's Fashionable Impures, an elite courtesan whose loveliness and engaging ways afforded her a life of high style and comfort.

She had recently withdrawn from London, she confessed, because she had committed an unfortunate indiscretion. In short, she was with child. As a trained physician, almost ready to practice his arts, surely he could help her remedy the situation? She had tried gin—which she detested—and scalding baths, but all to no avail.

Such was his infatuation and his indebtedness to the lady, he felt impelled to help. But after discreet inquiries, he knew it was far too late. He was trained to be neither butcher nor surgeon, he pointed out, but a healing physician.

Could he not at least secure some ergot for her? she pressed. He was, after all, four times a week at the county hospital. Surely there was a dispensary? She had heard that ergot was infallible. Was it true?

A long night of desperate soul-searching brought him to an unshakable conclusion. His avowed aim would always be to preserve life, not take it away. Besides, by now he was her ardent lover and deeply devoted to her. He was even beginning to think of the stirring life in her body as his own.

"Dearest," he implored, "carry the child to term without further hindrance. I shall see you through this safely, and cherish the infant as my very own. When I am licensed, I shall be able to support you both in style. We shall marry, and this child shall be our firstborn. Shall we not both love him dearly?"

"My heart, my own," she replied tearfully, melting into his hungry embrace. "How can I refuse you anything?"

At the end of April, Phyllida's change of heart was rewarded by the birth of a perfect, vigorous baby boy. As he had promised, he acted as midwife. It was hardly a physician's task, but neither was it difficult; his anatomy classes stood him in good stead.

There lacked but a few weeks of steady application and Tarkington would receive his physician's license, so he plied his books eagerly, while the infant prospered and Phyllida recovered her strength and her slender figure.

The infant slept in a cradle beside their bed, and one morning, six weeks after the birth, Tarkington woke to unusually furious squalls. The pillow beside him was empty, save for a note.

My dear Patrick,

Since you bear such affection for your son, and since I find him a noisy and intolerable burden, I leave him to you. You may dispense with him as you see fit. (I understand there is a foundling hospital in Islip.)

Do not attempt to find me. I have gone back to London, to the life I know and love.

To clear any confusion you may have, I came to Oxford expressly to find a needy medical student such as yourself who would be skilled enough to abort my mishap in return for whatever rewards I could offer, such a course seeming preferable to the alternative: the ministrations of some filthy crone in the back of a greasy cookshop in Fenchurch Street. For adamantly refusing to perform the service I sought, your rewards have been nevertheless considerable—my undivided attention *gratis* for almost half a year, and the sharing of all my funds, now thoroughly depleted!

So do not repine or feel sorry for yourself, Patrick. I never had the least intention of marrying you, but you are a dear boy, and I shall always remember you with ungrudging affection.

A fond farewell to you, from Phyllida St. Regis.

It was twilight as the hackney approached the outskirts of London. Verity had listened, subdued and attentive, throughout the long recital and was no longer inclined to doubt a word. His narrative had been simple and unemphatic, but the controlled emotion in his voice had brought tears to her eyes.

Having explained the farewell note, Tarkington leaned his head back against the headrest and lapsed into silence.

"And that infant, of course, was Robbie?" Verity said in a small, shaken voice.

"Yes."

"So you did not choose to place the child in Islip. You could have."

"You forget, Miss Cox. I know those institutions from firsthand knowledge. No, I did not choose. I could not."

"Did you make no effort to find his mother again?"

He shrugged. "Such a parent was of no avail to the child. Besides, I had more pressing problems, and neither the funds nor the time to travel to London, search her out, and prevail upon her to soften her heart."

"So, what did you do?"

His eyes took on a distance as he stared past her in the deepening gloom of the carriage. "The infant needed sustenance and care. I had at my disposal the house, whatever food was left in the larder, and the clothes I stood up in. And I discovered in short order that the rent was sadly in arrears. The owner of the property held me accountable, as the remaining tenant, for the debt. I might add that he was not nearly so patient with me as he had apparently been with Phyllida."

He paused, and she saw him smile as if the memory amused him, before he continued.

Jack Reese had been his closest friend at St. Agatha's, and he had recently married. Jack and his bride had willingly taken the infant into their care. As a penniless student, Tarkington could pay them nothing for their kindness, so he tried the gaming tables in the town and enjoyed some beginner's luck.

"I had just enough sense not to push that luck," he said with a self-disparaging grimace. "With a winning of two hundred pounds, I stopped playing and—"

"Purchased yourself the colors, so that you could wear a peacock uniform and attract a wealthy female," Verity finished for him.

Tarkington threw back his head and laughed heartily. "No! I thought myself very shrewd with my master plan. I was green enough to believe that a soldier's life would mean quick advancement and a steady income. It was the spring of 1815, you see. Wellington was struggling against Bonaparte. Medical skills are precious on the battlefield, and commissions were far cheaper to come by during the wars."

His arms spread in a large comical gesture. "I invented this impeccable family tree and got myself a cornetcy in the Fifteenth Hussars, the finest of all regiments. It was an investment. What a blessed and tricky rogue was I! I had always been assured that I was exceptionally quick-witted. In no time at all I would become a colonel. One field promotion after another which would cost me nothing."

He turned on Verity an exceedingly wry expression, and lightly took her hand. "As you've guessed by now, I knew nothing of the militia, and nothing of what was to happen that June."

She let her hand rest lightly in his, so rapt in his story that she was aware of little but the slight comfort of it. "June? You mean the victory at Waterloo?"

He nodded. "I never saw a day's active duty. By the time I was invested, it was all over bar the parades. No heroic lifesaving acts. No plucking wounded generals from the jaws of death. I merely found myself a minor officer in peacetime."

His eyes widened in mild inquiry. "Do you know what that means, Miss Cox? No? It means I was stuck with the expense of outrageous uniforms, mess bills, valets, and a hundred other undreamed-of commitments—and a mere nominal wage. An officer could save his wages for three years and it wouldn't pay for one decent pair of Hessian boots. A hussar's boots must be made in Bond Street, you see, from the very finest hides. An officer is invariably a gentlemen of independent means."

Verity could not understand his genuine amusement. She detected not one trace of bitterness. Indeed, his shoulders were fairly shaking with laughter.

"I had led a very sheltered life, and my lack of worldly knowledge was not to be believed. I was well and truly hoisted on my own petard as a result of my monumental ignorance."

Gently, Verity removed her hand from his. "But you could have sold your colors again, could you not? They would surely have brought you something."

"Oh, they would have brought a trifle over what I paid for them, I suppose, but what then?" He shrugged. "I had by that time lost my Oxford endowment, of course, and I was somewhat chastened by my former rashness. If I'd learned one thing, it was not to act in haste. So I simply considered my assets for a while."

"Assets?" Verity frowned, pondering the predicament he had just spelled out to her. She couldn't think of one asset to be counted in such a fix.

"Oh yes. I had discovered a slight gift at gambling, and it was temporarily serving me well. It still does."

He began to study his fingernails rather studiously. In what little light was left, Verity thought she saw him color slightly.

"I also found that I had some unaccountable appeal to the ladies. I had already observed an officer pay court and eventually marry a lady of vast means. And Phyllida had given me a splendid schooling in the art of dissembling."

A great sadness washed over Verity as she thought of all the gifts, all the energy and determination of the man. All turned finally to nothing more than the

sordid endeavor of hunting down an unearned fortune.
Suddenly she was angry with him.

"But why set your cap at Laura, of all people?" she
asked shortly. "When it was so obvious she would
have none of you?"

"I thought she was young and inexperienced enough
not to see through me." He turned his head away. "I
don't have much experience at this kind of thing, you
know. I'm far from expert at deception."

"You are expert enough!" she retorted. "You've been
at it, by your accounting, for over four years. Four
years as a professional fortune hunter. You're hardly
a novice."

"Four years and still no wife to show for it," he
mused. "I'm beginning to think it is not my forte."

"But why waste six whole months on my cousin?"
Verity persisted. "In London, she made it clear enough
you were wasting your time."

Tarkington resumed the careful study of his fingernails, and took his time before he answered. "I had
counted on her fickleness passing, I suppose."

It was suspiciously unconvincing. Indeed, to Verity
it was no answer at all. "I don't believe you wasted
that six months, Mr. Tarkington. I think you were
playing the field—courting more than one heiress while
you toyed with my cousin's affections."

"No," he said hastily. "I cannot take credit for such
conscientiousness. I did nothing of the sort."

"Then where were you when you absented yourself
from London?"

"Visiting my son—and also retiring discreetly to
replenish my funds in the gaming hells, as it is frequently necessary for me to do."

"Why such discretion?" Verity asked cannily. "All
the officers gamble. They haunt White's and Tatter-
sall's and Gentleman Jack's, but they never feel
compelled to leave London at the height of the season."

"Those gentleman play for sheer sport, Miss Cox."
His voice was low. "I play for livelihood. It is an

altogether different exercise." His arm reached up and rapped the wall above the facing banquette, signaling the driver to stop.

It was with great reluctance that Verity realized they were arrived at the corner of Sloane Terrace. Discreetly out of sight of the windows of number 18, the hackney came to a gentle halt.

After they alighted, Tarkington paid the cabby and dismissed him. As the carriage rolled away, he stood on the street looking at her strangely while a lamplighter passed them, completing his round of the terrace.

"I came to bid you farewell, Miss Cox," he said simply. Reaching for her hand, he brought it lightly to his lips, then turned to walk away.

"One moment," she called after him.

He paused at the lamppost and turned his head. As he looked back at her, the gaslight played on his features, and she saw such ineffable sadness that it caught at her heart.

Why had he really come? Why had he told her this poignant story? He had certainly never breathed a word of it to Aunt Maria. Verity hoped she knew why, but she longed to be certain. As she closed the distance between them, her courage failed, and instead she asked an altogether different question.

"Mr. Tarkington . . . since my aunt has spread your infamy far and wide, what will you do now?"

He straightened his shoulders, and his tone became brisk. "Don't worry about me, Miss Cox. I shall simply remove myself from the Strathmore sphere of influence and proceed as before. With more success, I trust. There is plenty of wealth in the provinces—and far less fastidious mamas."

He had merely told her this pathetic story to gain her sympathy. Her blood cooled and a shudder seized her as the simple answer dawned. She herself was from the provinces. But now she was exposed to this heart-wrenching story, she was unlikely to spoil his chances.

Perhaps that tale was nothing but another ingenious pack of lies after all. Yes, perhaps by gaining her sympathy, he even hoped to enlist her aid. Oh, what a conniving heartless rapscallion! *I don't have much experience at this kind of thing, you know. I'm far from an expert at deception.*

He was an adept at deception. A past master! And she was simply a wretched, stupid pawn in his game.

It took all her strength to remain calm while she voiced her outrage. "If you have told me this heart-rending pack of lies in order to enlist my sympathetic aid, let me assure you before you go, sir, I am no fool. I will not be a party to your trickery." Tightening her cloak about her, she walked stiffly toward number 18.

An iron grip on her shoulders stopped her progress, then whipped her around to face him.

His eyes flashed a brief, hot anger. "You seriously believe I would submit myself to this ordeal in order to find an accomplice? I have bared my soul to you!"

"What possible other conclusion could I reach with any brains in my head?" Unsuccessfully, she tried to shake off the odious hands that gripped her arms so painfully.

"If you had any brains in your head, Miss Cox, you would know that I cannot bear to have you think so ill of me. The Strathmores, the de Lyons—the whole silly pack of them may think what they choose. I simply rearrange my plans. But you!" At last his grip relaxed and his hands slid upward to cup her face softly. "You are the one woman of all women—"

He drew her face closer, crushing his lips to hers. Then his arms encircled her with such fierce-tender passion that her suspicions fled, and she gave herself up to his embrace with a heedless, rejoicing heart. When he finally released her, he held her at arm's length, gazing down at her as though he would engrave her face forever in his mind.

"Laura was nothing more than an excuse to be near you," he whispered. "How could you not have guessed it?" He placed a slow kiss on her brow, then turned away once more, this time quickly disappearing into the falling night mist.

As she mounted the entry steps to the house, she felt utterly bemused. Grimshaw opened the front door to her, and mercifully, she managed to reach her room without being detected by any member of the family. There was no way to avoid the consequences of her afternoon's disappearance, but she was at least able to postpone them for a few precious minutes.

The fire was lit in her boudoir grate, and she stood before it warming her hands and watching the glow of the coals as she tried to clear her dazed mind. After a minute, she removed the letter to Papa from her reticule, dropped it onto the red coals, and watched it curl, blacken, and writhe into ashes.

—11—

Tarkington's revelations shook Verity so profoundly that she was unable to marshal her thoughts on the subject with any degree of clarity for the space of two days. She was, however, able to scrape together a weak story to account for her long absence that afternoon. She had slipped out to post a letter, she explained, and then had strolled about the shops taking the air, becoming so completely rapt in the window displays that she lost track of the time. It was quite the best she could come up with at the time, and to her astonishment her veracity was not put in question.

In the end, the dire consequences of her disappearance were not so dire as she had expected. There were torrents of words from Aunt Maria, of course, sighs, implications of fecklessness, threats, gesticulations, and many reproachful glances. But what punishment could her aunt possibly inflict? To confine her niece to her room? To send her packing back to Briarley? Any such measures would only have defeated the purpose of the season.

It therefore occurred to Verity that her personal freedom was in reality far greater than she had assumed. She was not, in truth, obliged to attend every function without question. Effectively she was at liberty to come and go as she pleased, always provided she could withstand the moral pressure of tell-

ing an occasional falsehood. She had no wish to cause
undue anxiety in the household. In future, she would
inform her aunt of her comings and goings. It all
sounded very plausible in theory. But she had yet to
put it into practice.

The core of her predicament lay not in her desire
for greater freedom of movement, but in the discovery
of Tarkington's regard for her. No, it was far more
than regard; his embrace had informed her of a depth
of passion no words could adequately describe. And
that passion, she acknowledged, was mutual. There
was no question but that she was hopelessly in love
with the man, and at last able to see that she had been
thus afflicted for many weeks. But Papa had sensed
her *chagrin d'amour* from the very day he had arrived
in London. But how would Papa feel if he knew what
manner of fellow it was who had caused her sleepless
nights and sudden tears? *A fortune hunter blacklisted
all over London!*

Would it count that Mr. Tarkington was a man of
sincere and admirable sentiments, of brilliant wit and
high courage? Alas, had not papa already voiced his
suspicions of the man?

Apprised of all the facts, Verity could no longer
reproach Tarkington with anything worse than audacity in the face of desperate straits; his was no crime.
His charade, all his pretenses, they were but peccadil-
loes now. Papa perhaps could be persuaded to view
them thus ... but to reconcile the Strathmores to her
opinion? Impossible! What then was to be done about
it? Thus far, she hadn't the least idea. She knew only
that something, unquestionably, must be done.

It was at the Strathmore dinner party two evenings
later that a plan of sorts began to germinate. The seed
was, of all things, a stray glove.

Bennington-Jones was Verity's dinner partner. He
was utterly unaware of her last setdown and sat at
table regaling her with an eyewitness description of
the wondrous new Indian domes on the Brighton

Pavilion. "His Highness's favorite summer palace, don't ye know! And, indeed, a veritable splendor to behold."

The doings of the Regency Court were one of his perennial topics, providing him as they did with unlimited opportunities for pointing out the Bennington-Jones's longtime ties with the Hanovers, and for deploring the upstarts who pressed around the Prince.

Verity had learned that boring his listeners into a stupor was by no means the captain's only accomplishment. Bennington-Jones had a talent for malicious gossip and the worst kind of snobbery, which he exercised often. His was more than mere class consciousness; rather, it was an acute awareness of the inadequacies of all who were not blood-related to the Hanovers, the Tickberrys, or the Bennington-Joneses.

Verity had heard it all before, and her mind was free to ponder her plan.

It was while mounting the stairs earlier that evening that she had picked up one of Uncle George's white gloves. The chambermaid had apparently dropped it from the linen bag on her way down to the laundress. Verity had meant to give the glove to Sarah to take belowstairs, but before she reached her room, she changed her mind for some reason and cached it in the drawstring reticule she was carrying at the time.

If the glove were still in her room, she reflected, toying with her haricot of mutton, it could be the perfect vehicle. But had Sarah by now emptied the reticule of its contents and dispensed with the glove?

When the ladies repaired to the drawing room, Verity flew to her room to find out. In the top drawer of the tallboy, the reticule she had used that afternoon lay nestled innocently beside others, its only content a lavender sachet. But casting about the room, her eye caught the stray glove. It lay carefully smoothed out on the top of her chiffonier. She smiled broadly. One gentleman's white glove was very like another, and finding it so secreted, Sarah would not have guessed it was only Uncle George's. She must have thought it had some touching romantic significance for her mistress. Now, it *would* have!

Tearing a fold of notepaper in half, Verity scratched out a brief message, then folded it small and slipped it inside the glove. "For Mr. Tarkington," she wrote on an envelope, then sealed the glove inside it with a light wafer of sealing wax.

By the time she rejoined the ladies, the envelope concealed in her evening sac, the gentlemen had joined them in the drawing room.

From her tall-backed chair, Lady Strathmore eyed her flushed niece chatting prettily with Bennington-Jones. The child was so animated and responsive to him for once that her hopes for a fruitful conclusion to the season began to bloom anew. Vastly encouraged by the promising sight, Lady Strathmore left the couple to bill and coo on the far side of the room.

Verity was nodding and smiling and paying no attention whatever to the captain's discourse. She was busily considering her chances. Could Bennington-Jones be her unwitting messenger? Blind as he was to all things outside his narrow interests, he might yet be ignorant of Tarkington's disgrace, she thought. She prayed it was so, for if he knew it might quite easily shipwreck her entire plan.

But what if Tarkington had already left town? If word had reached the colonel, he would surely be stripped of his rank by now and drummed out of the regiment. Could word have reached the colonel? Aunt Maria's only concern was the parents of "unsuspecting gels," and it was doubtful she would feel impelled to protect the ranking officer of a crack regiment from his own carelessness.

She would simply have to chance it, she decided, hoping against hope that Tarkington had not yet changed his status or his quarters—somewhere in Albemarle Street, she believed—and that her message could still reach him. Didn't all the officers of that regiment lodge in Albemarle Street? One of

Laura's stray remarks jogged her memory, and she was sure that they did.

The message so crucial to her future happiness lay heavy in the sequined sac suspended from her wrist. As she sipped black Kenya coffee from her demitasse, she ran through the brief urgent words in her mind.

It is imperative that I see you, but it cannot be here or anywhere where we might be recognized. I shall therefore present myself at the house in Somertown, Thursday next at ten in the morning. If you have any regard for me at all, please be there.   C.V.C.

Verity discarded her demitasse on the console tray; the time had come to act.

"Oh, I almost forgot," she said, clapping her hands together in dismay and disrupting the captain's monologue. "I wonder if I might beg a favor of you?"

"Of course, dear lady," clucked Bennington-Jones. "How may I be of service?"

"Mr. Tarkington dropped a glove here yesterday." Opening her sac, she withdrew the envelope. "I was unable to catch him before he left the house. Would you be so good as to see that he gets it?"

"Delighted to be of some small service," he said. "Tark shall have it first thing in the morning." Placing the envelope in his waistcoat pocket, Bennington-Jones picked up on Prinny and Mrs. Fitzherbert at the Brighton Pavilion where he had left them moments before.

Verity breathed a sigh of relief. So Tarkington had not yet left, and the captain apparently knew nothing of the scandal. Vastly grateful, she rewarded the captain with her rapt attention for the remainder of the evening.

It was only late that night as she tossed in her bed that she turned her thoughts to the next problem. Exactly how would she manage to be in Somertown at ten o'clock on Thursday? Should she perhaps confide in Laura? Her cousin's wildly romantic streak would ensure willing aid in the arrangement of a tryst. Laura, she knew, would not fail her. But would she be shocked? Possibly. Would she be jealous to know that Tarkington's courtship of Laura signified no more than a pretext to be near her companion? Oh, hardly. She scarcely noticed the man's existence anymore! Most critical was the question of whether Laura was up to such responsibility. And was it at all fair to press a mere child into the most grave duplicity?

Before she fell asleep, Verity had firmly resolved to act entirely alone. She would take a leaf from her beloved's book, and act boldly.

"We have nothing particular yet for Thursday morning, do we, Aunt Maria?" Verity ventured the next day at breakfast.

"I don't believe so, dear. Why do you ask?" Aunt Maria grimaced as she pushed away her dish. "Too much sugar in the stewed pears. Mrs. Johns is very good at some things, but not at compote."

"It's just that Mr. Bennington-Jones was telling me last night that Kew Gardens is quite lovely, and I really should see it. I thought perhaps if I rose early, I could visit the gardens and be back before two."

Aunt Maria drew back the compote dish and decided to give Mrs. Johns's pears a second chance. "Ah, I'm glad you two are hitting it off better. Good girl! I've no objections if the captain wishes to drive you down to Kew, but don't expect Laura to accompany you. You'll have to leave by eight at the very latest." She inclined her head toward Laura's empty seat. "She's hard put to get to breakfast in her peignoir before ten-thirty, as you can see."

"As a matter of fact," Verity said in a small voice, "I was proposing to go by myself, so I shouldn't need a chaperon."

"You mean he didn't invite you?" Aunt Maria puzzled over this. "Mr. Bennington-Jones simply extolled the beauties of Kew and never suggested escorting you there?" Her smile turned down at the corners, settling into a disgruntled *moue*. "There's nothing in flower this time of the year, in any event. What on earth would possess you to rise at dawn the morning after Almack's? You know how late it is when we get home. It's absurd."

"Not entirely absurd, Aunt," Verity murmured. "You see, I believe Mr. B-J is on the point of proposing to me. It will come any moment, I think. I do so need to be quite, quite sure of my answer, don't you think? I have a feeling that a few tranquil hours in natural surroundings will bring me to a happy conclusion on the subject at last." Dismayed, she felt a flaming blush suffuse her cheeks, betraying the enormity of her falsehood. But it was that very blush that saved her.

To Lady Strathmore, her niece's sudden color spelled a girl about to become betrothed, and if it took all day in Kew in the dead of winter to bring the child at last to her senses, so be it!

"There *are* orchids and fuchsia in the conservatories," Verity ventured, hoping to tip the scales in her favor. "They bloom all year round, and I'm told they're quite a show."

"Yes, of course, the conservatories." Lady Strathmore smiled. The very word was balm. It was in the conservatory at Lionsgate, amid the overwhelming fragrances of ginger blossom and freesia, that George had offered for her so long ago.

Verity did not mention that she would not be riding in one of the family carriages. No driver in the Strathmores' employ could be entrusted with the secret of her destination. She would simply have to walk down to Sloane Street, she resolved, and hire a public vehicle. Her aunt would draw the line at her niece's hiring a common hackney, but the family would all be abed when she left, and thus blissfully unaware.

As far as Verity was concerned, Tuesday and Wednesday were vast wastelands of time, save for one momentous event, whose very nature was such that she was unable to share the joy of it with a living soul. A letter in the Wednesday-afternoon post. The envelope bore no hint of the sender, but she knew instantly it was from Mr. Tarkington.

The letter had been written only hours after he had kissed her, for it was dated Saturday last. Its belated arrival suggested that he had agonized over sending it at all. How overjoyed she was that he had at last decided to run that risk and be damned! She feasted on it, repeatedly retiring to her room at every opportunity to reread it, until at last she had committed it to memory.

My dearest Miss Cox,

I have abducted you, burdened you with the heaviest secrets of my heart, then topped it off by forgetting myself so far as to embrace you wildly on a public thoroughfare. And, alas, all without ever declaring an honest intention. Will you ever forgive me?

In my defense I can only say that it has been hard for me to suppress the dictates of my heart ever since I first laid eyes upon you in Denning. Were it not for my lack of prospects, I would not hesitate to fly in the face of London society, and the world for that matter, and beg for your hand in marriage, as I have always longed to do. But I am sensible that your father is a man of modest means. Never would I presume to place upon him the added burden of my poverty. I wish only for you what he does, a life of the utmost refinement and daintiness, unmarred by material anxieties.

Please know, however, that you can never be replaced in my affections, although for Robbie's sake, I must follow a grievous path and steel myself to a marriage of convenience. I hope you can find it in your heart to think kindly of me, for I wish you a lifetime of happiness and prosperity such as I, regretfully, cannot offer.

Discretion demanded that she burn the letter, but she could not bring herself to destroy the evidence of such tender sentiments.

How natural it was for Tarkington to have assumed she was a poor relation! He had met Papa and, of course, noticed his austere simplicity of dress and manner. How touching, how searingly honest Tarkington was at heart! And how glorious that moment when she could disabuse him. Now, even in the face of the formidable Strathmore barrier, her heart spilled over with hope. If Mr. Tarkington was prepared to fly in the face of society, well then, so was she. She would let nothing stand in her path.

When she had seen him again, pointed out to him that money was no object, she would immediately write to Papa and tell him everything. No longer did she have a moment's doubt that Papa would give them his blessing.

Leaving the sleeping house at dawn on Thursday, Verity made her way to Long Acre, hours too early. She idled away the time watching the women unload baskets of turnips and cabbages and pile them up on the stalls. A little before eight, she wandered down to Charing Cross Road and purchased some sugared almonds for Dora and a picture book for Robbie. Then she retraced her steps back to Covent Garden and hired a hackney outside the Royal Theatre.

She blessed the London cabbies for being so well versed in the city's thoroughfares. Without that knowledge, she would never have found her way to Somertown. But she had no difficulty picking out the white house once they arrived in the village, and, stopping the driver, she bade him wait for her. It lacked but a moment to ten o'clock. Her eyes swept eagerly up and down the narrow street. There was no sign of him, no other vehicle in sight. For a moment she doubted he had received her message. Could he fail to come if he had?

As she approached the door of the cottage, Tarkington emerged and strode down the footpath to meet her.

Relief flooded through her. "You came," she said gratefully. "I thought, when I saw no other hackney—"

"I rode my horse." He inclined his head toward the saddled gray at a tethering post across the street. It was an abrupt gesture, not overly friendly. "If there is something you wish to discuss, Miss Cox, I suggest we walk. There is no privacy in the house."

"But I have a little gift," she protested, holding up her packages.

"That was not necessary." As he widened the door and followed her into the house, she wondered what ailed him. He seemed so displeased, so impatient with her. After the briefest exchange with Dora and the child, he hurried her out of the house with a muttered excuse to his hostess.

At the end of the village street was a narrow lane where they walked between tall hedgerows that bordered fields on either side. The day was chill, but it was quiet and sheltered from the wind. She walked beside him in silence for a while, so disconcerted by his manner that she knew not how to begin.

"You should not have run this risk," he said at last. "I have caused enough agitation to your family, I should think. You should be more mindful of their feelings, Miss Cox."

Stony-faced, he fixed his eyes straight ahead on their path. "And as for me, you bestow no blessing upon me by opening a fresh wound."

Laying a hand on his arm, she stopped and made him look at her. "But I *had* to see you. I had already made up my mind to that, but after your letter there was no question." Her voice became soft in an effort to gentle him. "You see, Mr. Tarkington, like you, I am not in the least what I appear to be."

His brows lifted slightly, but he remained silent.

"Not at all," she went on. "Far from being a poor

relation, I am exceedingly well provided for—if anything, rather better even than my cousin."

"I see," he muttered, still frowning, and Verity laughed joyously.

"You saw Papa dressed very plain and came to a natural conclusion. But he happens to be one of the two richest men in all Lancashire. He is not a man of modest means, dear Mr. Tarkington. He is simply a Quaker."

"A Quaker," he echoed. His flat tone betrayed no interest, indeed no emotion of any kind.

"Yes! Quakers avoid finery like the plague. It is quite understandable that you were deceived. But at least one of your assumptions is quite correct; you *will* fare splendidly in the provinces!"

She waited for him to clasp her triumphantly to his bosom, but he merely asked, "Does that not make you a Quaker too, Miss Cox?" in a voice so detached that she felt he had failed to take her point.

It seemed impossible to jar him out of his woodenness. Why was he so slow to rejoice? Did he not realize how much was at stake? She reached up and laid her gloved hand tenderly on his cheek. "I was raised in the Church of England according to my late mother's wish. She was a Strathmore, of course. My parents' marriage was a romantic misalliance, as they say. There, there, my dear Mr. Tarkington. I beg you not to look so woebegone. It is splendid news I bring, not disaster," she chided.

But he appeared stricken, his facial expression evidencing such torture that she became concerned. She could not imagine what ailed him.

She took his arm and continued their walk along the lane. "Do you not see? You can now follow the dictates of your heart, *and* have the Cox Mills fortune into the bargain. I fail to see any cause for distress!"

But his gloom, for which he offered no explanation, was impenetrable. He was fast becoming a great trial to her patience.

"Only ask for my hand," she blurted out, "and you shall have it." One could hardly speak plainer than that! Catching her breath, she awaited the embrace that would surely come now. Instead, he disengaged her arm and turned very stiffly to her.

"*Please*, ma'am. I shall now escort you back to your hackney."

Much too astonished to protest, she walked beside him as they retraced their steps back to the street. This was utterly bizarre. In the prolonged silence that lay between them, she struggled to find a rational explanation for his behavior.

"Have you nothing to say?" she asked as the end of the hedgerows came back into view.

"I should have thought it perfectly obvious," he said hotly. "I can't possibly marry you for money."

"But you won't! You will marry me for love. It is simply an added good fortune that—"

"That nothing!" he exploded. "Unthinkable! Out of the question!"

"But you said in your letter that were it not for your lack of prospects, you would fly in the face of society. I can hardly believe you've changed your mind."

"My prospects, Miss Cox, have not changed."

She stamped her foot. "Indeed they have. You have won my affections and you have my fortune at your disposal. If that is not a vast change of prospects, I pray, what is?"

He remained obdurately silent, gripping her arm to speed her slowing steps, hurrying her toward the hackney as if he could scarce wait to be rid of her.

Furiously she shook off his hand. "What nonsense is this? You claim nothing holds you back but your reluctance to place a burden on a poor man, and I am informing you quite unequivocally that my father is so far from poor that your trifling temporary lacks are nothing to him. A mere bagatelle."

He froze, as if her words stunned him, and simply

stared at her. "You amaze me, Miss Cox," he said after a long silence. "Do you credit me with no sensibility whatsoever?"

"Rather, I credit you with no *sense* whatsoever." Again she stamped her foot, this time so hard that she felt the sting of it through the sole of her leather boot. But he was not in the least intimidated.

"And what of pride, dear lady? Am I to have no pride? Would you have me marry you with the whole family knowing what they know? Believing that I married you solely for support?"

"A pox on pride!" Verity snatched at a low-hanging sycamore branch and gave it a vicious tug. It snapped off clean. "You profess to love me as you can never love another, and you are an unabashed fortune hunter. Yet you refuse to marry me poor, and refuse equally to marry me wealthy." She kicked the dead branch out of her path and hastened away from him to the waiting hackney.

He quickened his stride to catch up with her, and opened her carriage door. She cast over her shoulder a withering look, then mounted the step. "I do believe your professions of undying love begin to sound exceeding hollow, Mr. Tarkington."

He slammed the door hard enough to set the carriage swaying. "You must believe whatever you choose. You always do." Turning to the amazed driver on the high perch, he bellowed, "Back to London, driver." Through the glass, she saw the furious set of his mouth as his head inclined in a wordless farewell.

It was the last thing she saw for some time, because, as the cabbie took off, Verity buried her head in her hands and allowed the welling tears to fall freely.

A pox on him! He'd never meant a word of it after all. He had simply been amusing himself with her. No! No! It wasn't possible! Only his beastly, obstinate pride stood in his way. Oh, but what a fearful hurdle that would be to overcome, more formidable even than coping with the Strathmores! She despaired of ever arriving at a happy outcome with such fearful odds against her.

When she had thoroughly soaked her handkerchief, she raised her face. For the first time, she noticed the blanket on the facing banquette; it was suspiciously lumpy, and it had not been in the carriage before. Gingerly, she leaned forward and lifted a corner. The blanket stirred. Stripping it away, she revealed a small figure curled into a tight ball.

"Robbie! Whatever are you doing here? Running away?" They must be some two or three miles from the house by now, she guessed. Stopping the hackney, she directed the driver to turn back to Somertown, then fell back against the seat rest with a heavy sigh. The child's expression made it hard to scold him.

"What an adventurer you are, Robbie," she said, dabbing at her eyes. "But it's time to go home now."

Quickly deciding that he was not about to be thrashed, Robbie became conversational.

"It's not my real home, miss. Aunt Dora is not my mama."

"I see."

"My real mama went to heaven a long time ago, but Pappy says he will get another soon. Then I shall go to my real home with my real parents." He paused and examined her curiously from the toe of her boot to the crown of her head. "Why were you crying? Are you my new mama?"

"No, I am not," Verity said with emphasis, then, after a moment, "Would you like it if I were?"

Robbie folded his arms across his blue shirt and thought about it, fixing his eyes on the carriage lamp that swung from the ceiling. Then he smiled and nodded his head.

The ingenuous gesture set her sobbing helplessly again. Confused, but moved to pity, the child climbed into her lap to comfort her wordlessly.

Verity found consolation in the warm clinging little body, and by the time they were back at the house, she was calm. She released herself from the child's embrace and opened the carriage door.

"Robbie, I want you to go straight back inside and tell Aunt Dora that you are home. I shall sit here and watch until you are in the house."

"Come with me," he said, holding out his hand to her.

She shook her head. "I don't want Pappy to see that I've been crying," she said simply, as Dora burst from the cottage and came running out to the hackney. Pulling Robbie out, she swept him up in her anxious arms and let forth a torrent of shrill reproaches.

"Oh, I'm so grateful to you, Miss Cox. We've been frantic. Wherever did you find the little rascal?"

"Right here under this blanket, Dora. He was a stowaway. Is the blanket his?"

"Yes." Dora leaned into the hackney to take it, then saw Verity's face. "Why, you're overset, Miss Cox! Not on account of Robbie, I hope?"

Verity shook her head. "It's nothing," she said, attempting a watery smile.

Dora's eyes narrowed. "Then it's Patrick! Did that big good-for-nothing make you cry?" She put out her hand. "Why don't you come in? You need a cup of tea at the very least."

"I really must be getting back," Verity protested.

"Don't worry about that lummox. He's not here anyhows. He's gone off looking for Robbie." Dora's face broke into a grin. "He won't be back for some time, will he?"

Suddenly, there was nothing Verity wanted more in all the world than the warmth of the cottage, and a cup of Dora's tea.

Seated at the kitchen table, she was soon unburdening her woes. It took very little time; Dora knew everything except what had passed between them that morning.

"Well I never," Dora said at last. "So your father's a Quaker, is he?" She took Verity's cup and refilled it with tea. "I can tell you one thing for sure, miss. Pat's lost his heart to you and no mistake."

"Oh, I thought so too, Dora. But when it comes to Mr. Tarkington, I find nothing is sure." Verity frowned. "Did he tell you so?"

Dora gave a little snort. "He didn't have to. It's written all over his face. Even Robbie's noticed how foolish and moony he's acting lately. And he's never brought a lady here before. That tells *me* all I need to know."

"Is it then only his pride that keeps him from offering for me?" Verity asked.

"No doubt of it." Dora shot a speculative glance at her fancy city visitor and stirred her tea thoughtfully. "My Jack at least knows who he is. His parents died in debtor's prison, and an ailing great-aunt had him admitted to the home. But Pat was just a babe in arms left on the steps of St. Aggie's. You wouldn't know what it's like to be a foundling, miss—but pride is all he's got. It won't be easy to get around it."

"You don't have to tell *me* that," Verity said with feeling, then looked uneasily toward the door, as if she expected the topic of their conversation to walk in and discover her any moment. She would die of humiliation. Never could she face him red-eyed and pleading for help. Never must he know that she had wept for him.

"Rest easy, miss." Dora leaned across the table and patted her hand. "Pat went off on his horse, and he don't plan to come back without finding the boy. I'll have to send Jack after him tonight, very like. But let him stew for a while. Serves him right, the fool, turning down a beauty like you."

The sympathy of Dora's touch brought Verity dangerously close to sobs again, but she fought them down. "What am I to do, Dora? I love him hopelessly."

Dora rested her chin on her hands and thought about it. The room was still but for a stew bubbling on the hob. Robbie had been banished to his room—a punishment somewhat softened by the fact that he was allowed to take a shortbread with him, and the fine new picture book Verity had brought.

"No point in doing anything until you tell your pa," Dora said skeptically. "Not if you expect his blessing."

"Oh, Papa is not the problem. He is a man of compassion and liberal ideas. His own marriage was a county scandal, but he never regretted it, and neither did my mother, I believe."

"You'd still best ask him first, though." Dora rose to give the stewpot a stir, releasing a warm, savory cloud as she lifted the lid. "In any case, it'd all work out easier if you went back to your pa straightaway."

"Back to Lancashire in the middle of the season?" Verity's eyes were wide at the thought. "Oh, what a hoo-hah *that* would create!"

"But you could do it, if you wanted, couldn't you?" Dora persisted.

Verity shrugged. "Oh, I suppose so, but to what purpose? It only increases the distance between us."

"Never mind the distance, miss." Dora returned to her chair and leaned forward emphatically. "One thing's certain, Pat'll never budge an inch so long as you're in the midst of the Strathmores. It's hopeless. Hardheaded as a mule he is."

"But if I left London, I'd never see him again," Verity wailed. "How on earth could I persuade him to follow me to Briarley?"

Dora laced her fingers together in fierce concentration and thought about it for a while. "I don't rightly know yet. You could go to his colonel and unmask him ... he'd get cashiered out of the silly regiment for a start. Yes, that'd clip his wings as far as this fortune-hunting nonsense is concerned."

"I could never do that! What are you thinking of, Dora? It would only make him more furious with me."

Robbie wandered into the kitchen holding his picture book, and was promptly sent back to exile with a swat on the rump.

"Your hour's not up yet, my boy," Dora called after him as he disappeared behind the chimney breast. Then her ruddy face brightened suddenly. Hurrying back to the table, she clutched Verity's arm. "I've got it! The very thing to send Patrick galloping up north as fast as you can say Jack Robinson."

"What, Dora? How?"

"No, never you mind. Just trust me. You just worry yourself about getting home to your pa, and getting his blessing. Leave the rest to me. I won't let you down, cross my heart."

Verity stared at Dora dubiously, wanting to believe.

Dora became brisk. "You're hackney's running up a fortune out there, miss. You'd best be going." After walking Verity to the door, she darted back into the house to fetch something and returned with a letter. Removing the contents, she handed the empty envelope to Verity.

"This is our address: five Hunnicut Row," she said, walking out to the hackney. "You be sure and send word to me when you're home and all's well with your father. I'll do the rest."

Dora, her smile aglow with confidence, watched Verity climb into the carriage. "Chin up, Miss Cox. The sooner you've talked to your pa, the sooner the wedding bells. Trust me!"

What choice did she have? Verity wondered, leaning back in the hackney as the horse took off. There was comfort, to be sure, in Dora's words, but she was far from reassured. What on earth could the woman do to persuade Tarkington to follow her to Briarley?

Idly, she examined the envelope Dora had thrust in her hand. The address was written in an elegant script, a decidedly educated hand. Turning it over, she examined the broken seal at the closure. The wax was chipped, and she could only make out part of the impression of the seal, which was quite an intricate design. Indeed, it was unexpectedly highfalutin—certainly not the kind of penny seal one could buy from any stationer's. Somehow, it was familiar to her, but she could not quite place why. In any case, far more critical matters demanded her attention; she was too overwrought to give much heed to the trifling question of how the humble Reeses came by such stylish correspondents.

—12—

It was a little before two o'clock when Verity arrived home. The house was quiet with that expectant hush that precedes the arrival of guests. A light trace of jugged beefsteaks scenting the air as she passed the empty dining room reminded Verity that she had missed not only luncheon, but breakfast too. She had refused Dora's repeated offers of food, but the innumerable cups of strong tea she had consumed were beginning to sour her stomach and shorten her temper. She was glad to reach her room without encountering any of the family. Above all things, she needed a sandwich, and was approaching the bell pull to ring for Sarah when she caught sight of herself in the mirror, and promptly decided against it. She looked a fright. Her face was pale and exhausted, her hair unkempt, for she had not awakened Sarah to coif her before she left that morning. And worse, there were telltale traces of redness about her eyes. She would do without the sandwich, and without Sarah's clucking and speculating about her sorry-looking condition.

With the ewer of water on the washstand, she set about repairing her face. Slipping off her dark green wool, she picked a primrose silk tea gown from the garderobe. She brushed her tangled locks until they shone, then mended her red nose with dusting powder, and her pallor with the lightest touch of rouge. Peering critically into the mirror, she thought it would do.

She wasn't exactly radiant, but she would at least pass now without undue notice.

Down in the drawing room, platters of macaroons and ratafia would be laid out as usual on the punch table for Laura's guests. She hurried down to join them for the two-o'clock.

But she had taken longer than she realized, and the room was already crowded. Her entrance was nevertheless instantly spotted by Bennington-Jones. He positively pounced on her before she was two steps through the open double doors.

"Ah, here you are, wandering lady. Lady Strathmore tells me you went to Kew this morning. All that way, alone!" A firm arm at her elbow, he guided her inexorably past the sweetmeats on the table and imprisoned her by the despised bay window.

She stood restless under his gaze, her eyes straying toward the faraway refreshment table.

"Won't you sit down? You never sit while I'm talking, Miss Cox." His voice was petulant. "I have much to say. I wouldn't want to tire you out by having you stand all through it."

Verity felt the last frayed thread of her tolerance snap. "I don't doubt you have much to say, sir, but you have already tired, me, *infinitely* tired me."

His smooth, blemishless features creased with effort, as if he were groping for abstruse meaning in the remark. "Well then," he said uncertainly, "if you are already tired before we have even begun, you must by all means sit down."

Behind the fullness of her skirts, Verity's hands squeezed into tight fists. "Captain, you warn me that you have much to say, and I'm quite sure I've heard it all a dozen times before. Therefore I have no intention of standing through it all. Neither do I choose to sit. You see, I have quite decided that I will not stay here and listen a moment longer."

To be quite sure she had made herself clear, she added, "I am this instant returning to my room to surrender myself to the far more agreeable company of Mr. Percy Shelley and his latest volume of poems."

The captain reddened, and blustered, "I—hem—I say, Miss Cox, are you not feeling yourself today?"

There was more that she did not catch as she turned away and hastened out of the room.

Verity went directly to her boudoir, quite expecting to be pursued by Aunt Maria. At any moment she expected the lady to storm in, girded for battle, and berate her niece for an unwarranted lapse of manners. Surely Aunt Maria had not failed to mark the captain's red-faced displeasure? If *that* had escaped her all-seeing eye, she would at the very least demand to know what decision her niece had reached after communing with nature all morning in Kew Gardens.

But the minutes passed without interruption, during which Verity tried to divert her attention to writing a careful letter to Papa. If she were to turn up at Briarley two months earlier than planned, Papa must be apprised of it.

After an hour's struggle, Verity looked up from her escritoire and gazed with frustration out the casement. It was much harder to explain than she had imagined. She turned back to the latest version as the ink dried.

Dearest Papa,

My affections are engaged irrevocably by the dearest man, who has already professed his love for me, and with whom you have some slight acquaintance—Patrick Tarkington. I have discovered that his former suit to Laura was the merest nominal gesture, forced upon him by the most grievous of circumstances . . . of which more later. First, let me assure you that he is without doubt a man of integrity, of keen mind and industry, and above all, he possesses the most generous, the tenderest of hearts. All those qualities which you most admire in a man

No, it wouldn't do. Scrunching up the sheet, she consigned it to the pile of false starts. The writing surface was littered with aborted attempts to explain herself—a sorry catalogue of failures screwed up into tight little blue balls of the best linen stock, which were beginning to uncurl.

What could she tell Papa, after all? That a confessed fortune hunter had declared his love for her? That he had asked for her hand in marriage? But he had not! In fine, all she could say was that she had good reason to believe Mr. Tarkington would eventually propose, based on the strength of the word of someone called Dora, who was foster parent to his son, who was in fact not his son at all, but merely the child of his ex-mistress. It was an impossible challenge. Hopeless.

And yet this letter was the very first and simplest step she must take. She groaned and covered her eyes. No letter could begin to justify the course she proposed to follow. She gave up.

Failing a letter, she would have to arrive unheralded and simply tell Papa in person. The next step then would be to announce as much to the Strathmores. She quailed at the idea.

For a few minutes, she toyed with the notion of slipping away early one morning with Sarah, and leaving a note. Sarah would hold her tongue if pressed. But it was the coward's way out, an admission that what she was about to do was shameful. Of course, she could never reveal to Aunt Maria the true reason for her departure, but she would at least be frank enough to announce her intention of going home.

It was almost five o'clock by the time she came to that conclusion. The Strathmores would be sipping beverages in their various dressing rooms while they dressed for the evening. They were all expected at the Lievens' dinner and ball tonight, where the strapping blue-eyed Russian diplomats fresh out of St. Petersburg would charm the ladies with their broken

English and fluent French. At the residence of the Russian ambassador and his lady, they could always count on a sprinkling of young lieutenants and captains from the Tsar's household guard, their dazzling uniforms and jingling decorations enhancing the general color of the spectacle. Countess Lieven's receptions were famous, the embassy in St. James's considered no less than an adjunct of the Russian Winter Palace.

Exactly how and when would she broach the subject? Verity asked herself, trying to picture a scene in the family phaeton, as they all rode toward the embassy. If she did it on the way to the Lievens', who knew what might happen? Aunt Maria might just choose to faint, Uncle George would turn purple—and they would surely turn about for home, incapacitated. Not fair. Laura had talked of the Lieven dinner for days. Verity sighed. Decency demanded that she allow the entire family a grand evening, and bide her time until the morrow.

Sarah cut into her chaotic thoughts by rattling a tea tray as she walked past with it into the dressing room. "Tha' said tha'd ring for tha' tea when tha' was ready," she said reproachfully.

"I know, Sarah, but I've been trying to write a difficult letter, and it's not done." Carefully, Verity swept the debris off the escritoire into a white wicker basket.

"Well, it's high time tha' stopped, then. This is no run-o'-the-mill dinner, tha' told me. Russian embassy! Tha'd better come right this minute, if tha' don't want to disgrace the family before all them furriners." She eyed Verity's face and hair acidly. "There's much to do."

The champagne was French, the caviar from the Caspian, and the *saumon fumé* plucked from the finest salmon waters of the North Sea, but it was the venison that commanded the conversation at the banquet table that night. The gamy meat was a personal gift to Count Lieven from Tsar Alexander, bagged by His Majesty at his northern dacha on the Taymyr Peninsula and shipped all the way to London by the Imperial Fleet by way of the Bering Straits. It was a rare feat that could only be undertaken in early winter, when the temperatures were cold enough to preserve the venison, and before the ice floes had closed off all northern shipping routes. The guests were duly impressed.

Hung to perfection in the kitchens at St. James's, the game was declared an unprecedented delicacy. To Verity, ravenous by the time it was set before her, the wine-sauced haunch meat was delicious, but scarcely distinguishable from the country venison that came off Mrs. Budgitt's roasting spits at Briarley.

This might be her last taste of such grandeur, she reflected, and although she felt no reluctance at leaving London elegance behind her, she decided she might as well enjoy her last evening here.

Surprisingly, she soon found she was enjoying it all very much. The Lievens were munificent hosts. The Russian officers were expert at the waltz and charmingly inexpert at English, their halting words inhibiting excessive conversation, but encouraging gestures, expressive glances, comical grimaces, laughter, much kissing of hands, and the liberal use of first names. And, best of all, Bennington-Jones was blessedly absent.

Laura promptly caught the twinkling eye of dashing Prince Mikhail Ilyich Zukov, archduke of some unpronounceable territory in the Balkans (which territory, Lady Sefton assured Aunt Maria, was slightly larger than France, adding behind her fan that the prince was a direct descendant of Catherine the Great).

After dinner, Verity was swept into the strong arms of one blue-eyed charmer after another, waltzing with such zest and to such irresistible rhythms that she felt she could willingly whirl on forever. The secret happiness she hugged to her heart was something quite new, an intoxicating blend of the gaiety of the evening, the blissful freedom from Bennington-Jones, and the slowly blossoming conviction that Mr. Tarkington adored her.

Or was it merely the effect of too much champagne? Later, as she struggled wearily out of her orchid satin, she thought it might be. She drew back her bedroom curtains and saw night paling into dawn. She had been up almost twenty-four hours at a stretch, and the euphoria was rapidly fading. She had bid Sarah not to wait up for her, but as she wrestled alone with slippery satin buttons and the clasp of her amethyst choker, she regretted it.

Yes, of course it was just the champagne. There had been so many toasts before the dancing began. *God Bless King George! To His Highness, the Prince Regent! Her Majesty, Queen Charlotte, long may she live! To His Imperial Highness, Tsar of all the Russians! To the beautiful Tsarina! May they reign forever!* She had finished three tall glasses of the bubbly before they even got to the Bourbons—*de rigueur*, since the French ambassador was a guest.

Through the entire evening she had danced on a cloud, like a starry-eyed bride. More like a perfect idiot, she amended as she laid her pounding head on the pillow.

Why on earth had she thought it would be easy? *Amor vincit omnia*, she had thought blissfully all evening. But in the cold light of dawn she feared that love conquered all only in the kind of romantic reading that Laura favored. What had love managed to conquer so far? Why, she hadn't even brought herself to tell the Strathmores she was leaving yet. And what had made her think for one minute she would overcome Tarkington's monumental pride? For that matter, why was she so calmly sure that he did indeed love her? She only had his word for it—and hadn't he proved himself to be a most accomplished liar?

There *was* Dora's word too, of course ... and Dora appeared to know him very well indeed. On that tiny ray of hope, she fell into an exhausted sleep.

—13—

When Jack Reese came home to supper that night, Tarkington had still not returned from his search for Robbie, although the child had been safe at home since noon. Dora sent Jack straight out again to find him. Jack spent a futile hour combing the neighborhood, inquiring and leaving messages, then gave up.

It was another two hours before Tarkington staggered into the Reese kitchen, ashy-faced and disheveled. Robbie was already in bed and asleep. Sagging with relief at the good news, Tarkington tiptoed into the back room to reassure himself, and when he saw the sleeping figure curled up under his blankets, apple cheeks rosy against the pillow, he was at once dizzy and nauseated.

"You look proper shaken about, Pat," Dora whispered as he came back into the kitchen. "You've not eaten a thing all day, and you've fair worn yourself out. Worrying over nothing! Don't take sick on me, now."

Dora fussed over him with cups of broth and insisted he stay the night, making up a pallet for him in the big, warm kitchen. Tarkington did not protest. In any case, his stallion was spent and would carry him no farther that night.

Jack sat at the table, his supper eaten at last. Lingering over his ale, he watched Tarkington stretch out exhausted before the hearth, his head propped on one hand.

"You take on too much over the boy, Pat," Dora scolded. "Boys will be boys, and there's no cause to go tearing half across the country for the little tyke, as if you'd fair lost your wits. You'd have found him back here inside half an hour."

"I didn't think of that. He's all the family I have, aside from you and Jack," Tarkington said, and grinned sheepishly. He had been rather witless, not checking back with the Reeses all day. "But what would you have me do? Shrug my shoulders and walk away as if he were just one chicken less in the barn?"

"What *I'd* have you do," Dora stressed, "is find yourself a wife and have a real family." And stop all this folly about Robbie and leave him to us, she thought to herself.

"I'm trying, Dora." Tarkington sank back and clasped his hands behind his head.

"Are you?" She pursed her lips. "What about this nice Miss Cox, then? Why don't you ask her?"

He shut his eyes and shook his head, his face pale and expressionless.

"That's no answer!"

He gave a hoarse laugh. "That's no *question*, Dora. That's a joke. She's a Strathmore first cousin. I told you, I'm a special kind of poison to the Strathmores now."

"Well, you asked for it! Parading as nobility and all. I told you no good would come of it. Haven't I told him, Jack? But Miss Cox seems to stomach the poison well enough, for all your shenanigans." She grinned. "Coming all this way to visit Robbie, and all. I'll lay a turnip to a gold guinea she'd have you if you humbled yourself a bit."

His face hardened. "Enough, Dora. I told you *no*. It's not possible. And even if it were, she's far too good for the likes of me."

"Rubbish!" Jack, who had contented himself with

merely listening to this point, now rose from the supper table and set himself down in the rocker by the hearth, opposite Dora. He made a small ritual of lighting a long-stemmed briar pipe, and for a while there was no sound save his sucking on the mouthpiece and emitting a fragrant cloud of tobacco smoke.

Tarkington opened one eye, then sat up grinning. "Let's have a puff, Jack." He reached out an arm as Jack handed it to him. "And let's stop flogging a dead horse."

Jack Reese had the weathered look of a farmhand, tough and leathery, but the pale blue eyes were sensitive as he searched Tarkington's face. "We've taken to thinking of the boy as our own," he said slowly. "Dora's in no hurry to lose him. We don't have no others, and even if we did, Robbie is always—" He broke off, his body tensing forward and his voice pitched low.

"Why don't you go back and finish what you started? You worked so hard for it, and you talk like a gentleman now. You should have a gentleman's calling. It don't make no sense, Pat. Giving it all up overnight for a lad that ain't even your own kin."

Tarkington fixed his eyes on the rafters. "Not again! We've gone over it and over it, Jack. It's too late. It's finished and done with years ago. A student can't support a growing boy, so let's drop it."

"A practicing physician could. We'd manage fine until then. So would you. You did before." Jack took back his pipe and clamped his lips over the stem angrily. "You give us too much for his support anyways. It's madness. He's only one small boy, not a regiment we're feeding. We've saved most of it and put it in his name. And look what you have to do to get it! Not a penny that doesn't come from the gaming hells. How long do you think your luck can last?"

"Until I find the right woman."

"I'd say you already found her," Dora put in. Her voice became teasing. "Took a real fancy to the boy, she did, taking him for a ride in the hackney like that."

Tarkington sat bolt upright with the motion of a jackknife. "She *took* him? But you told me he stowed away and hid himself under a blanket!"

"Wee-eell." Dora rocked back and forth in the pine chair. "She took her time about bringing him back here, didn't she?"

Tarkington turned to face her squarely with a suspicious scowl.

"Anyways," she said quickly, "what will you do now, Pat? You'll not find a rich wife in London with Lady What's-er-name passing the word out like bird droppings all over the town."

"I'll start over in the Midlands. Lots of money there."

"No," Jack said fiercely. "Enough's enough! You're no fancy Johnny, and you're no faker. Look, I can't stop you—it's none of my affair—but you're stuck in London anyways with the regiment. You're still a hussar, ain't you, Pat?"

"Ah, Jack." Tarkington sighed. "You know as much of the army as I did three years past. There's more liberty in the regiment than at Merton College! As long as you've a good second to watch your cornet for you, you're free as a lark. A pair of colors in the Hussars is a gentleman's passport to pleasure."

"You've had little enough of *that*—or success either."

Tarkington's jaw tensed. "As you say, Jack, it's none of your affair." He reached out and gave his friend's arm an affectionate squeeze to soften the remark. "You'll see, man. I'll take a provincial leave and one of these days I'll be coming for Robbie with a wealthy lady on my arm from Leicester or Darby, most like."

"You've got a terrible hard head, Patrick, boy," Jack muttered through his teeth. "I told you, we don't care if you never pay no more for Robbie, and never come for him. We love him like our own."

"None of that!" Tarkington shook his head. "This is strictly a business arrangement, and you've always

known it and so has Dora. You're kind and you're
good to him, both of you, but I'll not burden you like
that. I'll always be grateful, but a boy should be with
his parents."

Jack and Dora looked hopelessly at each other.
What parents had Robbie ever had except for them?
Would this wooden-headed clodpole never come to his
senses?

Tarkington missed the look that passed between
them, for he was deep in his private thoughts.

A boy should be with his parents.

How that had stayed with him, that sharp reproof
from a young mother scolding her restless little son.
He had heard it many years ago in Bridlington Church,
where they were taken on Sundays, and where he had
caught his first glimpse of real families. . . .

The noisy bundle that appeared on St. Agatha's
steps came with no recognizable possessions save a
signet ring tied to one grimy ankle, a ring of such base
metal that no one had thought it worth stealing. A
nameless bundle was not unusual. Its designation was
as arbitrary as most procedures at the foundling home.
The new admittance was recorded on St. Patrick's
Day. Embroidered on one of the rags wrapped about
the infant was a monogram of some sorts, already
disintegrating. It looked somewhat like the letters T
RK GT N as far as one could guess.

Patrick Tarkington? A bit high-stepping for such a
little ragbag, but it tickled the fancy of the admitting
registrar, and thus he entered it in the rolls.

At St. Agatha's, a child was set to work in the
nursery as soon as he was five years old. Jack was five
at the time, and he was charged to watch over the
new bundle.

Ever since Patrick could remember, Jack had been
his brother.

The staff boasted often that every child at St.
Agatha's was given an opportunity to learn reading,

writing, and arithmetic. It cost nothing above the five hours of wasted child labor each week, for the volunteer ladies of the town provided their teaching services and brought their own materials.

Jack did well enough at his lessons, although he much preferred to work in the vegetable garden. But at two years of age, Patrick was impatient to begin, jealous that he couldn't follow Jack into the classroom. He would press Jack to tell him exactly what went on in there on Wednesdays and Fridays, and he would make Jack show him his slate.

Patrick could read and write better than Jack long before he was old enough to go to Mrs. Colfax. When he was allowed in the classroom, Mrs. Colfax was very surprised. Soon she was giving him special attention, bringing him all kinds of books to read and assigning him extra lessons.

At the age of nine, St. Agatha's dismissed its charges and sent them out into the world with a dire admonition not to sin, and a pittance of half a shilling.

But when Patrick reached nine years, Mrs. Colfax went to the director, George Collis, and made a fearful scene. It was against all the rules, but she stormed and she threatened until she got her way.

Patrick stayed on at St. Agatha's until he was what Mr. Collis termed a "great useless lout" of eleven, learning Latin and Greek and history and a great many other things that would never turn an honest penny. One had always to humor Mrs. Colfax, because she was no ordinary volunteer. Her husband was Bishop Colfax, a trustee of the institution, and a substantial donor to the general fund which paid Mr. Collis's stipend and kept open the doors of St. Agatha's.

Patrick knew that he was an incredibly fortunate fellow who had never lifted a finger to merit his good fortune. He knew, because Mr. Collis told him so regularly until the day he left for Eton College.

There were ten scholarship boys at Eton. Among them were the sons of younger sons, nobility with depleted patrimonies, the sons of impecunious vicars and ambitious solicitors. The scholarship boys were an ignominious group, for the normal Etonians were the sons of earls and archbishops, of grenadier guard officers and ministers of the realm.

Singular among all the sons of Eton College, Patrick Tarkington was nobody's son. The chasm between himself and normal folk yawned deep and wide for the first time.

He tried to bridge the chasm. Unconsciously, he emulated the speech patterns he heard, the manners he observed, and consciously, he excelled in his lessons. The more he succeeded, the less popular he became. That he survived those years whole in body and spirit was a tribute to his physique and his sportsmanship, particularly in sprinting and boxing.

Mrs. Colfax died while he was struggling through Eton. She had served him well, but she had kept her distance, never bestowing upon him her personal friendship.

Phyllida St. Regis, therefore, was the first lady ever to befriend him. His life had been too rigorous to be anything but innocent, but meeting Phyllida was more than first love. It was undreamed-of bliss. It was the explosive culmination of his full manhood; it was a woman's warmth, and bounty, and affection. It was his first breathless introduction to a hearth and a home.

He poured out his adoration on the fragrant, beautiful goddess, not merely with a young man's ardor, but with a religious intensity born of years of starvation. He never blamed Phyllida for her desertion; he merely suffered, recovered, then transferred to the child his wrenching need to love and belong. Giving up his cherished dreams of healing the sick seemed a small price to pay for the precious gift of Robbie's smile of recognition. . . .

*   *   *

During the heart-stopping hours when he'd searched high and low for the boy, he had not given one thought to Miss Cox. Now, at peace in the knowledge that the child was safe, he let the memory of her glowing beauty flood through his closed eyelids like sunlight. *Caroline Cox—Verity.* From this day, he knew he would always think of her as Verity. Reality returned like a leaden weight dropping on his lungs. He must learn not to think of her at all.

He returned to his rooms off Albemarle Street the next day, to spend ten days in shiftless idleness. Except for his regimental duties, he went nowhere, saw no one. He made no plans to remove himself to the provinces; he did not even return to Somertown to visit Robbie. He would ride alone through the city streets and the park, and he would walk to tire himself sufficiently to sleep. Then he would return to sit in his rooms, staring at nothing.

Why had he wasted his chances for three years? He knew the glance of encouragement when he saw it. Time and time again he could have brought off a marriage. And each time, when the moment was ripe, he had backed away. Always an excuse to himself. This one was too shrewish, that one too old, another too young. Jack was right, of course; he was simply not made of the stuff of fortune hunters. He didn't have the dedication.

At last he had found a woman who made the words leap from his throat, and he must choke them down. He was a nobody. God only knew what kind of wretches his parents must have been to cast him away as they did. He was the progeny of two people he would never know, and would never even want to know. Mr. Collis had always said that foundlings had bad blood. Bad blood . . . never would he taint her with it.

Resolutely, he cast all thought of Verity aside. For Robbie's sake, he must redeem himself. His son's future must not lie forever in the fickle turn of the dice.

After ten days of brooding, he got out pen and paper one evening and began to make certain calculations.

—14—

"I shan't stop you, Caroline." Aunt Maria's face betrayed no feeling, save for the rigid set of her mouth as it bit off the words. She had greeted Verity's breathless announcement with nothing more than shocked terseness and a slight loss of color.

At the breakfast table, Verity had simply drawn breath and taken the precipitous plunge.

"My mind is made up, Aunt. I do not intend to accept the captain's proposal, or even stay to entertain it. I shall cut short the season and depart for Lancashire as soon as arrangements can be made."

It had seemed extraordinarily effortless at the time, but now, as she looked at her aunt's face, Verity's relief at finally unburdening herself was overshadowed by a terrible sense of guilt. She had been prepared for blistering anger, but not this painful resignation. Indeed, had she endured the verbal onslaught she had fully expected her conscience would have been salved, but apparently there was to be none.

Aunt and niece sat along at table in sharp silence, the smoked haddock untouched, the coffee cooling. So intense was the quiet that the ticking of the clock became thunderous. When at last Aunt Maria spoke again, Verity jumped.

"I don't know what you expected. This isn't the Dark Ages. The more's the pity! I can neither clap you in irons nor send you to a nunnery. My only duty

193

now is to see that you get home safely. You will take Sarah with you, of course, and we shall hire a private vehicle from the post house. They complete the journey in four days now."

"I expected to be railed at." Verity's voice wavered.

"Railed at?" The light snort was closer to disgust than amusement. "I'm fully aware that you are quite set to do this, and I know better than to waste my breath." Aunt Maria sat ramrod-straight and grim. "You are regrettably like your father, but at least Josiah credits me with more sense than you do."

The warm ties of blood and affection—bonds which Verity had taken for granted all her life—were unraveling before her eyes. She was desolate.

"Would you like me to inform Uncle George?" she asked.

"No. You shall leave that to me."

Verity rose from the table, acutely distressed. What a monster of egotism she was, laying so dire a task upon her aunt's shoulders! "Oh, dearest Aunt, it is so unfair that you should be saddled with telling Uncle George." She laid a sympathetic kiss on the cold, unbending cheek.

Aunt Maria did not stir at the embrace. "Yes, unfair." She rose stiffly, disengaging her shoulders from her niece's hands. "Need I say I am bitterly disappointed in you?"

With leaden heart, Verity returned to her room and rang for Sarah, whose reaction to the news of departure was uncannily like Aunt Maria's: shocked silence, then a sullen obedience to orders, docile, but laden with quiet fury.

Taut-shouldered and efficient, Sarah came and went in the performance of her duties, informing the laundress, itemizing articles, ordering the trunks sent upstairs for packing. It was a classic exercise in silent reproach, and after half an hour, Verity could abide it no longer and fled to Laura's room.

Her cousin was still asleep, but it was high time she

roused herself, Verity decided, tiptoeing into the room after several soft raps on the door. Laura's hair trailed dark and luxuriant over the pillows and spilled over the counterpane. She stirred at the sound of Verity's approach, opened one eye, then closed it again. "Mmmm," she murmured. "What time is it?"

"Almost noon, layabed!"

If Verity had felt robbed of her due from Aunt Maria, Laura's reaction made up in full measure. Verity's news shocked her into instant wakefulness. Heartrendingly, Laura exercised a veritable concerto of emotions, from staggering disbelief to tearful pleading. With arms entwined, they wept together for a few minutes, Verity aching to share with her the true reason for her sudden departure.

How consoled Laura would be, how ecstatic to be party to such a romantic secret! But she could not share it. Verity's common sense informed her that her cousin was too young and too flighty to be the guardian of so delicate a matter. It was far too grave a burden to place on a mere child. The simple fact of Verity's defection was causing intolerable domestic vibrations as it was; if they were to know precisely why . . . dear God!

After a touching scene, Laura resigned herself to tragic acceptance. "How *could* you, co¬, how could you!" And Verity made one last attempt to comfort her.

"Come, love. We shall all be reunited in Lancashire come spring, and it's hardly the end of the world that I don't find London my favorite milieu."

Uncle George reacted to the news by assiduously avoiding the sight of his niece. He took a solitary ride in the park, then confined himself to his rooms the rest of the day.

Their evening was spent at the Royal Theatre. They had come to see Kean play Macbeth. It was Lord Strathmore's favorite Shakespeare play, possibly because it was the shortest, but that night he decided to absent himself. Instead, he persuaded his cronies from White's to join him in the Sloane Terrace library for a tray supper of cold pheasant and Rhine wine and a night of dicing and brandy and reminiscing.

"I believe Papa sees it as something of an Irish wake—just as if we'd had a death in the family," Laura whispered to her cousin, while on the stage below their loge the great Kean's eyes fairly started from his head in frozen horror at the sight of Banquo's ghost.

Verity did her best to concentrate on the tragedy behind the flickering footlights, but the gloom in the velvet-lined box where she sat, her aunt on one side, Laura on the other, vied all evening with the stage performance.

She was to bid them all a last farewell that night, it was decided, for the carriage would come for her before dawn on the morrow. Aunt Maria had actually gone so far as to send regrets to the Seftons regarding the late supper party that was supposed to round out their evening. She simply wasn't up to it.

It was a deplorably dismal farewell, Aunt Maria stony-faced on the second-floor landing as she bid her niece goodnight and goodbye, and Laura once again reduced to tears. Verity felt all bright hope and joy shrivel under a cloud of self-loathing and guilt, as she witnessed the misery she had willfully caused.

Uncle George was still in the library when they returned from the theater, but when Verity inquired whether she should enter to bid him adieu, Aunt Maria thought not. From the muffled sounds of revelry escaping the closed oak doors, Verity could console herself that he at least was successfully drowning his sorrows.

When Sarah disrobed her, she fairly tore the amber silk gown from her mistress's body, actually ripping off two buttons, which rolled across the carpet and had to be retrieved from under the clothespress. Sarah placed the buttons on the chiffonier, and let her eyes rove over the bandboxes, hat bins, and trunks that lay packed and strapped for the morning. Taking the limp amber gown, she laid it angrily over the empty press.

"Ah'm not packin' this! The chambermaid can sew back the buttons and give it to the laundress. The Strathmores can bring it back at the end of the season." Sarah's spirits were at their nadir. "Tha'll never be needing finery again where tha's going!"

Sarah was deliberately making it sound as if they were exiles, about to be driven into some howling wilderness.

"Tha' won't be wantin' this neither," Sarah announced, marching over to Verity's bedside table and snatching up her book. "This goes in the cloak bag. No reading for you tonight. Ah'm rousing tha' at five o'clock sharp. The chaise will fetch us before six."

Verity's expression was wry. Sarah's tone suggested nothing less than a tumbrel arriving at dawn to fetch them to the scaffold. But Verity was limp as a dish rag, and couldn't even laugh at Sarah's melodramatics.

The huge post chaise which arrived in the dark of the morning was comfortably appointed. The well-upholstered banquettes were wide and long enough for two passengers to stretch out and sleep, and behind each headrest was a cache for blankets. Indeed, such vehicles were often hired for an express run, with regular stops long enough only for a change of team, passenger relief, and the purchase of food baskets. In such fashion, a two-hundred-mile journey such as they were now undertaking could be completed in a scant forty hours.

But surely it was rare for any traveler to be that pressed, Verity reflected as she watched the sun rise over Hampstead Heath. The coachman drove a four-in-hand, and they had already passed the outskirts of the city and were fast approaching Luton.

Two carriage lamps swung from the ceiling. The driver had offered to light them when they embarked, but Verity had declined. Sarah was still half asleep, and she herself was so exhausted that she wished only to lie down. But as the first harsh rays pierced the side glass, she sat up, turned to the cloak bag beside her, and drew out her book. Sarah snored lightly.

But Verity's eyes refused to fasten on the printed word. Instead she cast a restless eye about the interior. The very comfort of it filled her with a sudden sense of sin. Was it sin? Or was she merely following her heart as Papa had urged her to? But, oh, to what depths of deception she had sunk!

"I just want you to be happy . . . God knows it won't be easy," Papa had whispered to her before she left Briarley. She had always known her problem when it came to finding a husband. She had never expected it to be simple, but she had always sensed a solution was waiting hidden, to reveal itself to her somewhere, some time. Was this in truth the solution? To pick a man who might be anathema to both sides of the family?

Well, you goose, he hasn't chosen *you* yet—and maybe he never will, she thought grimly. Suddenly she remembered from her childhood another one of Sarah's gems: "Tha' can never 'old a funeral without a corpse, love." And you couldn't hold a wedding without a groom, either, Verity observed glumly.

Racked between optimism and despair, Verity became so moody as the day wore on that Sarah soon tired of it. During an afternoon stop, she forsook the warm interior of the coach and climbed up to the windy perch to sit beside the driver in search of more congenial society than her mistress could offer. The weather being dry, Sarah chose to remain outside through the daylight hours for the four days of the journey. On their night stops, Sarah kept herself aloof in the antechamber of Verity's inn room.

It was therefore an infinite relief to both maid and mistress when, as dusk fell on the fourth day, they found themselves driving through the tall gates of Briarley. Papa was welcoming, but not confounded. He had received Lady Strathmore's curt letter the previous day, and expected his daughter.

"I have found the man I wish to marry, Papa," she blurted out after their embrace.

"Good," he replied with simple contentment, for all the world as if she had just found a mislaid umbrella.

Was it after all going to be easy? she wondered foggily, and promptly tumbled into a disjointed, incomprehensible discourse, fair tripping over the words in her haste to get it out.

Papa laid a calming hand on her shoulder. "Hush now, my dear. Go to your room and refresh yourself. Mrs. Budgitt's baking a fine carp for our supper. Time enough when we sit down to eat."

It was such a comfort to be home! Easily and with far more clarity, Verity poured out her heart to him at the dining table. He listened kindly, his face betraying no distaste.

Only when Verity came to the end of her tale did she falter. As she described her planned tryst in Somertown, it struck her that she had shamelessly pursued Mr. Tarkington. At the time, it had seemed she had only sought him out to tell him the truth, but as she related every detail it sounded as if she had thrown herself wantonly at the man. How vulgar it must have appeared!

Her shoulders sagged. "Oh, Papa. I thought at first that it was only pride that held him back. Now I fear it was his distaste at my boldness." A sob shook her. "I pursued him!"

"Just as your mama pursued me." Papa stroked her bowed head. "Don't fret, child. You were right the first time. It's only his pride."

Verity's head rose slowly, and her eyes grew round. "Mama?"

Papa grinned at her look of utter astonishment. "Oh, yes. I loved her more than life itself, and I was a bold enough fellow, but before your mama I quailed. She was not just my heart's desire, you understand, she was also the daughter of a viscount, a member of one of the five leading families in the shire. It was a formidable barrier for a self-educated squire's son who had simply made good in the mills. What did I have to offer? No title, no high-stepping airs, no coat of arms. In those days I would no more have dared to ask for your mother's hand than I would have presumed to walk on water. Yes, indeed, your mama pursued me, and pleaded and stormed and protested and wept. It was only when she wept that I was persuaded of the incredible fact that she would have no other but me. Where else would I have found the courage to wed her?"

Verity dabbed at her wet face. "But I'm no formidable titled lady, Papa. Surely Mr. Tarkington feels no awe of me?"

Papa rose from the table and clasped his hands behind him, frowning into space. "You're still a viscount's granddaughter, child. Tarkington does not even know whose son he is, and he hasn't a penny to his name. But pride he has in good measure."

"You're not suggesting I run after him, Papa!" Her voice failing, the words came out as a croak.

He struggled to achieve a sober expression. "Lady Strathmore isn't the only bloodhound in the family. I made my own inquiries when I returned from London in the New Year, and I can tell you this. Every word Mr. Tarkington told you is true. What he failed to mention is that there are medical professors in Oxford who are certain he was the most gifted student ever to pass through their hands. He would make a distinguished physician. But he's stiff and he's proud, and he has a good deal more brains than he has plain sense, this genius." His mouth stretched at last into a frankly wide grin.

"You may *have* to run after him, Verity. If you think him worth the chase. But you'll have to beat some sense into him, too. He must prove he can do better than gambling and masquerading if he wants my blessing."

"Papa, you had him investigated?"

"I did indeed." He paused, enjoying the play of lively emotions on his daughter's amazed face. "When I left London, I knew you'd set your heart on him. At the time he struck me as a very odd fellow indeed, the way he was behaving to Laura when he had eyes only for you."

Verity could only shake her head back and forth in silent awe at her father's wisdom.

He ruffled her hair teasingly and fairly shook with laughter. "It didn't take a magician, my love. I may be old, but my eyes are still good."

The following morning, Papa was obliged to leave on urgent business. He would be gone for ten days, and as soon as she had bidden him farewell, she wrote to inform Dora that all was well.

"My papa knows all, and he is not averse to Mr. Tarkington," she wrote, still rather dazed by it all. Then she braced herself for an intolerable siege of waiting. It was all in Dora's hands now. The mail coach took two days to London, so she knew she could not look for a reply from Dora before four or five days.

Verity occupied herself with the household affairs, but the days inched forward at tortoise pace. A week passed, and she began to fear she would drown in the ocean of immeasurable hours.

Relief did not arrive until the day Mr. Cox was expected home. A letter from Dora came in that morning's post. Verity tore open the envelope with trembling fingers and consumed the message. She read, and reread, first in disbelief, then in growing horror. Without so much as a by-your-leave, she had been thrust into the role of an abductress!

Dora had led Tarkington to believe that Robbie was missing from home, and that Verity had actually carried the child off to Lancashire with her. Surely

Tarkington couldn't believe such an utterly implausible story. But according to Dora, he did.

Once more Verity read Dora's unlikely message, the words jumping crazily before her startled eyes.

I was plannin to go to London and tell him the day after i got your letter. But i didn't have to go anywares. Pat came to Somertown the very next mornin. Jack had took Robbie out on his rounds with him, as he does when the wether is nice. It was providence i am sure of it. Pat swallowed my story & is on his way to Lancs. He left here like the divil was after him. He is so sure you got Robbie and his rage is terrible. So i hope you get this to warn you afore he comes. I promisst he would come and he is commin. Good luck.

Verity let out a groan. *I promisst he would come and he is commin*—not as a suitor, but as an outraged father pursuing a kidnapper! She slumped in her chair, watching her dreams turn to dust. *Oh, not this way!* She had never dreamed it would be this way. "Trust me," Dora had said. Perfidious Dora. Now Verity was stripped naked with no retreat, no decent facade behind which to hide her motives. *Dear God!* Was she to be reduced to abasing herself? To blurting out the shameful fact that she had manipulated him like a chess pawn in order to throw herself at him? It was worse than chasing after him. It was shameless harassment. If he came now, it would be her undoing.

Mercifully, she had only the remainder of the morning to agonize. The chess pawn arrived at noon.

Verity sat perforating her fingers as she tried to work her needlepoint. The sitting room where she sat was in the west wing, but there was such a prolonged jangling of the front door bell and it was followed by such a *fracas* that it sounded all the way to the back of the house and brought Verity hurrying toward the entryway.

Mr. Tarkington stood on the threshold, fairly terrorizing Mrs. Travers. When he caught sight of Verity, he pushed past the housekeeper in a black, towering rage.

"Where is he?" he demanded, striding ominously across the hall carpet toward Verity. "Where is my son?" He was a formidable sight in his disheveled riding habit, his buckskins splattered with mud, his head bare and windblown. And in his right hand, he clenched a riding crop as if he fully intended to use it.

Verity gave what reassurance she could to the nonplussed housekeeper. "It's quite all right, Mrs. Travers. Just a friend from London. I'll take care of the gentleman."

Mrs. Travers fled, for Dora had not exaggerated. His rage was indeed terrible. He had ridden as fast as the mail coach, and he looked like the wrath of God.

"Robbie is quite safe," she said quickly. "Please don't distress yourself. Would you care for some tea?" Verity gave what she hoped was a placid smile, thinking to calm him.

"Don't trifle with me, Miss Cox! This is no social call. I want my son and I want him now! Where is he?" He stressed his words with an unnecessarily menacing crack of his whip. In the imposing entryway with its marble flooring and high vaulted ceilings, the crack resounded like the promise of divine retribution.

"I have no idea where he is, Mr. Tarkington. And you certainly won't find him by standing here in the hall bellowing in this fashion," she snapped. She'd been prepared to assuage an overwrought father; she'd expected to offer reasonable apologies to a wronged man. But she had not been prepared for an utterly incorrigible boor. Had she not this very moment assured him that the child had come to no harm? He refused to listen. In fact, he looked quite capable of proceeding to ransack the house if she did not produce the child instantly in a puff of smoke.

"I have just assured you that Robbie is safe and well," she said stiffly. "And if you care to come, *civilized*, into the house, I shall explain as best I can."

His face darkened, but he followed her without another word through the corridors and back into the west-wing sitting room where she had just left her needlepoint. She motioned him to sit. He refused. Shrugging her shoulders, she rang for Mrs. Travers, then resumed her own fireside seat on the sofa.

He glowered down upon her, rocking back and forth on his heels until she was so unnerved that she picked up her embroidery in order to avoid meeting his eyes. How on earth could she begin to explain? But in all conscience, she must say something. His distress was acute, and she could not torment the man.

She gave a nervous laugh. "It's all too silly, you see. Just one big misunderstanding, Mr. Tarkington. I promise you there's no cause for alarm. Robbie is not and never has been missing from home. He is not at Briarley, but—contrary to what you have been led to believe—"

"God's bones!" he exploded. "I didn't come here to listen to your equivocations, woman. I came for my son! Now fetch him this instant."

"I shall *not* fetch him, you stubborn, ill-mannered lout!" Her sympathy for him had vanished. Could he not see that her own ordeal was by far worse than his? He was making this intolerable. Why would he not hold his tongue and listen?

"I shan't move until you *bring* him to me," he shouted.

"Then you will have a *very long wait!*"

Whatever retort he had planned, it was stopped by the light rap on the door. His head whipped around at the sound, as though he fully expected Robbie to walk in. It was only Mrs. Travers, of course, and Tarkington sat so suddenly on the sofa at his back that Verity suspected his knees had simply collapsed under him in shock.

She requested a tray of tea, but after the housekeeper withdrew she thought she might have been better advised to have called for a decanter of brandy. At the sight of Tarkington's stricken gray face, her anger dissolved and her heart went out to him. It was the most monstrous trick to play on so devoted a father. She had no right to her own anger at all. She had lost all hope of winning him now. All she could do was reassure him, and prove to him that at least she was no child stealer.

She swallowed hard to clear the sudden obstruction in her throat. "I cannot produce Robbie for you because he is safe at home with Dora and has been all along. She deliberately misled you. And since you have every right to doubt my word at this point, I shall fetch Dora's letter, so that you may read it for yourself. Please excuse me," she murmured, rushing out of the room before he would stop her.

In her room, she leaned against her writing desk. For a moment she tried to mend the ripped shreds of her dignity, but it was beyond repair. She reached into the desk drawer and drew out the letter. He would believe when he read it for himself. She would not weep, she would not tremble, she would not blame Dora. She would simply walk back into the sitting room without a word, and hand him the letter to read.

By the time she returned to the sitting room, a tea tray lay on the side table. Tarkington still sat where he had dropped. He seemed both less strident and less sure of himself as he glanced up at her entrance.

Avoiding his eyes, she handed him Dora's letter, then turned to the teapot and concentrated on keeping her hand steady enough to pour. But as she filled the second cup, his howl of outrage made her tremble and spill tea on the mahogany table.

"But why, in God's name?" Tarkington crumpled the letter in his fist. "Why would Dora suddenly conspire against me like this, knowing what anguish she would cause me? Was it at your urging?"

Verity's heart constricted at the wrenching break in his voice, but she busied herself mopping up the spilled tea with a serviette and kept her face averted. "I wanted only to have you come here," she whispered. "Dora offered to arrange it. I didn't know—I never dreamed she would go to such lengths."

Abjectly, she gazed at the carpet, then from the corner of her eye she saw that he had risen, was standing over her silently willing her to look at him if she dared. At last she looked. He was a tall pillar of cold disdain.

"You were determined to demean me further, and would stop at nothing to do so." He let the crumpled letter fall from his hand, and turned to leave. "I have made it abundantly clear that on no account will I be your kept man, Miss Cox. I meant it."

An instant later he was gone, and she stood frozen, staring at the door he had just slammed and hearing his boots pounding the parquet. She knew that if she did not follow him now, she would never see him again. She must go after him, but her feet were leaden and refused to move.

As the sound of his footsteps faded, she summoned her last strength and wrested her feet free. Then she ran down the hall as if her life depended on it. When she reached the front doors, he was under the porte cochere, already untethering his mount.

"No, you should not be my kept man," she called after him, running down the shallow steps. "I have no intention of keeping any man, ever!" Her breath was obstructed and her throat was on fire, but she forced out the words. "If you completed your studies—if you ever finished anything you started—you could follow a noble calling and keep *me!*"

One foot in the stirrup, he stood clutching the bridle and staring at the hindquarters of his stallion. "I have already made up my mind to that. I'm returning to the university. I didn't need you to point out the error of my ways." His voice was so low she was forced to strain her ears. "I have found a purchaser for my colors. The price will keep me for a few months. Then, provided the tables don't fail me, I shall have enough funds to complete my courses and qualify. When I succeed in doing that, it will only be a matter of time before I can make a decent home for Robbie."

Her heart lifted as she listened, coming closer as he spoke. But he had not quite finished.

"My plans do not, of course, include you, Miss Cox," he said, swinging into the saddle as she reached his side.

It was the *coup de grace*. Despite her fierce resolve to salvage what pride she could, her self-esteem crumpled. For one fleeting moment all her hopes had been revived. But she'd misread him. Even Papa had been wrong. His pride was far more precious to him than she could ever be.

In a voice that could no longer hide her abject desolation, she whispered, "Forgive me. I was mistaken," and dissolved into helpless sobs.

"No, don't, please don't . . ." Instantly he was dismounted and at her side. "For pity's sake, don't cry. You were not mistaken. I shall always love you, my precious, dearest girl. And that is precisely why . . . why . . ." His voice faltered as if he himself were close to tears.

Her grief was devastating to him, so intolerably painful that at last he could take no more and his arms went out to comfort her.

"You are a princess," he murmured into her tawny hair. "You deserve far better than a foundling and a rogue."

She shook her head, then let it sink onto his chest, weeping as if her heart were past mending. "If I cannot have this foundling and this rogue—then I shall never marry," she gasped, sobbing ruinously.

Quite beyond stemming her flood of tears, she let

them fall and soak his cambric shirt, feeling through her wet cheeks the wildly erratic thudding that shook him from within as he held her.

"Please don't say that, my darling. You will marry, and it will be someone worthy of you. Please, I beg you . . ." He stroked her hair and hushed her, raising her face and pressing his words against her wet eyelids. But he could taste the agonizing salt of her tears. It was more than a man could withstand, this angel brought to such depths of despair, and he drew back his lips from her face. "*Please* . . ."

"Then—I shall marry—" For a moment she choked, her throat convulsing as she abandoned herself utterly to the eternal pit. "Mm-mm-marry—I-sh-shall marry Ba-Ba-B-B-Bennington-Jones!"

She felt it then, the terrifying lurch in his breast, as if a great bird battered its wings to escape. "*Not if you want him to live, you won't,*" he said, and stopped her stammerings with his lips.

—15—

The kiss was his undoing. After weeks of agonizing strength of purpose, Tarkington was at the end of his resolve. With Verity so pliant in his arms, and desire for her raging through his blood, he could rein his feelings no more. So total was his surrender to the leap of wanton joy that, as Verity was to tease him later, it was fortunate indeed that Papa came upon them when he did. For Mr. Cox's arrival at his front door was greeted by a scandalous tableau, equally visible to two gardeners, the coachman, and a face at a second-floor window: an oblivious couple engaged in passionate embraces right out on the carriage sweep. It was so compromising a scene that Papa had little choice but to give a prompt blessing to their betrothal and salvage what propriety he could for his feckless child.

Order restored, and the lovers duly reminded of their respective duties, Tarkington's future plans were laid out before Papa. With astonishing indelicacy, Verity insisted on remaining in the study while the two men conferred. Under such odd circumstances, it did not of course run smoothly, and Verity soon began to despair that their marriage would ever come to pass.

Tarkington's everlasting pride was the rub, of course. Would she never see an end to it? she wondered. It threatened to drag out their betrothal interminably, for despite Mr. Cox's generous offer of support until

he was established, and despite Verity's pleading,
Tarkington was obdurate. He would accept not a penny.
He must make his own way entirely, he insisted.

"But you just gave your solemn word to Papa that
you would forsake the gaming hells," Verity said, her
eyes heavy with reproach.

"And I'll keep it. There are other ways to support
myself at Oxford. I'll do as I used to do."

"Haul coal!" she exclaimed. "You've lost your wits.
Besides, with most of your time wasted in menial
labor, your studies will crawl at a snail's pace. Papa,"
she appealed, "for pity's sake!"

But Papa chose at that moment to keep his counsel.
Verity's eyes grew dark with horror as they turned
on her betrothed. "Why, it could take years before you
are established. What am I to do in the meantime?"

"Might she not do what she has always done, Mr.
Cox? Live with you here at Briarley?"

"And *wait indefinitely*?" Verity squeaked. "And leave
you prey to every predatory female eye in the southern counties while I languish in the north? Never!"

"I shall start as I mean to go on," Tarkington
announced, his voice menacingly low. "If I cannot
offer you an illustrious name, I shall at least provide
you with a home and fair prospects. And until I can
do so *entirely of my own purse*, I will agree to no
wedding date—and there's an end to it!"

To Verity that was no end to it at all. Quite clearly,
she would be counting gray hairs before she could
ever count the days to her wedding. But this time not
wiles, not threats, not even tears could breach the
impregnable wall of his pride. For that singular victory,
she had none but Etienne de Roncy to thank.

Unassailable in his last stand, Tarkington left for
Oxford with his insufferable pride intact, and Verity
found herself obliged to submit to his rigorous terms
or lose him.

"His grit is to be admired," Papa said soothingly as

they saw Tarkington off on his way. "For it will go hard with him after the ease of London, and he knows it. Come, child. Why so down in the mouth? The time will pass pleasantly enough at Briarley. It always has before."

But this was not before. It was now, and Verity was not to be consoled in this, her first irreversible defeat. The long separation was unconscionable, she reflected. And quite unnecessary. She resolved to suffer in deafening silence.

Although it seemed as if long months had ground away, it was not two weeks after Tarkington's departure that the Frenchman came to call.

Mrs. Travers came into the breakfast parlor to announce the visitor to Papa, who, after inviting de Roncy to join them, did a most unprecedented thing. He withdrew from the room to consult with his bailiff, no sooner had the Frenchman sat down at the table.

Verity poured coffee for their unexpected guest and eyed him speculatively. It was not a proper hour for calling, and she was thinking of their last encounter in London. Lost sons of France at the British Museum. Papa would never have left her thus unchaperoned if he knew what a slippery fellow this was—even if she was officially affianced. But dear Papa was so purely good that he saw evil in no one. He saw only the honorable French nobleman whose trade dealings were always fair and honest—never the opportunist, the womanizer, the would-be adulterer.

"What keeps you in England so long, monsieur?" she asked him blandly. "Is it trade, or is it still the mysterious business of your King and country?"

His dark eyes widened, then lightly swept her bosom, but did not linger overlong. "Why, the business of the King, mamselle. Surely the news has reached here? I had it by runner eight days ago. The poor Duc de Berry."

Verity felt chastened. "Yes, I read about his assassination. Shocking news. You have my sympathy."

"He was heir to the throne, you understand," de Roncy said gravely. "The succession is a trifle uncertain at the moment. As a result, I have been requested to remain here awhile longer and exert all my efforts. You see, mamselle, to ascertain all possible claimants to the throne is no longer merely desirable; under the present circumstances, it is imperative."

"Ah, and you have reason to believe there may be some Bourbon heirs to be discovered in England?" she asked, exerting her best efforts to remain straight-faced.

"Yes, mamselle." His face glowed with patriotic zeal.

Verity lowered her gaze to her coffee cup. Oh, such high-sounding flights of fancy! Nothing was too preposterous to sound quite plausible on his tongue. Still, she reflected, the murder of the Duc de Berry was no invention. The newspapers had been full of it. But could de Roncy truly have been charged to scour England for missing Bourbons? Stuff! It belonged with Cinderella and other children's stories. And it reflected sadly on his estimation of her. Did he really think she could be beguiled by such romantic nonsense?

"So you are promised to Mr. Tarkington, " de Roncy said as he stirred his coffee. "My felicitations, mamselle."

Astonishment bereft her of words for a moment, her coffee almost choking her. No one except Papa knew of their betrothal yet, for they had agreed upon discretion until Patrick was set up.

"What an amazing man you are!" she said when she recovered. "You waft back and forth like thistle-down—across the Channel, up and down the Great North Road on such lofty affairs of state. And you know simply everything that goes down! Not only are you aware of my betrothal, but you show not the least surprise."

She concentrated on buttering some toast she didn't

want, hoping his response would satisfy her curiosity. *How on earth could he know?*

His only response was to tuck his silk neckcloth into the velvet revers of his jacket and bend to his coffee with an inscrutable smile.

How infuriatiing he was! "You do not even cock your noble brows at the fact that I am 'marrying beneath me,' as they say?" she asked, probing again.

His smile became broader as he glanced over the rim of his china cup. "If you speak purely of rank, mamselle, I am tempted to suggest that the reverse may be the case."

"The *reverse*?" For a moment she was at a loss. Was he hinting that she might be marrying above her station? The man seemed addicted to fairy tales! He was quite incorrigible, but this time she could not help but laugh at his outrageousness.

"Ah, you take *that* tack again, do you? You still insist that Patrick is the missing piece of one of your aristocratic French puzzles. Please spare me your elegant inventions. Heavens above, monsieur, I plan to marry the *man*, not his parents! Deplorable as it may seem to you, I have become quite bourgeois. I don't give a fig for his lack of family."

From under her eyelashes, she watched his expression while she called his bluff. "Besides, if there were the slightest grain of truth to your case, instead of paying us courtesy calls at Briarley when you clearly have no errand in this shire, you would certainly be taking the matter up with the gentleman himself."

"That is precisely what I have done, mamselle." He gazed at her earnestly, and she detected no sign of chicanery in his eyes. "I have informed Mr. Tarkington of the nature of our search. He is now fully apprised of my investigations, and my findings. But although he was cooperative enough to let me have his ring, he has no intention of pressing a claim. *Tant pis!*"

De Roncy shrugged and, leaning back in his chair, expelled a heavy sigh as if the end of a long and exhausting journey were at last in view. "Well, at least his ring will allow the courts to confirm or deny—and I shall have done my duty."

"Ring? Claim? You have spoken to Patrick?" Verity began to feel less and less sure of herself. "If you have something to say, please say it," she snapped, "or I shall have no reason to give weight to your mystifying remarks. You say you have spoken to my fiancé, but he has told me nothing of this."

"Undoubtedly he will, mamselle. He has hardly had time to come to terms with the news himself. I arrived in Oxford hard on his heels. But"—he rose politely as his host came back into the breakfast parlor—"I am now quite satisfied that the signet ring is rightfully his own, and it will suffice."

Noting the utter frustration on Verity's face, Mr. Cox patted her shoulder as he passed her chair. "What Monsieur de Roncy is telling you, my dear, is that Patrick owns a signet ring—of no intrinsic value to be sure, but it identifies his family." He paused to clear his throat. "A family at least as well connected as the Strathmores, I might add." He looked across at de Roncy and gave him a slight nod.

"Your father and I crossed paths in our investigations of Mr. Tarkington," de Roncy told her. "Our motives were quite different, but our itineraries similiar: Bridlington, St. James's, Oxford. We were able to pool our resources and aid each other, as it were."

Then it was no hum after all? Her spirits rose as she digested the news. If Patrick was truly an heir, he would surely have money of his own. They would not after all have to wait forever to wed.

"Does he stand to come into a fortune?" she asked eagerly.

"Alas, no," the Frenchman told her, dashing her hopes for a timely marriage. "That is to say, not unless—" He stopped abruptly as though he had almost betrayed a confidence.

Her glance darted in vexation from Papa's uncertain expression to de Roncy's. "Papa, tell me if he will not."

"It would be—indiscreet, my love," he answered. "The knowledge is very—that is to say—the facts are strictly in Monsieur de Roncy's domain. I know it not from his lips, but by the merest happenstance. As he explained, our paths crossed. He has my word of honor I will say nothing, but if *he chooses* to tell you . . ." He offered de Roncy a steadfast look, then gave his daughter a most uncharacteristic shrug of helpless regret.

Was there a conspiracy to keep her in suspense? Her eyes turned to the Frenchman, imploring. "Come, monsieur. I am to be his wife!"

De Roncy gave an indulgent nod. "The Duc de Berry was murdered two weeks ago, and he died without sons, as you—"

"Yes, I *know*," Verity cut in furiously. "We've been all through it. Have the goodness not to change the subject!"

In the awesome silence that followed, something in de Roncy's expression told her that he had not exactly changed the subject, and her heart began to knock at her ribs in a startling fashion. "I beg you to speak out," she said, her voice more breath than sound. "If you know anything of significance about my future husband, I surely have the right to know it too."

De Roncy seemed to grope for delicate words before he drew breath to speak. "Mr. Tarkington may have a claim in the royal line of succession."

She was unsure whether to laugh hysterically or faint clear away. Fighting down both urges, she managed to gasp, "Are you telling me that Patrick Tarkington may be a Bourbon?"

"Yes, mamselle, a bit far removed from the throne—but a big step nearer to it since the duc's demise. I'm afraid the duc has no issue. His widow believes she is with child, but it is too early to be sure, and she is so stricken by her sudden bereavement that her physicians doubt she could carry the child to term."

Verity caught the edge of the breakfast table, no longer able to follow his words. She was wrestling suddenly with the direst possibilities.

Had she just plighted her troth to one man to find she was marrying another? Would Patrick even wish to stand by his promise to her if the tables were turned? And if he *were* to remain true to her under these circumstances? *Dear God!* Could she then be in danger of finding herself consort to a French monarch? The color drained from her cheeks, and she began to tremble violently as the horrible relics of the guillotine rose up before her eyes.

"My dear! Are you unwell?" Papa took her chilled hand in his and chafed it.

De Roncy jumped up from the breakfast table and hurried to her chair. "Please do not distress yourself, mamselle. I understand. The news is a shock, no? But I assure you, Mr. Tarkington abjures all claim. He wishes only to procure a copy of his baptismal record, if his identity is confirmed by the court—which is little more than a formality as far as I am concerned. You see, the design of his signet ring is a match."

Again, she lost track of his words, her mind tripping in and out of half-forgotten scenes that swum past her inner eye.

A wet balcony. De Roncy's arms about her, and then an intruder. "Mais le comportement, le menton . . ." *De Roncy unaccountably fascinated by Tarkington's features. The comportment? The chin? Had he even then recognized some familial likeness? A markedly royal bearing?*

An unmasked impostor standing bareheaded in the rain, daring to invite her into a hired hackney—and yet so commanding in the way he held himself that she was powerless against his authority.

Aunt Maria, struggling so against her suspicions. "Not in Collins' . . . I don't think the printers are at all conscientious when they compile these genealogies."

*The hall of the Elgin Marbles . . . two griffins and a
serpent drawn on a sheet of fine linen. But she had seen
that cipher before. No, no. Later. Days later. The broken
seal on the envelope Dora had given her. How she had
stared at it, not knowing why she had cause to!*

Dear God, she wasn't dreaming, and neither was de
Roncy inventing. It was true. And she was cold as ice.

Papa was stroking her hair and murmuring comforting sounds. And now de Roncy was speaking gently.
She made an effort to listen.

"You must understand, he has no sense of duty to
France. He feels himself to be an Englishman and
thinks of nothing but establishing a medical practice.
No law can oblige him to take his place in the line of
succession." He smiled at the utter relief in Verity's
dazed eyes as his words struck home. *"Eh bien, petite!*
Have no fear. Your future will not be in the least
affected."

Verity raised her eyes from her writing to glance at
the moonlit snow piled up against the casements. It
was so cozy that she loved to leave the curtains open.
They said it was far colder here than in Lancashire.
Perhaps it was, but she had yet to notice it. Seeing
Patrick's nose still buried in his books, she smiled.
What was it de Roncy had said, two months ago?

*Have no fear. Your future will not be in the least
affected.* Thank goodness de Roncy didn't know everything. Her future had been deliciously and irrevocably affected. How could it fail to be?

Patrick could hardly argue further that he had no
decent name to offer her. Jean-Louis Chrétien de Bourbon et Chambord was a very decent name indeed
whether he decided to avail himself of it or no, and
regardless of whether the issue was ever sufficiently
settled to make public. She returned to her letter,
reading the latest page carefully to make sure she had
given nothing away.

Oh, how I longed to tell you sooner, dearest coz, but you can surely see what an extraordinary predicament was mine when I left London. I could not expect you to share it.

I can't begin to describe how hard it was for Patrick to accept help from Papa. In the end, he consented to a loan in his own name, with Papa as guarantor. I am so thankful he at least agreed to that, for had he not, I would have been obliged to wait Lord only knows how long, until he had established his medical practice before we married. On that score, I was positively adamant. I was not prepared to wait another year. Not even another month. After all, I was about to turn twenty-one at the time, as your mama so oft reminded me. It was like melting granite. But I prevailed. (I do win quite often.) Patrick's pride is monumental about some things, but on the rare occasions when he yields, he is gracious and ungrudging and never refers to it again.

Verity smiled to herself at the half-truth. It was trying to be obliged to omit the richest part of it, she thought, reaching for more notepaper and taking up her pen.

So, my dear, here we are married and in Edinburgh until Patrick is licensed. It will mean an extra year, but Papa has persuaded him to study under Dr. Ian McClure, the master of lung diseases. Patrick has long been conversant with McClure's work in this field, and is aware of the surge of ailments arising from the cotton-milling industry. Only his lack of funds had prevented him from considering the specialty before, but now at last he no longer spurns Papa's help. When he is qualified, he will practice in the mill country, and I shall never be too far from Briarley to visit Papa, or you, if Aunt Maria will allow a physician's wife to call at Strathmore House.

I have also managed to persuade Patrick of the senseless cruelty of taking Robbie away from Dora and Jack Reese. Papa has corresponded with them, and Jack has agreed not to renew his lease on the acreage in Somertown. Instead, at the end of this year, he will move north and buy some acres of his own adjacent to Briarley. Thus Patrick will have his beloved Robbie at hand when we return, and the child will have two sets of parents. I hope he can withstand the strain of it!

Gradually, Patrick is realizing that a woman cannot nurture an infant for four years and expect to maintain a purely detached business attitude. Poor Dora! It would have broken her heart to lose Robbie. I hope Patrick's obsessive hold on the child will relax when we have children of our own, but I too have already come to think of Robbie as "our son."

At present we are living entirely on Papa's loan to Patrick, and I shall not touch a penny of my own allowance until my husband is earning his way. This was my own resolve, not his. The arrangement stems from an argument we had when he came to Briarley last February, and one day I shall explain.

The point of it is, I have come to Scotland without out a single servant, and apart from a woman who comes daily to clean the house, and a weekly laundress, I do everything. Imagine, Laura! Patrick doubted I would last out the first week, and frankly, so did I. But I am amazed at how much pleasure I derive from the simple chores of cooking and planning menus. Neither of us has the time or the inclination to participate in the doings of Edinburgh society, and although our life will be more leisurely when we return to Lancashire, I shall always cherish this time here in our little house. It is an extraordinary feeling to know, after the servant leaves, that we are quite, quite alone.

To answer your question, the wedding took place in the music room at Briarley. It was quite beautiful, the room banked with daffodils, and you can assure Aunt Maria that it was a Church of England ceremony. My only regret is that you could not be present, but, of course, it had to be broken very gently to your parents.

I trust by now that your papa is no longer purple, and that your mama is recovered somewhat. You might point out for her comfort that at least I did not marry a Quaker. At some future date, I may be able to smooth her ruffled feathers still further, but I'm afraid that must wait on our return to the shire.

When we do come back, I shall be wife to Dr. Patrick Tarkington—a title that will have to suffice until the Prince Regent sees fit to bestow a knighthood on my husband in recognition of the splendid healing work and marvelous medical discoveries with which I have no doubt he will soon distinguish himself.

He is quite brilliant, coz, and avid for his studies. He is even more avid for me! Modesty forbids me to be more specific, but no doubt you will find out about such delights for yourself one day. Suffice it to say that Patrick is now an altogether different man from the bored, aloof creature of Mayfair.

Verity came to the end of another sheet, and paused to read what she had written. It was her first really detailed letter to Laura. So much had happened so fast, she scarcely knew where to begin. And then, of course, there was so much she could not say that it was hard to write coherently.

Having hungered so for a decent name to offer her, Patrick was now in no hurry to claim the illustrious one which de Roncy assured him he was entitled to. How strangely perverse he could be! And how adorable. "As long as I can feel worthy enough to marry you immediately, my darling, I don't give a tinker's curse for titles and rank."

Nor did she, when she searched her heart. If she were never able to tell the world, she would still be utterly content to be simply Mrs. Tarkington. But it *was* rather delicious to contemplate a day when the Strathmores might learn of it. She looked across the table at his place, and discovered he had left his chair and stolen up behind her. A delicious tremor went through her. He still had cat feet when he chose.

His hands touched her shoulders and his lips brushed her ear. "So, I am avid for my studies, am I, love? If only you knew what a trial it is not to raise my eyes and look across the table at you! For when I do, I am undone."

Immediately she placed a hand over the letter. "One is not supposed to read another's private correspondence."

"Not even my wife's?" His chin played with the nape of her neck.

"No, not even your wife's." Verity bent her head and smiled to herself. He was such a child in the ways of family etiquette, and it was her delight both to instruct him and to tease him mercilessly on the subject.

"Then how may I know you are not writing to a lover?" His voice was fierce, and his caress became bolder as it swept across her shoulders and throat.

"You don't! You have to trust me."

"*Can* I trust you?"

"Not for a moment!"

"Wench!" Laughing, he took her by the waist and lifted her out of her chair, holding her close to him. "Is one supposed to kiss one's wife?" His eyes were wide and bland.

"Only if one asks," she said, her voice silken with longing. With their wedding night two months past, her pulses still skipped madly at his intimate touch.

"And if one *fails* to ask?" His grin was villainous as

his arms tightened possessively about her waist. He began to trace the path of her spine with lingering fingertips, and it was her undoing. Raising her arms and locking them tight about his neck, she drew down his smiling mouth to hers.

But his head drew back out of her reach. "And if one *fails* to ask?" he insisted. "Answer me."

Her laughter rang out joyously. "Then a poor wife has no recourse at all. She must suffer the embrace."

"For a woman so intent to marry me," he complained to the ceiling above his head, "she has become the coolest of wives."

She was unable to reach his lips if he would not bend his head. He held back only for the sheer pleasure of seeing her longing for him, she knew. But two could play at that game.

Spreading her palms over his shirt, she smoothed the fine white lawn against his thudding breast. "Ah, so even the blood royal can pound, *seigneur*. Quite extraordinary! Mayn't I even tell Laura? She'd never breathe a—"

"No! It may never become official. And even if it does, I shall never accustom myself to it."

"But you must simply practice believing it, my darling." She pulled away from him to sweep into a low curtsy, fit for a king. "I shall call you *seigneur* with great frequency, and you will soon become accustomed to it."

"How are the mighty fallen!" He gazed ardently at the gleam of white neck as she bowed her head. "You, who would not bend an elbow to allow your waltz partner to approach you, now bend your knee?"

Her shoulders shook with laughter, but she held the deep obeisance at his feet.

"Baggage! If you persist . . ." he murmured, scooping her up into his arms and carrying her out into the hallway. He began to mount the stairs, more intent on reaching their bedchamber than continuing the conversation.

"What if I do?" she pressed, touching her lips to his ear.

His only response was the quickening of his breath as he raced to the landing and down the corridor of the upper floor.

"Answer me," she demanded, aping his own imperious tone.

His eyes flamed as he kicked closed the door to their room, and passion rasped in his voice. "Then you will have my *droit de seigneur* to reckon with."

"I was counting on it, my lord," she purred.

His fingers were bold and nimble as he unbuttoned her dress. "Be warned," he growled. "If I am to practice believing it, it will require the constant exercise of my rights."

"As constant as you wish," she whispered ecstatically, as at last his lips met hers.

About the Author

Mollie Ashton's interest in the Regency period began with a teenage fascination with Napoleon and Lord Byron, but it was not until she wrote her first Regency romance that she discovered the significance of her eldest child's birthday—the 150th anniversary of the Battle of Waterloo. "For some reason," she says, "it suggested to me that I was destined to write about that period."

Under various pen names, the author writes contemporary romances and historical novels. An English transplant, she now lives in Southern California with her husband and two daughters, and writes a minimum of forty hours a week.